Saving HOLLYWOOD

by Katherine Adair

TATE PUBLISHING,

For Granddaddy

"Some trust in chariots and some in horses, but we trust in the name of the LORD our God."
Psalm 20:7

Dear readers, let us never forget that God is the Author of our lives. Even the best fictional stories are only a shadow compared to the amazing story of which He has made us a part. He has weaved such wonderful people into my life. Thank you Mom and Jennifer Emery for reading and re-reading my book from start to finish, praising every effort I made along the way. Thank you all of my first readers: Carol Scott, Tracey and Kayla Keller, Karissa Roy, Beth Dunlop, Dr. Johnny Wink, Dr. Marvin Pate, and Alyse Vandyke. Thank you Dad for always reminding me that no dream is out of reach. Thank you Grandmommy for giving the story of my life significance by always being willing to listen.

Thank you Ashley Moore and Amy Welch for inspiring me to live the life I once thought was only possible in stories.

I have been blessed with a wonderfully biased grandfather who has doted on me my whole life. He is my biggest and dearest fan. Granddaddy, my story is dedicated to you.

chapter one

Now, now, now! Now was the time for her escape. Just a few more stairs and she'd be out of sight. *Phew, I made it,* she thought when she reached the second floor, but her triumph was short lived. *What was that?* There was someone coming out of the door to her right. *Move!* shouted a voice inside of her head. She quickly bolted through the door on her left and then pressed her ear against the wood to listen to the footsteps fade down the servants' stairway. She felt her breathing slowly returning to normal.

When a person looked at Hollywood Rose Johnson, it was through eyes of envy and wonder. Her parents were divorced, but that only added to her renown. On one end of the country, she was known as the daughter of Anne Tricony, one of Hollywood's brightest stars, and on the other end, she was the progeny of the prestigious multimillionaire, Tres Johnson. She was also beautiful. Holly had inherited her mother's frame and dark hair. With her father's striking blue eyes added to the package, she was a knock-out by age twelve. Even if she hadn't been born a celebrity, people would have noticed her. On top of her wealth and beauty, she was brilliant. Her mother's photographic memory coupled with her own desire to learn gave her the title of a genius. She was born to succeed and to turn everything she touched into gold.

At the moment, America's favorite whiz kid was hacking into her father's PC. At sixteen, she was more beautiful than most ever dreamt of becoming. Had she not promised herself that she would never become like her mother, she might have considered acting or modeling. There were easier ways to make money, though—such as pilfering some of her father's funds into her own account. She was bored. Holly sighed when her hair fell into her face for the hundredth time that evening. She hated wearing it down, but her father would not tolerate his only child looking like a "ragamuffin" by wearing it in a braid. Go figure. Usually if he remembered that he had a daughter, he couldn't care less what she looked like, but tonight was Victoria's birthday.

Victoria was Holly's spoiled grandmother who refused to be called "grandmother." Therefore, Holly called her Victoria to her face and "Torie" the rest of the time. The joke would have been lost on her anyway. Holly wasn't sure that her grandmother knew anything about the American Revolution.

"Miss Rose!" Holly jumped when she heard the housekeeper, Natasha, hiss at her from the hallway. Within the blink of an eye, Holly had her father's account closed and Minesweeper up on the screen. Natasha was the only one who called Holly by her middle name. Holly figured that it was a form of endearment. Holly's father, Steven Johnson III (Tres), had practically given his daughter over to Natasha to raise when Holly was four. Tres did spend some time with Holly, but whenever it came to discipline or, heaven forbid, "girl stuff," Holly was left in Natasha's capable hands.

Nevertheless, Victoria saw to it that Holly never became too close to the frumpy, old housekeeper. Holly could hear her grandmother's shrill voice in her head. *It is not suitable for someone of your standing to become emotionally attached to the lower class.* Holly wondered what would happen if her grandmother ever woke up and realized she was living in the twenty-first century. The old hag would probably suffer from heart failure.

"Miss Rose! What in heaven's name is you doin' in here? You is supposed to be down stairs with your grandmother's guests." At five feet, Natasha didn't look very intimidating compared to Holly who was just shy of five ten, but Holly knew better than to argue with Natasha—at least not when she was already furious.

"Your father's been askin' where you was, and I've been lookin' for you for a half hour. And here you is playing that game. Honestly, you is always playin' that thing. Every time I comes in here you're playin' it." Natasha put her hands on her hips to make herself look more imposing. It worked. "Now git downstairs like a proper lady before I take you down there myself, and you know you don't want that." Holly was proud of herself for not gulping, not audibly at least. She hadn't had a spanking since she was eleven, but she wasn't about to put the idea past her old nanny. Holly did as she was told and walked down the main staircase to the ballroom to watch the circus act led by her father, the ringmaster.

"Now you behave yerself!" Natasha yelled from the top of the stairs. Holly couldn't help but smirk. Did she ever misbehave? Holly had always figured that it was easier just to do what grown-ups expected; only then would they leave you alone. She had long given up misbehaving for attention from her father. He simply didn't have the desire to deal with a problem child. All attempts to win his attention in that way had led to a spanking from Natasha, or even worse, a lecture from Torie. Holly figured that the best way to deal with grown-ups was to be what they wanted you to be. In Salem, that was a reserved, socially adept young adult. In Hollywood, it was a vivacious, beautiful teenager. Holly realized that she could play both parts exceedingly well. Maybe it was because of this that she was adored by everyone and known by no one. Holly couldn't say that she was happy, but she was definitely content. That was better than most people her age, wasn't it? Holly forced a smile as she was sucked into the inner ring.

Salem, Oregon…7:30 PM (Pacific Time)

Joshua Timberlaigh knew two things. There were two seconds left on the clock, and his teammates would crucify him if he missed this shot. *Oh please, God! Let it go in. I'll do whatever You want me to do, just please let it…*Josh sucked dry air when the ball hit the rim. It bounced up, hit the other side of the rim, and went through the net with that satisfying swish all ball players dream of at night. Josh heard the crowd explode. He'd done it! His team was going to the finals!

Suddenly, Josh couldn't breathe. All of his teammates smashed into him to give him one huge victory hug, but Josh didn't care if he ever breathed again. No little thing like oxygen could make him feel this incredible. *Thanks, God.*

After the game, the euphoric feeling of a nail-biting victory hadn't worn off, but Josh began to feel the fatigue from school and his game catch up with him.

"Yo! My man, Josh, hold up!" Josh kept himself from grimacing when he heard one of his teammates run up behind him.

"Hey, Bret." Josh tried to sound enthusiastic but to no avail. Everything about Bret rubbed Josh the wrong way, from the trash he talked to the trash he did. Yet except for teasing him about "that God thing," Bret had never actually done anything to Josh. Other guys messed around with him about being a Christian too, but it had never really bugged him. Bret bugged him.

Completely unaware of Josh's inner conflict, Bret ran up and gave him a high five. "Dude, that shot was killer!"

"Thanks." *Now leave.*

"Hey, I just wanted to say something. Now that we're going to the finals and everything, I wanted to get this off my chest." All of a sudden, loudmouth Bret was astonishingly quiet. "I, um, I'm sorry about giving you such a hard time about that God thing. I really am." There he'd said it. Maybe now his conscience would leave him alone. The stupid annoyance had been bugging him lately.

"No, it's okay . . ." Josh started. He was already beginning to feel guilty about his earlier thoughts.

"No, it's not okay. I've given you a rough time this season. All of us have, but what gets me is that you took it as if it was nothing. I would have cracked by now and pummeled one of them." Bret grew quiet again. Josh noticed Bret didn't sound as confident as he usually did. "Anyway, I was wondering. Do you think that after the game tomorrow you could talk to me about that Christian stuff?" Bret felt like an enormous weight had just been lifted off his shoulders.

"Sure!" Josh hoped that he didn't sound too enthusiastic. That tended to scare people away. "I mean, sure." He tucked his thumbs into his front pockets. "I'd be glad to talk to you, if you want me to."

Bret's face lit up. "Thanks! Well, I've got to go. Get some rest, Timberlaigh. We've got a big game tomorrow." And with that, Bret ran off.

Josh rubbed his eyes in amazement as he watched Bret disappear. *Thanks God. Please use me to show him You.* Josh walked away with more joy than he'd had after making the winning shot.

11:30 PM (Eastern Time)

Holly gazed around the spacious ballroom. She was already looking for another opportunity to bolt. Did these people think that she actually enjoyed listening to them talk about the stock market? Or even worse, a few of them gushed on about how "lucky" she was to have Tres as a father. Holly could see right through their carefully laid compliments. Assuming that she and her father were close—and they weren't—the guests thought that she would repeat their good feelings back to her father, and he would in turn increase their bank accounts. Holly looked around the room. The only interesting people at the party were the caterers, and strictly speaking, she wasn't supposed to talk to them.

Holly groaned audibly when she saw Albert Bergenstein heading her direction. *Here comes the slime ball.* Of everyone at the party, he was one of the closest to Holly in age. *Is he nineteen or twenty?*

"Hello, Holly, you look beautiful tonight."

And you look like a slug, she wanted to say but restrained herself. "Hello, Albert, I hope that you are enjoying yourself." *Stop looking at my shirt,* Holly finished silently.

"I always enjoy myself when you're around." He took her hand and kissed it.

Holly hoped she didn't laugh…or puke. She was certain that her father would not approve of either one. In Holly's way of thinking, the best way to get his mind, and hopefully his eyes, off her was to distract him with business. "I hear that your father and you have expanded the family business to Tokyo."

"You heard correctly. I . . ."

"Is he here?"

"Who?"

Bless his stupid soul. "You're father—I was hoping that I might be able to say hello."

"Oh yes," Albert said with the slightly bored expression he always wore whenever the limelight was taken off him. "He's around here somewhere. Well, if you'll excuse me, I'm going to get another drink."

Holly thought vaguely about the fact that he already seemed a bit drunk. Oh well, it was not as if he were driving home. In fact, Holly wasn't sure that Albert had ever owned any car aside from a limo. It was a shame, really; then he could get himself killed and save her the trouble of strangling him. Holly glanced in his direction once more and saw the clock overhead. It was nearing twelve; the perfect time for her to make another, and hopefully her last, escape.

"Oh, Holly, darling . . ."

Drat. Holly turned and saw Mrs. Vancouver, one of Torie's more bubbly friends. All that Holly could think of was that she looked like a cherub stuck in a plum. Holly knew that purple was the color of the season, but did everyone have to dress in it from head to foot? Not that Holly could say much. She, herself, was sporting a light purple blouse. Natasha had won that argument. Still, she would not have agreed to wear it if it hadn't looked fabulous with her eyes. At least, that's what Holly told herself.

Mrs. Vancouver did indeed look like a plum, from her purple eye shadow down to her purple tights and shoes. The only relief in color was the priceless jewels that she wore, compliments of Mr. Vancouver. Holly adored Mr. Vancouver. He was a skinny little man of seventy who was afraid of his own shadow, or so it seemed. Next to his wife, he all but faded into the wallpaper, but he was one of the kindest, most good-hearted men that Holly knew. She sometimes wondered how such a shy, reserved man could ever marry a talkative social butterfly like Mrs. Vancouver. How had the man proposed? Perhaps he sent her a telegram. *Were there telegrams back then?*

"Right, Holly?" Mrs. Vancouver suddenly asked.

What is she talking about? Holly panicked. Had she been paying any attention, she could have replayed the conversation in her head. Unfortunately, she had completely zoned out, and to make matters worse, her grandmother was standing right there. *Better just smile and nod.* Holly slowly nodded.

"You see, Victoria, even Holly thinks that the color of mourning should be orange."

Huh? Holly looked at her grandmother. Torie did not seem pleased.

"Well, I've never heard of such foolishness," Victoria huffed, "everyone in this world wears black for mourning, and that's the way it should be."

Holly didn't think it was a good time to inform Torie of Indian or Chinese mourning rituals. Besides, she highly doubted that her grandmother considered anyone who lived farther east than the Europeans as part of "this world."

Seeing the conversation was going nowhere, Holly said the first thing that came to her mind. "I'm terribly sorry, but I promised Father that I would say 'hello,' and I haven't had a chance to all evening, so if you would excuse me."

"Of course, darling, run along now and come back to see me later so that we can discuss your love life." This, of course, came from Mrs. Vancouver.

"Oh, um, sure. I'll be back later." *I'll be back after you've gone and can't embarrass me!* Holly shot one last glance at her grandmother before she left. *The old hag is probably already plotting my "love life."* Holly was fairly certain that if Torie had it her way, she would arrange her granddaughter's marriage.

Holly spotted her father. He was deep in conversation with the elder Mr. Bergenstein. At the moment, she knew that she could start singing "Jingle Bell Rock," and he wouldn't notice her. A waiter walked by, and she saw her chance to escape. Holly ignored the man's curious stare and walked beside him until they reached the stairs. The moment they were there, she charged up the stairs, taking two and three at a time.

Once upstairs again, Holly went to her study. Holly loved that room. It was two stories and open in the middle so that you could look onto the lower level from the top. The upper level was filled with thousands of books and nothing else. The lower level had the latest in computers and video games. Holly kept all of her outdated games and game players behind a glass cabinet for sentimental reasons. She couldn't bear to throw away what she considered to have been her childhood friends. She still enjoyed playing the original Mario Brothers from time to time. Her favorite gaming machine, though, was her Game Cube.

Holly flopped down onto a beanbag chair and started playing a game. It was harder than she'd expected, but she was determined to beat it in less than a week. After a while, her eyes became so tired that the colors on the screen began to blur. She reluctantly turned off her game, walked up the steep spiral staircase to the upper level, and looked around for a book to read. She chose a sci-fi thriller she hadn't read yet and was about to sit down again when she heard the door open. Holly looked over her shoulder expecting to see Natasha, who would undoubtedly try to coerce her into going downstairs, again, but it wasn't Natasha.

"Are you lost?" Holly recognized the dark figure looming in the doorway. It was Albert. Even with the bad lighting, Holly see could that something was different about him. He looked drunker than she'd ever seen him before. He always drank, but she'd never seen him plastered. The sight was not a pleasant one.

"I followed you up here to your little cave."

"Oh, well then, I'm sure that you know your way back down." Holly knew that her father wouldn't approve of her being rude to the son of one of his wealthiest guests, but Albert was beginning to scare her. Holly clutched her fingers tightly around her book.

Albert took a step toward her. "Do you know what you do to me, Princess? Every time I see you, you flirt with me and then walk away just to make me need you more. Don't deny it. You want me just as much as I want you."

"I'm flattered, Albert, really," she tried to soothe his ego so that he would stop walking toward her, "but I don't think I'm ready for any kind of relationship."

"You tramp! Do you really think I'm going to buy that? I'm a Bergenstein. We take what we want, and that, for the moment, is you."

Albert lunged at her. He was bigger than her, but the alcohol made him slightly slower. Holly did the first thing that came to her mind. She slammed her book into his face and ran through the door. She'd barely gotten into the hallway when he smashed her, full force, into the wall.

"You're going to pay for that," he whispered harshly into her ear. She looked at him and saw blood running down his face. The edge of the book must have done that. Out of the corner of her eye, she saw Natasha running up the servants' stairway.

"What's going on?" Natasha yelled once she reached the top of the stairs. Albert shoved Holly to the ground, and she hit the side of a lamp stand on her way down. The last thing she saw was Albert shoving Natasha. As if in a dream, Holly watched Natasha slowly lose her balance and tumble head first down the stairs. She flailed her arms, trying desperately to grab a hold of something, anything, but her hands only met air. The clock chimed once.

10:00 PM (Pacific Time)

Josh rolled over in his bed, wide-awake. Out of the seventeen years he had lived, he could not remember one time when he'd suffered from insomnia. Until now, he had thought insomnia was just another one of those "disorders" people made up in their minds. Josh tried to remind himself of this as he strangled himself further in his covers.

Josh was raised in a Christian home, a Christian home that taught God was more than just some nebulous spirit wandering around somewhere in the universe. His parents taught him that God wanted to have a personal relationship with the humans He'd created. Josh did have a personal relationship with God, but at the moment, all he could do was complain. He punched his pillow in frustration. *God! Why won't You let me fall asleep? I have the most important game of my life tomorrow!* After his little tirade, Josh started to feel guilty. If God was keeping him awake on such an important night, then there had to be a good reason.

Trying not to grumble, Josh sat up in bed and turned on his light. *Okay, God, I'm sorry for losing it. What do you want from me?* he asked sincerely. Suddenly, Josh remembered a sermon from way back. He remembered the preacher saying that sometimes God kept him awake at night to pray. *Is that what You want God? Who do you want me to pray for? Bret?* Then Josh remembered another sermon. It was one about how it was never too early to pray for your future spouse. *Well,* Josh thought to himself, *it couldn't hurt.* Momentarily, he considered praying for his wife to be a supermodel. *If you don't ask, you don't get.* Josh began to laugh at himself until he was hit with a sudden urgency to pray. So he prayed desperately, but not knowing why. Fifteen minutes later, Josh was fast asleep.

Back East

When Holly woke up, she felt herself being half-carried, half-dragged into her bedroom. It took a split second to remember what had happened and what was about to happen. He was going to rape her! When she yelled out for help, Albert shoved Holly into her room and then locked the door.

"Why are you doing this?" she sobbed, as he pushed her onto the bed.

"It's the price you pay for being beautiful." He jumped on her. She heard men's voices and loud banging on the other side of her door. Yet all that she could think of was getting away from Albert, but even drunk, he was much stronger that her. The pain in her head was blinding, and Holly finally gave up trying to get away. Every muscle in her body was maxed out. She couldn't fight him anymore. Holly looked up in time to see the mirror above her bed shake and then come crashing down on Albert. She watched in astonishment as his eyes rolled into the back of his head, and then he fell off her onto the floor. As if in a dream, Holly got off her bed, stepped over Albert's limp body, and opened the door. It looked like it was about to break under the pressure of pounding fists. Her father and another man rushed in.

"What happened?"

Holly looked from Albert's limp body to her raging father. "He tried to . . ." she stammered. Holly tried desperately to say something more, but darkness swam towards her. She didn't feel herself fall to the ground.

chapter two

Holly awoke two days later in the hospital. At first, she panicked because she didn't remember why she was there, but it didn't take long to recall exactly what had happened. *Looks like that jerk didn't get what he wanted.* Holly looked down and saw an IV in her arm. *How long have I been here?* She peered around the drab room and caught sight of a mirror. *Not long enough for the swelling in my face to go down.* She had a black eye and could make out a small gash just above her right temple. Holly realized that if she had hit the lamp stand just a little lower, she could have been blinded or even killed. Holly kept gazing in the mirror at her bruised complexion. She heard Albert's voice ringing loudly through her head, *"It's the price you pay for being beautiful."*

Holly shuddered. She certainly wasn't beautiful at the moment. She didn't even recognize the pale girl staring back at her in the mirror. *The mirror! How did it fall off the wall?* For a moment, just a moment, Holly thought that maybe something supernatural had been at work. Then she reminded herself she didn't believe in stupid things like that. *I'm sure there is a perfectly logical explanation. Something must have shaken the mirror off its hook, or maybe the hook came out of the wall.* Holly promised herself that the second she got home she would check to see if the hook was still in place. *That has to be it.*

She completely forgot about the mirror when she heard the door swing open. An old man, whom she assumed to be her doctor, walked in.

"Oh good, you're awake. How are you feeling?"

"Like someone hit me over the head with a sledge hammer, and you?"

The doctor chuckled and then put on his half-moon spectacles. "Oh, a bit better than that, I'm relieved to say. Now, do you remember what caused your fall down the stairs?" The doctor clucked his tongue. "You were quite lucky, you know, that you didn't break anything on the way down. Aside from your concussion and a few bumps and bruises, I believe that you came off on the better side of things, Miss Johnson."

Holly blinked, "Did you say that I fell down the stairs?"

"Yes, don't you remember?" the doctor looked a bit worried. He hoped that his patient didn't have memory loss. That was always a messy business.

"I can't say I remember that, but . . ." Holly suddenly remembered who had fallen down the stairs. "Natasha!"

The doctor jumped at her sudden raised voice. "Pardon me?"

"Is Natasha all right?"

"I'm sorry, but I don't know who that is. Perhaps one of the other . . ."

The old man cut himself off when another man stepped into the room. "Hello, Holly." Holly turned towards her father's voice. Tres was looking at the doctor. "How is she?"

"Well, she seems to be doing just fine, though she is having some problems remembering what happened to her."

"Yes, of course, that is to be expected." Tres inspectehis finger-nails, implying he found the whole matter quite a nuisance. "Would you please excuse us, Doctor Lester?"

"Certainly, sir, just let me know when I can come back and check on her. Now that she's conscious, I want to do full x-rays to assure myself that nothing is broken. Your daughter is very lucky. Being a religious fellow, I'd say God had His hand of protection on her." Saying nothing else, the doctor quietly exited the room. Holly glanced at the newspaper in her father's hand. The date told her she'd been unconscious for over twenty-four hours.

Tres checked to make sure that the door was closed, and then with his back to his daughter he asked, "How much do you re-member?" Holly looked at her father's face when he turned back around. It was the first time she had ever seen him look stressed. Was he concerned about her?

"I remember enough to know it was Natasha, not me, who fell down the stairs. Dad, is she okay?" Holly would have given any-thing to be able to read her father's face, but she couldn't. She'd never been able to.

"I'm terribly sorry, but she died in intensive care yesterday. The funeral will be Wednesday." Tres cleared his throat. "I have spoken with your grandmother, and we have decided you will be allowed to go." He looked at his watch, apparently undisturbed by Natasha's sudden death.

As for Holly, an earthquake couldn't have shaken her more vio-lently. Holly bit back the tears that threatened to fall. If she cried, then she would be at her father's mercy. She would wait. For now, she quickly replaced her grief with anger. "How good of you to allow me to go to the funeral of the one person who actually cared about me. A person who, might I add, would be alive today if it wasn't for you!" Holly had never allowed herself to lose her temper in front of her father, but now that she had, she felt the power of it almost consume her and was loathe to do anything to stop it from taking complete control.

"If you do not speak to me with more respect then I'll . . ."

"You'll what? Fire me?"

"We will speak about this later once you have calmed yourself. Now, about what happened last Friday, Albert's father and I have spoken concerning the matter. We believe that it is in the best interest for all of us if this little incident is kept quiet."

Holly couldn't believe what she was hearing. *He really doesn't love me.* "So what am I supposed to do? Just pretend nothing ever happened? He tried to rape me!"

Tres' entire face hardened. "Holly Rose Johnson! Keep your voice down. There is nothing else to be done. I am sorry that this happened, but what were you doing upstairs in the first place? You should have been with the guests."

"I'm sorry," Holly ground her teeth, "but I didn't realize I had to protect myself from being taken advantage of by your friends in my own house!"

"That's it. I am tired of you raising your voice to me. I will not tolerate it. Just remember that you fell down the stairs, and, oh yes, Natasha died of a heart attack. I don't need any trouble from her family, though they will be richly compensated for their loss." Tres' face relaxed into his typical regal expression. "Call Giraud when you are allowed to come home from the hospital. He will pick you up.

"Does Anne know I'm here?"

"Of course not. There is no need to send her into a panic."

Indeed, of course not, Holly thought bitterly as her father calmly walked out the door. When it closed, Holly grabbed her Styrofoam cup filled with ice and threw it at the closed door. Seeing the ice crash against it did nothing to ease the pain. Holly turned her face into her pillow and sobbed for Natasha and for herself. *"It's the price you pay for being beautiful."* Holly shivered. The world had never felt so dark.

Holly arrived home the next day and set to work immediately.

It took her all of fifteen minutes to secure an airline ticket to L.A., first class of course. She was scheduled to leave directly after the funeral the next day, which gave her about twenty-four hours to come up with a plausible excuse not to ride home with Giraud. Holly thought a few moments about luggage but then figured that everything she needed could easily fit into her backpack. She could just buy more clothes once she arrived in L.A. Shopping was like yoga for Holly. It relaxed her.

At the age of twelve, her father had given Holly her first credit card. It was easier for everyone if she didn't have to ask him for money directly. Father/daughter communication had never been a big thing for either of them. The ticket almost maxed out her credit card, but without too much effort, she was able to raise her limit. Holly Rose Johnson was now the proud owner of a Platinum Discover card.

Holly leaned back in her chair and sighed. Tres would find her sooner or later. *Probably sooner.* It was not as if her father gave a darn where she was, but it would be bad for his reputation if word got out that his daughter had run away from home. The media would have a field day. Holly chuckled at the thought.

Holly logged off her father's computer, stretched, and headed toward her bedroom. She couldn't stall forever. She had to know what had caused the mirror to fall. Holly opened her door and stood in the doorway, suddenly petrified of going in. She knew that it was stupid, but she thought that if she stepped inside, someone might come up from behind and lock her in. Holly's hand trembled on the doorknob as the flashbacks rolled through her all-too-perfect memory. She could feel Albert's hands on her. Holly's hand fell from the handle. She couldn't take it anymore. Holly ran away from her room as if a demon were chasing after her, but then screeched to a stop in front of her study.

After everything that had happened, she didn't want to go in there either, but it was where she kept her hard cash. Holly took a deep breath. She couldn't be afraid of her own house. She would not allow Albert Bergenstein to control her life like that. Holly strode boldly into her study. She refused to look over her shoulder to see if anyone had followed her in as she made her way to the steep staircase. So what if she gripped the guard railing a bit harder than usual? At least she wasn't shaking anymore.

When she reached the top, Holly smiled in satisfaction. It wasn't a big accomplishment, but it was something. Holly was about to reach for her fake copy of *Pride and Prejudice* when...

"Holly? Where are you, girl?" A voice floated in from in the hallway.

Holly briefly considered not answering, but she decided against it. She couldn't hide forever. "I'm in here, Victoria."

Victoria gracefully walked into Holly's study and glared up at her. "Child, what are you doing?"

"Looking for a book to read. Is there a problem?" Holly could see the suspicious look in her grandmother's eyes. Yet considering that Torie had always had that same look on her face since the time Holly had been born, she didn't think much of it. In fact, Holly would have been concerned if Victoria didn't glare at her.

Torie's scowl deepened. "No, there is no problem, except it seems that there is no one around to call you to dinner, therefore I have to." Natasha had always been the one to tell Holly when dinner was ready, not that Victoria cared. She was just complaining that she had to come all the way up to the third floor. There was an intercom system in Holly's study, just like in every other room in the grandiose house. However, when Holly had been ten, she'd gotten tired of being interrupted without her permission; therefore, she removed a section of the wires behind the speaker in both her study and her room. Her father had been too lazy to have the system rewired. On-demand contact with Holly was not high on his priority list anyway.

"Actually, I'm not hungry," Holly said with a dismissive flick of her hand. She waited for her grandmother's retort.

"Fine then, don't eat." Victoria walked out and left Holly in a semi state of shock. She knew her grandmother didn't care if she starved to death, but Victoria had always been adamant about

Holly being present at the dinner table if for no other reason than the fact that it gave her a scheduled time during the day to lecture Holly on the finer points of society.

Holly pondered her grandmother's strange behavior for a few moments but then shrugged her shoulders. What did she care if her grandmother's body had been taken over by alien life forms? Not giving Torie a second thought, Holly pulled out three thousand dollars and started packing her bag. It was exciting, really. Holly had never done anything like this before. It was a grand adventure, and for the first time in the past seventy-two hours, Holly felt like a kid again.

Natasha's funeral was beautiful. Holly tried not to cry, but she couldn't help it. Natasha had been well loved by both her family and coworkers. There was no doubt about that. Holly was not surprised that neither her grandmother nor her father attended the funeral. In Holly's mind, that made the service more genuine. She didn't want to see her grandmother's crocodile tears or her father's "sorrowful" reserve. At least they had had the decency to pay for the funeral. Holly supposed it was their way of making up for what had happened. Nothing, though, could change the fact that Natasha was never coming back. Holly wondered if her heart would ever stop hurting.

Toward the end of the service, Holly couldn't help but think that in many ways her life was changed forever. It terrified her because she detested change, but in a way, Natasha's death freed her from the confines of her father's world. Natasha had been the one person who didn't treat her as if she were different because of her money, her intelligence, and—her beauty. Still, Natasha had always made Holly act the way she knew a refined young lady of society was supposed to act. Holly now understood that, in her own way, Natasha had done the same thing to her as her father and grandmother had. They had all tried to make her into the type of person who best suited themselves. Now there was no reason to continue on with the charade. Natasha was dead and so was the daughter of Tres Johnson.

Holly was so deep in thought that she almost forgot about her escape plan. It was nearly three and Giraud would be leaving the house soon to pick her up. Holly took a split second to berate herself and then went to the restrooms for privacy. When she was sure no one was around, Holly pulled out her cell and called Giraud. The phone rang only once before being answered.

"Giraud speaking."

"It's me. I forgot to tell you that I will be going to a reception at the home of one of Natasha's relatives. I have a ride over there and back home, so you don't have to worry about driving me."

Giraud sounded suspicious. "Is this okay with your father?"

"Of course. I just spoke to him. He thinks it will be better for our image if they see someone from the Johnson family at the reception. He's also the one who suggested I ride with someone else to the party. He wanted you to take the night off. Well, I'd better go."

That should keep him from talking to Father any time soon. Holly hung up and dialed a taxi service. After they'd assured her they would be there in no later than fifteen minutes, she quickly changed into normal clothes. Holly looked in the mirror. The girl staring back at her could easily have appeared on the cover of *Seventeen.* Holly had always known she was beautiful, but it had never meant anything to her until now. *"It's the price that you pay for being beautiful."* Holly learned at a very young age to use her wealth and intelligence to her father's advantage, but had *he* also been using her looks? The thought repulsed her. Look at where being beautiful had gotten her. She shuddered and opted not to reapply her makeup.

chapter three

There was a one-hour layover in Chicago, which was good since she had to walk from one end of the airport to the other, no small feat. Though she hated herself for it, she stopped at a tourist trap and bought an ugly, oversized T-shirt to replace the chic blouse she'd been wearing. Holly felt like the entire population of males was staring at her, just like Albert. Some were. She hated it most when she saw their eyes move slowly from her face, to her chest, to her legs, and then back up again. It had never bothered her before. Yet now she had trouble keeping her eyes off her feet. What had happened to the All-American girl who had it all? Holly couldn't help but think that that girl had been an illusion, one who would never come back, even if she wanted to. Yet wasn't "the perfect life" just one big fantasy anyway? People seemed to think hers was perfect, which just proved how gullible humans were. They believed what the media told them to believe and would fight to the death to defend the lies they were told.

Holly arrived in L.A. at six o'clock. It was raining, but she didn't mind. Holly loved the rain, especially when it stormed. The bold excitement of it never ceased to thrill her.

It was fairly easy getting a taxi. Her driver was nice enough. He spoke primarily Spanish. Holly could speak Spanish fluently, but she didn't let the driver know that. She wasn't in the mood to speak in any language.

Holly watched the cars speed by on the other side of the highway, and for the hundredth time that day, she asked herself what she was doing. Finally, she came to the conclusion that she needed someone. Maybe, for once, Anne would act like a mother, not just an eccentric aunt. It was worth a try. Robert wouldn't mind if she stayed with them for a while.

Robert Salvido was Holly's stepfather. He and Holly had a mutual respect for each other, but that was about all they could claim. Neither one wanted to develop a relationship that went beyond face value. Holly had been ten when Robert and Anne married. Robert had been directing one of Anne's movies when they decided to make a more lasting commitment. Unlike her first marriage, which had been done to spite an old boyfriend, Anne wanted this one to last. They seemed happy together, maybe even in love, if there was such a thing. After six years of fidelity, Holly thought that this one might just stand the test of time.

When they first married, Anne asked Holly if she wanted to live with them. It was possible that Anne had been ready to become a real mother back then, but Holly figured it was more likely that Anne had felt obligated to take care of her daughter now that she had a husband. At the time, Holly had been comfortable where she was and hadn't seen any reason to leave her father's house. Ever since then, Holly had spent one month during summers in Los Angeles, but she had never considered living with Anne year-round. Natasha had been at Holly's house in Massachusetts. Now that Natasha was gone, Holly thought about seeing if the offer was still open. Who knew? Maybe things would work out. She tried to squash the sensation of hope that coursed through her as the cab approached the gates of her mother's home. Holly felt nervous. Maybe she was more like a normal teenager than she gave herself credit for being.

Holly stood at the gate and peered up at the house. Even in the rainy mist, her mother's home did not reflect its owner. It emulated the image of Anne Tricony who Robert created for the public eye. The house was sophisticated and classy in an old-fashioned way. There was never a trace of dust or anything out of place. Holly wasn't fooled. Anne was as scatter brained as they came, and Holly loved her for it. It was like a breath of fresh air after spending months with her father in his elegantly masculine manor.

She dropped out of high school at seventeen and chased the American dream all the way to Hollywood. Her daughter recognized what she never would. Anne Tricony had been one of the lucky few to make it. *Though*, Holly thought to herself, *Anne hadn't been lucky running across Tres Johnson.* Then again, Holly wouldn't be around to ponder that; so, Holly supposed that it was a dumb thing to think about it. Holly wasn't a big fan of circular reasoning. It made her brain hurt trying to find the answer mathematically. She'd leave questions of the universe to the psychologists.

Suddenly, Holly realized she'd been standing at the gate for three minutes. What was she, a chicken? Holly shook her head. No, she had never been that. Taking a deep breath, Holly pushed the buzzer on the side of the gate.

"I'm sorry, little girl," said an irritated voice on the other end, "but Mrs. Tricony is not available for fans at this moment." With that, the sound on the line went dead.

Holly smiled at the guard's stupidity and rang again.

"Yes?" said the guard, even more irritated this time.

"Hello, you must be new. My name is Holly Johnson. I'm Anne's daughter."

"And I'm the Queen of England. Now buzz off, kid, before I have to come down there." The line cut out.

Now this was getting annoying. Holly rang again for the third time.

"Listen kid . . ."

"Wait a moment, sir. Before you say anything else, I would like to ask you one question. What if I am the daughter of Anne Tricony? Your very job could hinge on the way you act in response to this; therefore, if you have an ounce of common sense, you will go inside and tell my mother I'm here. The choice is up to you, of course." The line on the other end was silent, not dead. The man was obviously considering his options. On one hand, he could just call security and let them deal with her, but then again, there was always the chance that Holly was who she said she was. In that case, he could very well lose his job if he left Mrs. Tricony's daughter standing outside on the pavement, in the rain no less. Holly could almost hear the wheels slowly turning in his head.

"Hold on," he grumbled. Holly heard him cursing her in the back round. *No wonder he couldn't get a better job than this.* Holly knew that she had been rude, but she figured the guard associated snobbery with wealth; therefore, if she acted like a snob, as opposed to an intimidated teenager, then he might believe she was who she said she was. All the same, Holly felt her conscience creep in on her. *The man probably doesn't know that Anne has any kids, and people do play pranks all the time.* Holly tried to soothe her conscience as the gates opened. *Well, my plan worked, didn't it? What would Natasha think?* Holly bitterly reminded herself it didn't matter what Natasha thought because she was dead. Look where kindness had gotten her. From now on, Holly wouldn't care about anyone. That way, no one could hurt her again.

The inside of the house was like the exterior, except for Anne's powder room, which was more like its owner: messy, disorganized, and fun. Her mother greeted her at the door.

"Holly! Darling! What a pleasant surprise. I mean, this is a surprise, isn't it? You weren't scheduled to come here, were you?" Holly could see the anxious look on her mother's face. Anne, being herself, thought she might have forgotten her daughter was scheduled to come into town.

Holly forced herself not to roll her eyes. "Yes, Mother, this is a surprise."

"Oh good, you had me worried there for a moment." Anne's shoulders relaxed. "So are you on some sort of holiday?"

"No, actually, I'm not. I ran away."

"Oh," Anne said, not knowing what else to say. What could she say to this girl who looked like her but had never been able to understand? "Well," Anne continued on, not quite as bubbly as before, "you're welcome, of course, to stay here as long as you want."

"Really?" Anne saw her daughter's face light up and couldn't help but feel a tinge of contentment at her child's happiness. At that moment, Anne would have done anything to keep her daughter smiling.

"Of course you can stay," Anne said brightly.

Holly felt like two tons of rock had just been lifted off her shoulders. Maybe she could trust her mother after all. "Um, Mom, can I talk to you about something? It's about why I ran away. I'd really like to talk to somebody."

Anne didn't hear the desperate pleading in her daughter's voice. Her ears had never been attuned for it. "No, actually you caught me as I was just heading out. I have to go to one of those parties Robert makes me attend. I wish I didn't have to," Anne sighed loudly as if to convey to the heavy load she was carrying, "but you know how important it is for me to keep up my image. It's so difficult to stay on top with all of these young actors and actresses today. Not that they have any talent, of course. All they do is smile for the camera and let their stunt doubles do all of the work. Quality acting is a thing of the past, my dear. You on the other hand, would do very well, I think, especially being my daughter."

"Yes, you've told me," Holly responded curtly, "and my answer is still the same. No."

Anne was hurt by the coldness in Holly's tone. She thought that things had been going so well too. Anne didn't realize that the ice in Holly's voice was her way of covering up pain. Though Holly wouldn't admit it, even to herself, she wanted a mother. She'd almost had one in Natasha, but even that image had been brutally snatched from her. She wanted someone to confide in, but now she realized she had no one.

Breakfast the next day was anything but a cheerful occurrence. It looked like it was going to rain again, but the clouds only darkened the atmosphere. Holly was first downstairs. By the time she had finished her second bowl of Rice Krispies, Anne was up. Her mother yawned a good morning to her daughter, but didn't say anything else until she had her coffee. "I spoke to your to father last night."

Holly let her spoon fall into her bowl, splashing milk everywhere. "What?"

Anne stiffened. She hated confrontations. "Now don't get angry, dear. Tres is your father, and he needed to know where you were." Mistaking Holly's silence for understanding, Anne continued, "We discussed the matter and decided that you should go home and work things out with him."

"I don't believe this," Holly said mostly to herself and then looked up at Anne. "I thought you said I could stay as long as I wanted." Holly searched her mother's eyes looking for some sign that Anne would keep her promise this once. "I'm not ready to go back to him."

"Oh yes, I did say that," Anne was starting to get nervous at the way her daughter was looking at her. Was she actually hurt? *No, that can't be it. Holly's never liked staying here in California with me.* Anne chalked it up to teenage rebellion. "Well, Holly, I'm sorry, but you'll be coming back here for the summer. Then you can tell me what's on your mind. By then, I'm sure you'll be past all of this, and you and Tres will be friends again."

"Friends! We've never even been father and daughter."

"But I thought that . . ."

Holly cut her off, "How is it that I'm related to you? You are quite possibly the densest person on this planet! I hate you, and I never want to see you again!" Holly screamed at her mother and shoved away from the table. Her chair hit the ground with a loud crash. "From now on, consider me dead to you, just like Natasha is to me." Holly saw a questioning crease form between Anne's brows. "Who is she? She's the one person on this whole earth who actually cared about me, and now she's dead! Why is she dead? Well, let's see," Holly's whole body started to shake with anger and hurt, "there's this guy named Albert who tried to rape me in my own house. He pushed Natasha down the staircase when she tried to help me. She broke her neck on the way down."

Holly put her palms on the table to steady herself. She leaned forward and stared into Anne's eyes, which were starting to water. "You see, Father was downstairs with his guests; he was too busy to come to my rescue, just like you're too busy listen to me. And by the way, he isn't pressing charges on that creep. That would hurt his business reputation. So now I'm here at the last place I could think of, the last place where I thought I'd belong. I'm now talking to the last person who I thought might care about me. I don't know why I thought you gave a darn about me. I'm just your daughter, but in these last few hours, I've realized something. Either you're too stupid or you're too selfish to raise a child.

"Well, you should be excited because I'm not a child anymore. My childhood was ripped from me while you were at some stupid party on the other side of the world." Holly's voice broke, but she didn't stop. "I hope someday you realize that all your fans and all the people who you *think* admire you, don't care about you at all. Maybe then you'll have a tiny inkling of the way you have made me feel every day of my life!" Holly started sobbing so hard that she fell into a ball on the ground. Anne didn't know what to do. She walked over to her and tried to give her daughter a hug.

"No!" Holly pushed Anne away even as she wanted to hold on, "Don't try to be a mother now. I already told you. I don't need one anymore." Afraid she'd give into the temptation of going into her mother's arms, Holly ran from the dinning room and out the front door. She didn't know where she was going. All she knew was that she had to get away, far away.

Holly ran and ran until she finally collapsed under an old tree. She'd never felt so lost and alone before. Maybe she always had been alone but just didn't realize. After a while, Holly looked around and noticed she had no clue where she was. She had no money, no cell phone, and no way to get back. Her photographic memory didn't save her this time because Holly had been too emotional to watch where she was going. As if on cue, Holly heard the angry call of thunder. She looked overhead and saw the sun was completely hidden by dark clouds that were turning blacker by the minute. *Perfect,* Holly felt the first drops of what looked like another storm. Sure enough, a few minutes later it started to pour. There she was—lost, penniless, and drenched. Not wanting to add electrocution to her list of woes, Holly got out from underneath the tree and started walking in the direction from which she thought she'd come.

After about ten minutes of walking in the rain, Holly was exhausted in every way humanly possible. Out of the corner of her eye, she saw a beaten up old Cadillac slow down and stop. There was a person inside, a man she thought, but she couldn't tell with the lighting. He, as it turned out to be, rolled down his window and called out to her. Holly walked warily over to his window.

"Do you need a lift?" Holly estimated he was around sixty. He was balding and looked like your average grandfather and, therefore, harmless. Was it worth the risk? *Well,* Holly figured, *I'll probably die out here anyway. At least if I get in the car, I will have some chance of living through this. Besides, if he turns out to be a serial killer, then I guess I won't have to see my mother or father again.* Deciding it was a win-win situation, Holly got into the car and slammed the door. She secretly hoped she would be alive to open it again.

"Where do you want me to take you?"

"187 Pinefield, please." Holly stared at her car window and watched the rain pellets zip across the glass. She also noticed a police badge on the floorboard of the car. *So the guy is a cop, or he killed one and hid the body in the trunk.* Holly gulped. Maybe this wasn't such a good idea.

After a while the man asked, "What were you doing out in the rain?"

Holly sighed. *What do I have to lose?* Holly proceeded to tell the stranger everything that had happened to her in the past week. When Holly finished, she felt better. The man had actually listened to her, and he didn't seem to condemn her for what happened. He just seemed sad. Holly didn't want him to feel sorry for her; she was having a hard enough time not doing that herself. So she asked him a question that had been running around in the back of her mind.

"Why did you stop for me?"

"It's what Jesus would have done," he said simply.

"Who?" Holly searched her memory banks. The name seemed familiar. "You mean that guy who died on the cross and everything."

"And everything," the man repeated as if he found her statement amusing. "Yes, He's the one."

"Why do you want to be like Him?" Holly was utterly bewildered.

"Because He's like a dad to me."

"But the guy's dead."

The man shrugged, "He's alive to me."

It still didn't make sense. "But even if He is alive, why do you want to be like Him? I don't want to be like my father."

"That's because your father, if you don't mind me saying so, is a stupid idiot who doesn't realize the precious gift he's been given."

"What gift?"

"You. Children are gifts from God. Some people, unfortunately, don't realize that, and it's the children who suffer."

"You talk about God like He's real." Holly hadn't meant to say that aloud, but the man didn't seem offended.

"He is real, and He loves you."

"If He loved me, then why did all of this happen to me?" Holly asked bitterly.

"He didn't do this to you, and, honey, even though you can't see Him, He's hurting because of all of this too."

"That's my house." She pointed it out to him.

"That's not a house; that's a mansion."

Holly smiled at that and then asked another question. "How can you believe in something you can't see?"

The man smiled again. He had obviously been asked this question before. "Let me ask you this. Hasn't it been the things, the people you *can* see, who have let you down?"

Holly thought about it for a moment and then nodded her head.

"Let me ask you another question. Do you ever worry that the air you breathe or the gravity that keeps you tied to earth will fail you?"

"No, of course not."

"Then you have already put your faith in what you cannot see, simply because you know it's there and has never failed before. I can't see my God, but I've put my life in His hands because I know He's real, and He has never let me down."

Surprisingly, it all made sense, too much sense. *I'm losing it. Maybe I have a fever or something.* "Well, that sounds like a great thing for you, but I don't think it's for me. Thank you again for the lift. I'll never forget you."

"Anytime, and remember this: You will never be too bad for God to love you."

"Um, thanks." *I wish that were true.* Holly felt something stirring inside her, but she violently shoved it away. The man watched as Holly ran through the gate and out of sight.

"You have big plans for that one, don't you, God?" The man smiled. He had known the answer to that question the second the sopping wet girl sat down in his car. The wind roared, the rain fell, and the thunder blasted. The Heavenly choir was tuning their instruments. The music was about to begin.

chapter four

Holly's plane was scheduled to fly out the following day. From the moment Holly had walked in out of the rain, until the hour she had to leave, Holly had avoided her mother like the plague. It was not until she was walking out the door that Anne finally summoned the courage to speak to her daughter. "Holly, wait . . ." Anne said from the top of the staircase. She was afraid to move closer.

Holly turned at the sound of her mother's voice. She forced her face to remain solemn and void of all emotion. It was difficult because Holly could tell Anne had been crying, yet Anne's voice didn't falter when she spoke, "Holly, I'm sorry I wasn't a good mother. I really am." Anne searched her daughter's blank face, hoping she wouldn't find hate.

Holly didn't feel hatred. In fact, she didn't feel anything. It was as if her emotions had been sucked from her. She answered her mother with perfect ease, the kind that came from the complete separation of mind from the heart. Yet despite her will to stop it, something inside of her was moved. "I'm sorry too. I would have liked the chance to love you, but I never had that."

Anne had a lost expression in her eyes. "I never thought you wanted it. You've always been so much smarter." Anne stared up at the ceiling, looking for the right words. "I didn't think you needed me as a mother."

"Intelligence has nothing to do with love. Are babies smarter than the mothers who love them?"

Tears rolled down Anne's face. For the first time, she began to grasp the huge mistake she'd made and what she'd lost. "Is it too late now?"

"I don't know." Holly felt like her heart was a lone soldier facing an army of archers. How much more was she supposed to take? "We'll see when I come back for the summer."

"I'd like that." Anne walked down the stairs, and for the first time in Holly's memory, she took Holly to the airport herself. They were far from being mother and daughter, but it was a start. Holly wasn't ready to become an optimist, but maybe there was hope in this confusing world after all.

Holly had an hour and a half delay in Chicago, so she decided to eat lunch and kill time. It was either lunch, or she could stare at the ugly carpet in the terminal and listen to screaming kids. Holly liked kids, just not enough to sit through twenty of their temper tantrums. Lunch was a much better option.

It was twelve o'clock, and every place was packed. Holly hated lines with a passion, but she braved the hoards for a Big Mac. There wasn't a vacant table in the whole cave-like eating area, but she saw a girl around her age sitting by herself at a table off in the corner. Holly walked over to her. "Mind if I sit here?" The girl looked up at her and motioned toward the seat. Holly was in one of her rare talkative moods, so she decided to break the ice. "Where are you heading?"

It took the girl a moment to answer, as she tried to swallow a big bite of her hamburger. "Back to Salem, you?"

"Me too! What school do you go to?"

"Lakeland Christian Academy."

"I've never heard of that before."

The girl just shrugged and smiled. "Oh, well it's a pretty small school. Where do you go?"

"I'm home schooled." Holly wanted to find out how old the girl really was. She had never been very good at guessing ages. "What grade are you in?"

"Junior year, you?"

"Technically, I'm a sophomore, but I'm thinking of going into my senior year at a real school in the fall."

"Wow, you must be smart. What did you get on your SAT?"

"A 1560. What about you?"

The girl crossed her arms and pretended to glare. "I'm not telling. By the way, I'm extremely jealous." Holly laughed as the girl continued. "So how long have you lived in Oregon?"

"Oregon? The state?"

Both girls stared at each other confused, but then the girl started to laugh. "I think we're talking about a different Salem. I live in Salem, Oregon. It's the capital."

"Oh," Holly laughed, "I live in Massachusetts. Sorry about the mix-up."

"It's okay. All the time I have people ask me if I live near the courthouse where the Salem witch trials were held."

"What do you tell them?"

"I ask them what their definition of 'near' is."

Holly choked on her drink when she started laughing. That made the other girl laugh even harder. Holly couldn't help but wish that she did live in Oregon. She liked this girl. "What's your name?"

"You have to promise not to laugh."

Holly crossed her heart. "I promise." The girl still looked hesitant. "Now you have to tell me," Holly told her.

"Okay, my parents were major hippies, back in the Stoned Age. So they named me Sunflower," she whispered. "I go by Sunny."

Holly had to bite her lip to keep from breaking her promise. It really was a bizarre name. "Well, Sunny, my name's Holly, but I wasn't named after a plant like you were. Unfortunately, it's worse."

Sunny leaned forward in anticipation. "Spill."

"Well, my mother's an actress, so…she named me Hollywood. You're probably one of the handful of people who know that." Sunny burst out laughing, and some of the people around them turned and stared. "Hey," Holly complained and turned red, "I didn't laugh at your name."

Holly and Sunny stood up to throw away their trash. It was time to leave. "You didn't warn me first. Well, Hollywood, it was nice to meet you."

Holly jokingly glared at the girl and said goodbye and good riddance. That just got another laugh out of the girl as she walked off in the opposite direction and out of Holly's life.

When Holly arrived home, she had to sit through a lecture on the proper behavior of a young lady. It was torture to listen as Torie prattled on about upholding the family name—blah, blah, blah. She did her best to ignore her and count the panes in the stained-glass window. There were two hundred and ninety-six pieces. Holly's fingers itched to superglue four more sections of glass onto the magnificent piece to make it an even three hundred. She was weird like that.

The next day was much more eventful. She received an e-mail from her father saying, "You are to be downstairs at four. Victoria, you, and I are having our family picture taken." Holly stared at the impersonal words on the screen. *That's it? No, 'I was worried about you,' or even a 'Never do that again'?* Holly e-mailed her father back saying, "It's obvious that you don't think of me as anything but your 'biological offspring.' So why do you want me to be in your family picture? Isn't that a bit hypocritical?"

Prompt as always, her father returned her e-mail in less than fifteen minutes. "Your appearance adds to the presentation of this family. Don't e-mail me again. I have too much work to do to keep responding to your juvenile insolence. If you have anymore questions, then ask Victoria." Holly shouldn't have been shocked and definitely shouldn't have been hurt by the message, but logic did nothing to halt the blows to her heart. *I'm beautiful. That's all that matters to him.* Holly took a deep breath. It was time for her to let go of any fantasy of having a real father. Holly glanced at the ticking clock on the desk. She only had five hours before she had to be downstairs. It was enough time, Holly surmised, to change her entire future.

Holly descended the stairs at precisely four o'clock. Her grandmother looked up with her usual dour expression, but then her mouth dropped. All that came out was a high-pitched squeak. Holly's long, beautiful hair was now a thumb's length. It was up in spikes and her right eyebrow sported a gold ring. Holly's outfit was nothing more than ragged tennis shoes, guy's shorts, and the T-shirt she'd bought in Chicago. Her only regret was that she hadn't been able to wear a baseball cap and show off her new hairdo at the same time.

"What have you done?" Tres roared. It was the first time Holly could remember him yelling. It unnerved her more than she cared to admit, but Holly had enough of her mother in her to act unmoved.

Holly couldn't resist baiting him further. "What? You don't like it? It's the very latest." Holly put on her most bewildered, innocent face and carefully patted her spikes. Her father looked like he was about to explode, and even better, Victoria was still speechless. If she had any luck at all, the old bag would have a heart attack.

"You are not, under any circumstances, coming with us for the photo shoot," Tres said in a tone that would make a graduate from Harvard Law quiver, but Holly could duplicate her father's tone down to the last inflection.

Holly stared at her father's reddened face and simply shrugged. "That was the plan. Oh, yes, and since I have decided to continue to look this way, I can only assume that I will not be invited to anymore of your parties. Is that correct?"

Holly could hear her father's teeth grinding. After what seemed like an eternity, his jaw loosened enough to speak. "You will not look like this by the time I come back."

She had him right where she wanted. "Is that so?" Holly raised her pierced eyebrow. "I suppose you will have to choose then."

"Between what?" Tres' eyes narrowed.

Holly gracefully ran her hand along the banister. "Either I will no longer be required to be your little trophy daughter, or I will go to the media and tell them everything that happened. I can just picture the headlines now. 'Business Tycoon, Tres Johnson, Attempts to Cover Up Child Molestation and Murder.' " That got another squeak out of Victoria. Holly could see her father paling, but years of business had done its job on him. He was not ready to cave.

"I do not have time to listen to your childish ravings."

Holly almost smiled at how easily she could anticipate him. "Oh, yes, Father, I know how busy you are. Since you didn't want me to e-mail you again today, I faxed your office a list of my 'childish' demands. I know that you are in a hurry, so I'll make this quite succinct. Either you agree, in writing, to every single one of my requests, or I go to the police and then to the media, in that order." Holly looked straight into her father's eyes, daring him to call her bluff.

He did. "You can't prove anything."

"Let's not play these games, Father. We're both smarter than this. The media won't need anymore proof than my word, and all the police will need to do is an autopsy on Natasha's body to prove you lied to them. At best, you will walk away with a huge fine and an irreparable name."

Tres looked at Holly with such loathing that her stomach clenched. "What do you want?"

It was difficult, but Holly was able to hold back a victory smile. "You can read the list, Father, but at the top is for you to quietly give up legal guardianship to Anne. Oh, and by the way, I've decided to go to college in the fall of 2004." Holly sent them her brightest smile and glanced at the old grandfather clock. "Oh, look at the time. You don't want to be late for that important photo shoot. Be beautiful." Holly blew a kiss their way and then glided up the stairs and out of sight.

Holly looked at herself in the mirror for the hundredth time that night. She looked horrendous, but she'd never felt better. Cutting off her hair had been her way breaking off the chains her father had wound around her so tightly her entire life. Now when she walked by people, they didn't look her way. They just kept on walking, and she loved every moment of it. There would be no more pickup lines or blunt staring. She could just fade off into the crowd, which was exactly where she wanted to be. Yet even in her elation, Albert's voice floated though her head like a bad dream. *It's the price you pay for being beautiful.* Holly sent her reflection a forced smile. *Not anymore!*

chapter five

Eighteen months later…
Austin, Texas

Sunflower White had the confidence of an alumnus as she stepped onto the campus of the University of Texas. This was where she'd been heading her entire life! Unlike most freshmen at UT, the fact that she was attending one of the largest universities in the world didn't intimidate her. Sunny felt like the campus was alive. There was no place like it. UT was crammed together like an odd jigsaw puzzle, yet somehow the old Victorian buildings meshed perfectly with the new skyscrapers.

Sunny's joy didn't dim even as she walked around the overwhelmingly large grounds to find her dorm. Her stuff, along with her family, wouldn't arrive until the next day. She had wanted to drive down alone to get her first taste of freedom. Her parents trusted her, and to Sunny, that was a gift unto itself. So, armed with her backpack, Sunny roamed the campus streets. She didn't try very hard to find her dorm, eventually running across it. The dorm, like everything else at UT, had class, and Sunflower White admired class. Excitement bubbled up in her throat as she mounted the steps to her room. She hoped that her roommate was there. She had been dying to meet her all summer. Since none of her girl friends had decided to come to UT, she'd let the school do the picking and prayed God would put her with the person with whom He wanted her to be.

Sunny smirked when she remembered her friends' reaction to her college decision. "Texas? Sunny, you're majoring in psychology, not cow herding." Sunny had just laughed at them. Let them think Texas was all open terrain and the nearest McDonald's was a horse ride away. She knew the days when a man could stake his claim on the land for free and rely on a handshake contract were long gone. Sunny smiled when she remembered the "Don't Mess With Texas" bumper stickers she'd seen on half of the cars. The land might have been tamed and turned into suburbia, but the people still fiercely held onto their heritage. That's what Sunny loved about them. Where else, other than Texas, could you find a Yale scholar who said "y'all" and thought boots and a cowboy hat was the eternal fashion statement?

Sunny finally reached her room. All thoughts of Texas and its breed of people flew from her mind as she pulled out her key. Well, actually, it was one of those horrible little computer cards, but Sunny noted optimistically that it did have the picture of a key on it.

The first thing she noticed when she entered the dark room was smoke. The smog covered the room like a dirty blanket, and soon Sunny caught sight of the culprit. What was it?

What could have passed as an alien life form sat on the dorm bed nearest to the window. "It" had dark hair that stuck up in the front and was plastered down in the back. There was a tacky bow on top of all the gel that led Sunny to presume that "it" was a girl.

She was wearing shorts that went down to her knees, a sweat shirt, and black and white make up. This could not be her roommate. She looked like a gothic Statue of Liberty. The unsightly creature glared up at her. "What are you looking at?"

It speaks. "I'm looking at you." Sunny's gaze drifted from the girl's scowl to down to the cigarette in her hand. "You're not supposed to smoke in here."

It shrugged. Breaking the school rules before school even started didn't seem to bother her much. "I disabled the smoke alarm."

A smart, gothic Statue of Liberty. "Are you an engineering major?"

"No, linguistics."

"Lin...what?"

Even in the dim lighting, Sunny could see the girl roll her eyes. "You wouldn't understand."

Smart alec. "Try me."

"Linguistics is the scientific study of language and its structure, including the study of morphology, syntax, phonetics, and semantics."

Note to self: look up syntax and semantics. "Did you come up with that definition all on your own?"

Medusa smiled at her, "No, actually, it's located on the seven hundred and eighty first page in *The Oxford American College Dictionary,* the 2002 edition."

"Thanks, I'll remember that the next time I need to look it up. So do you memorize dictionaries as a hobby? I collect stamps myself." Sunny's ill attempt at humor only got her the silent treatment. *How many days until Christmas?*

Liberty girl caught Sunny staring at her. "Is there something on my face?" she asked with yet another scowl.

"Yes, actually, I've counted two earrings so far, but I can't see the other side of your face. By the way, my name's Sunny." Well, that got a reaction from her. It was bizarre because the girl looked shocked. She stared at Sunny so intensely that for the first time since she'd stepped onto the campus, Sunny was uncomfortable.

The girl pushed off her bed and walked over to her. Maybe it was just Sunny's imagination, but the girl's face seemed to soften.

The girl stopped walking once she was only a few inches away from Sunny's face. "My name's Rose." Saying nothing else, she walked out of the room, leaving Sunny with a very strange first impression. *What was that all about?* She thought to herself as she opened a window to let some of the blinding smoke out. Sunny remembered a famous quote spoken by some dead guy. "What is in a name?" *I don't know,* thought Sunny, *but I'm going to find out.* Speaking of names, how strange that Liberty girl had such a beautiful one.

I can't believe it's her! Holly looked at herself in the bathroom mirror. Of course Sunny hadn't recognized Holly, and who could blame her? Holly knew what she looked like. In fact, Holly had worked hard to look the way she did and hadn't regretted it, until now. Holly didn't know why Sunflower had ever had such a lasting impression on her, but she'd never forgotten the friendly girl from the airport. Holly could have kicked herself. Now Sunny was her roommate, and Holly had done everything she could to make Sunny revolted by her. It was all part of her brilliant plan to get a room to herself. She thought that the smoking, which had made her so sick she'd thrown up, and her outrageous getup would force any sane person to run screaming in the opposite direction.

Holly mentally groaned as she washed off her makeup, something she hadn't worn in months. The atrocious black and white paint whirled down the drain. She started to dry her face with a paper towel, and it was only then that she remembered to take out her fake earrings. When Holly had moved in with her mother, Anne had begged her to take out her eyebrow ring, and Holly had never had the guts to get another piercing. She hated needles and earring guns. As for her outfit, well, that was normal, and her hair was about two inches longer than it had been a year and a half ago, but without the right hair cut, her head looked like a mop.

Holly took one last look in the mirror. She knew her face was more beautiful than it had been when she was sixteen, but the clothing she wore was a huge turn off, which was the way Holly wanted it. Yet why did she dread going back to her dorm? *This is stupid. Even if she did remember you, she'd be just like everyone else. You're better off not having a friend. They never last, remember?* Holly sighed and trudged back to her dorm, resolved to get rid of Sunflower once and for all.

"I'm telling you, Josh. She's the roommate from hell. Seriously, I think that she might be the anti-Christ."

"Oh no! Do you think we should tell someone?"

"Josh! This isn't funny!" Sunny tried to hit her friend over the head with a magazine, but he blocked. Her eyes narrowed, and Josh sent her a superior look.

"Sorry, I rarely get the privilege to see you this worked up." When Sunny continued to glare at him, he shook his head in fake disapproval. "Most people don't get under your skin so easily, Sun."

Sunny clenched her jaw, "You're doing a good job of it."

"Yes, but I've known you since you were in diapers. So I've had lots of practice."

"Josh, we're the same age. Why is it that you always mention the fact that I was in diapers and never say a word about yourself?"

"Because it gets on your nerves when I word it that way."

Sunny shook her head at him and tried not to smile. "How is it that we're still friends?"

"I'm just too adorable."

"Too idiotic is more like it."

Josh put his hand over his heart and gasped, "You cut me to the quick, milady."

Sunny laughed. It felt so good after her past week of torture. What would she do without Josh? Sunny leaned over and hugged him. That was the way Holly saw them when she walked into the café. So far, she'd managed to execute her plan perfectly. She threw her stuff all over Sunny's side of the room. She played her radio so loudly that Sunny was forced to read her precious Bible somewhere else. Holly deliberately set her alarm for four o'clock in the morning, and best of all, she made sure the room always reeked of smoke. Of course, Holly didn't smoke. She just set the cigarettes on fire and let them burn. As long as Sunny didn't know, it worked out just fine. There was still one little problem. The girl wouldn't crack! After two weeks of waking up at four in the morning and breathing nothing but smoke, Holly realized she was either going to have to crank up the intensity in her little war or else surrender. That was why she was here. It was perfect; Sunny was snuggled up with her boyfriend.

"Hey, Sunflower!" Heads turned at Holly's raised voice.

Josh and Sunny jumped at the sudden noise and smashed heads.

"Hi," Sunny said, rubbing her head and looking very sorry to see her there. When Holly just stood there staring at the two of them, Sunny figured that at least one of them might as well be polite. Obviously, that person would not be her roommate. "Um, this is my friend, Joshua Timberlaigh. Josh, this is my roommate, Rose." Holly looked at Josh for the first time, and her mouth almost dropped. He was gorgeous! It took her about a split second to get over that strange observation and remind herself she didn't like males in general. They were the source of all the world's problems. *Well, them—along with stupid roommates.*

"Nice to meet you." Josh said, taking in the girl's appearance. From a distance, he might have thought that "she" was a "he." Yet despite the girl's masculine clothing, there was something about her that screamed "*Look at me if you dare!*" Josh didn't know if he dared. Girls like this one didn't like guys staring at them. It's what made them so mysterious—and dangerous—Josh reminded himself as he felt himself melting under the heat of her glare.

Not wanting to waste any more time with "the lower species," Holly turned her frowning face towards Sunny. "I told you to keep your junk off my side of the room." By now, everyone in the café was staring at them, anxiously anticipating a fight. It was a great way to liven up Monday morning.

"What! None of my stuff is on your side."

"Not now," Holly said with an icy tone. Holly took off her backpack and poured its contents onto the table. Out fell dozens of pads, tampons, and condoms. No one could tell who was redder, Sunny or Josh. Both just stared at the table in horror and disbelief. Josh jumped out of his seat when a tampon fell into his lap. Everyone started laughing. Everyone except Sunny, Josh, and Holly. Holly leaned over and whispered into Sunny's ear. "Get out of my room. This is nothing compared to what I can do." Holly sent Josh a cocky smile and then walked out of the café very pleased with herself.

"You're right," Josh told Sunny when the laughter died down, "she is the anti-Christ. What are you going to do?"

"What she least expects."

Josh's eyes didn't leave the mountain of mayhem on the table. "And what's that?"

"I'll be her friend."

Josh looked shocked. "Are you insane? The girl just humiliated you." *And me.*

"What would Jesus do, Josh?"

"Zap her with a lightning bolt."

"Josh . . ."

He held his hands up in surrender. "Okay, okay. He'd do exactly what you're doing. I just hope you know what you're up against."

"*I can do all things through Christ who strengthens me.*" Sunny quoted with a smirk.

"Don't you want to get her back?" Josh asked as he continued to stare at the table. He certainly wanted to get her back.

"Don't you get it, Josh? If I'm nice to her, it will drive her nuts. She won't know what to think."

Josh raised one eyebrow. "You were singing a different tune earlier."

"I know, but now I'm curious."

"About what?"

"Why she dresses and acts the way she does."

"Maybe she likes it."

"You really are a guy, aren't you?"

"Guilty," Josh admitted jokingly.

Sunny shook her head at him. "No normal female wants to be unattractive. Something happened to her to make her so violently opposed to looking good. I want to know what happened to her and why she's so determined to make me not like her."

"I knew you choosing to become a shrink was a mistake."

"Very funny," Sunny said dryly and then sent her friend a mischievous grin, "and by the way, I think she likes you."

That got Josh's attention off the table. "What?"

"Didn't you see the way she looked at you?"

"Yeah, like I was a two-headed dragon waiting to eat her." Josh glared at Sunny, willing her to shut up. Unfortunately, he'd never been able to intimidate his friend who happened to be half his size. It was degrading.

"When she first saw you, I thought she was going to start drooling," Sunny told him matter-of-factly.

"Great," Josh said with fake enthusiasm. "You know, Sunny, I really appreciate you trying on this whole matchmaker hat, but could you please find someone who's less likely to crucify me?"

"I'm not trying to set you up. I'm just telling you what I saw." Sunny smiled sweetly at him.

"Well, what I saw was a very ticked off roommate dumping tons of very scary looking things on our table. Objects, may I remind you, which are still here and causing attention." Josh looked around the room wishing everyone would disappear.

"Is that your way of changing the subject?"

"Yes, that and trying to get you to remove these little neon things from my sight."

"They're called pads."

Josh made a face. After he helped Sunny clean up the mess, he headed off to biology. On the way there, he couldn't stop thinking about Rose's eyes. They'd been so blue and so—sad. Josh mentally shook himself. He was sounding like Sunny, and while he knew his friend was right, Josh wasn't ready to let the girl off the hook. *I mean, come on. The chick dropped tampons on me.* Josh shuddered and tried to squash the feeling that the girl needed him. Chivalry was for beautiful maidens-in-distress, not the Wicked Witch of the West.

It took awhile for Josh to find his class. He loved UT, but it was so huge that a person needed a map to get anywhere. Unfortunately, directions had never been his strong point. Josh kept on reminding himself that everyone got lost the first day, but when he opened the door to his classroom, he found out he'd been wrong, dead wrong. It looked like every desk was filled, all three hundred of them. Stupidly, Josh didn't catch the door as it slammed back into place. Three hundred pairs of eyes turned to stare at him. Josh saw a hand waving him over to the left side of the room.

"Thanks for saving me a seat, Bret," Josh whispered and slid down into his desk as far as he could go.

"No problem." Bret smirked at him.

"What did I miss?"

Bret yawned to convey his utter boredom. "Oh, nothing much, just Professor Vine's longwinded speech about the difference between a college graduate and a wannabe, video-playing dropout."

"What's that?"

"A wannabe shows up late on the first day."

Josh paled and Bret laughed aloud. A few eggheads turned

around and glared. One girl even had the nerve to shush them. Bret made a face at her back and then turned to Josh. "Dude," Bret whispered, "you are so gullible."

"Bret!" Josh hissed. He hated it when people tricked him like that. He really was too gullible, and Bret loved taking advantage of his mistrust deficit.

"Man, everyone knows professors at big schools don't give a hoot if their students show up or not." Bret elbowed him. "So why were you late? Were you talking to some hot chick, or did you just sleep in?"

"I got lost."

"Not a chick then?" Bret sighed and shook his head. "I can't believe we're friends."

Josh remembered his conversation with Sunny. "I've been hearing that a lot lately."

"What?" Bret whispered.

"Nothing." Josh didn't want to talk anymore. He just wanted to listen to the professor and zone out on life. Unfortunately, Bret had a different idea.

"College should get this 'all work, no play' attitude sucked from you. So how many hot girls have you talked to today?" Bret stroked the beginnings of what Josh would have called "peach fuzz" on his chin. "I'm thinking none, except for Sunny, but she doesn't count. She's like your sister, which is also pathetic."

Josh glared at Bret and then tried to pay attention to the professor, who, as it turned out, happened to be the most boring man God had ever had the will to create. Josh blamed the professor's monotone voice and Bret's teasing when he started to think about blue eyes instead of the importance of cytoplasm.

chapter six

That night when Sunny walked into her room, she was relieved she wasn't hit with a blast of smoke. Holly was sitting on her bed hunched over her laptop and typing at a hundred miles per minute. The typing abruptly ceased once she realized Sunny had entered the room. Holly looked up and stared at her, waiting for Sunny's reaction. What Sunny first saw in her eyes caught her off guard. Was there something hidden beneath her contempt. Was it loneliness Sunny saw?

Before Sunny had a chance to respond, the look turned into disinterest, but Sunny would not be put off so easily. She walked over to Holly's bed. "What are you typing?"

Holly shifted her position on the bed to where Sunny couldn't see her screen. It was a subtle move, but Sunny noticed it nonetheless. "It's none of your business," she said with a scowl that seemed to have taken up permanent residence on her face.

Sunny smirked. "Interesting topic choice."

"That's lame," Holly said as she continued to glare at Sunny. How dare she try to make her laugh.

"I've yet to hear you come up with better," Sunny pulled an empty trash bag out of her backpack and shoved everything Holly had carelessly thrown onto her bed inside of it. Holly just watched apathetically while Sunny tied the bag and walked over to the widow. "It's always so smoky in here. By the way, did you know smoking's bad for your health?"

"Like you care if I live or die," Holly mumbled almost incoherently.

Sunny just smiled, "Actually, I do. Who would I have to fight with?" Sunny put the trash bag up on the window sill and looked down. They were three stories up.

"You wouldn't dare," Holly said, when she realized Sunny's intention.

"You see, roomy, that's the problem between you and me. The two of us are on completely different wavelengths, and therefore, we don't seem to understand each other. So allow me to tell you a little something about myself. I never back down on a dare, and if you push me, I push harder." Sunny shoved the trash bag out the window. It burst open on impact. Holly jumped off her bed and started yelling at Sunny. She couldn't believe Sunny had just thrown her stuff out the window.

"Oh, I'm sorry," Sunny said innocently, "did you still want that?"

Holly tried her best to calm herself. "Get out of my room now," she said steadily.

Sunny crossed her arms over her chest. "News flash, babe, it's my room too. So you're just going to have to live with that, but I will leave—this time. See you later, roomy."

"Goodbye and good riddance!" Holly yelled at her as the door quietly snapped shut.

Where have I heard that before? Sunny turned back around, but not in time. The door was already closed. Sunny racked her

brains as she walked to the library. Something about her roommate seemed familiar—but what?

The main library stood regally in the middle of the immense
campus. If anyone had asked Sunny, she would have said that this
was the heart of the UT. This was where generations of young
adults had grown to maturity. Adjoined to it were other student fa-
cilities, but the sacred spirit of literature carried itself throughout
the entire building. It was here where new students checked in, and
it was here where old students said their last goodbyes.

Sunny walked into the lobby and turned to her right toward
one of the studying areas. The room was filled with tables, books,
and students, all of which were working together for a higher goal.
She was tempted to look around at the books on other floors, but
she diligently sat down, ripped open her calculus book, and attempted to work some of the problems. She might as well have
been translating ancient Greek.

Sunny thought about her calculus teacher with faint disgust.
He was a nerdy little man, who spoke primarily in mathematical
jargon. Not that Sunny could really tell, since the man lectured at
the whiteboard. She sighed and shook her head. Her only consola-
tion was she was not the only one in her class who wore a blank face
throughout the terrifying lecture. Some of the other students had
seemed ready to cry. Sunny looked around the library and thought
she recognized someone from class. It was a girl with brown, curly
hair. Sunny took a chance and tapped the girl on the shoulder.
"Hey, do you have calculus with Professor Tanker?"

"Yes," the girl said with a sigh, "unfortunately."

Sunny chuckled. "Good, I thought you were in my class. Do
you want to work some of the problems together?"

The girl beamed. "Sure! You're God-sent."

Sunny made a face. "I don't know if you'll be saying that once
you find out how bad I am at this stuff."

"If you're worse than me, then you don't belong in college." The girl held out her hand. "I'm Elizabeth Warner."

"Nice to meet you. I'm Sunny White. By the way, I hope that you don't mind me asking, but are you a Christian?"

Elizabeth smiled. "I don't mind at all, and, yes, I am."

"That's great!" Sunny pulled out one of the wooden chairs from the table and sat down next to Elizabeth. "It's hard to find real Christians in this place. I'm not saying that the people are bad," Sunny thought briefly about her roommate and almost took her last comment back, "but I come from a small Christian school, and it's so weird not hearing about God all of the time. At least, whenever I talk about Him, people look at me as if I've grown another head."

Elizabeth shook her head and grinned. "I know exactly what you mean. I went to a public school, but I was really involved with my youth group back home. Now I barely know anyone, but I did hear about a church just a few blocks from here that has a good program for college students. Do you want to check it out with me next Sunday?"

God, why couldn't she have been my roommate? Sunny instantly felt guilty. Who was she to question God's plan? "I'd love to. Can I bring some friends of mine?"

"No," Elizabeth said jokingly and then smiled. "Of course you can. In fact, I was thinking about bringing my roommate. She's totally into all that New Age stuff, but she says she's willing to give God a try."

"That's cool."

"What about your roommate? Is she a Christian?"

Sunny hesitated before she said anything. "Um, I don't think so. If she is, then she has a weird way of showing it."

Elizabeth shrugged. She'd obviously been around non-Christians much more than Sunny had. "Why don't you bring her then?"

Sunny doubted that would be a very good idea so early in their "relationship." Besides, the girl might burn the church down. That wouldn't be good. Sunny glanced at Elizabeth who was waiting for an answer from her. Sunny was once again perplexed about how much she should say about her roommate. "I'm still working on getting her to talk to me like a normal human," she finally said. Elizabeth shrugged and then squinted at her calculus book willing it to give her the answer. Sunny thought about her roommate again. *I wonder if she's still steamed with me for throwing her clothes out of the window?*

"Steamed" was putting it lightly. Holly Johnson had never been so infuriated in her entire life! Well, at least not since Christmas last year with her dad. That had been when she'd informed him that she was going to UT, not Princeton as he had. With one hard kick, Holly sent her backpack flying across the room. *Who does she think she is to threaten me? I'll show her.* Holly set to work. After fifteen minutes of tearing Sunny's side of the room apart, Holly crashed onto her bed. She was exhausted.

Thirty minutes later, Sunny walked into the dorm very pleased with herself. Elizabeth and she had plowed their way through half of their calculus assignment. She thought they deserved a victory party. Of course, Sunny wasn't going to think about the English paper due next Monday, for which she had yet to pick a topic. She hadn't even bought the new MLA handbook. In Sunny's opinion, it was the rulebook from down under sent to torture students.

When Sunny stepped into her room, it was dark, but light from the hallway gave Sunny a vague picture of what had happened. Her side of the room was completely trashed. Sunny didn't think Holly had actually hurt anything, but it would take her over an hour to clean the mess up. *That does it.* The anger welling up in Sunny threatened to explode. *Breathe in. Breathe out.* Sunny saw her flashlight next to her foot. She quietly picked it up and made her way over to Holly's side of the room. She found the stereo and saw that a CD labeled "Pink" was already inside. *Perfect.* Sunny cranked up the volume and hit the power. Hard music blasted through the speakers so loudly that even Sunny was startled, but it was worth seeing her roommate jump three feet in the air and then land hard on the ground. Sunny calmly walked over and turned on the main light.

"What are you doing?" Holly yelled over the stereo.

"Waking you up." Sunny didn't care how bad of a mood her roommate was about to be in. She was used to it.

Holly reached over and turned off the music. She didn't have the energy to glare at Sunny. "Well, now I'm up. What do you want?"

"I want you to help me clean up this mess you made. I'm pretty sure we can get it cleaned up in about thirty minutes."

Holly crossed her arms. Her bed looked so comfortable. "Why should I help you?"

"Because you won't get any sleep otherwise. I've never actually listened to that CD before, but I'm sure I could learn to like it." Holly knew she was losing this battle, but she was too tired to care. She picked up one of Sunny's notebooks and put it back on the shelf.

"Thanks."

"Do I have a choice?" Holly grumbled.

"You always have a choice."

"Whatever." Holly knew there must have been some hidden meaning behind what Sunny had said, but she'd never been very good at picking up on those things, not to mention she was too tired to give a darn.

They worked in silence for the next few minutes. Neither one had the energy or the will to speak.

Sunny picked up her camera. "Now where does this go?" she asked herself aloud.

"Top shelf on the left, behind your lamp."

Sunny looked around the room, "Where's my lamp?"

Holly looked up at the ceiling, as if she could see the desk lamp glowing up there. "It's under your bed, pushed behind a pile of clothes, next to your flowered make-up bag." Sunny blinked. A skeptical look crossed over her face even as she bent down and crawled underneath her bed. Low and behold, she scooted back out with her lamp in hand.

Sunny put the lamp back where Holly said it went, "How did you remember that?"

Holly shrugged. "I have an eidetic memory."

"A what?"

"Oh sorry," Holly said sincerely, "that's the scientific name for a photographic memory."

"Wow. That must be nice."

"I guess so, except when there are things that you want to forget." Holly wished she hadn't said the second part. What was getting into her?

"Like what?"

"It doesn't matter."

"Come on," pleaded Sunny. "Hearing about a…what's it called again?…an eidetic memory, is the closest I'll ever come to having one."

Maybe if I tell her, she'll leave me alone, Holly thought to herself. Truthfully, though, she didn't know what she wanted Sunny to do, back away or draw closer. "Okay, if you're dying to know. I can remember one time when I was three years old, and I was staying with my mother. She was complaining about how much trouble a toddler was and how she wished she'd never had a child. She said if she'd known better, then she would have had an abortion." Of all the memories Holly could have told her, she didn't have a clue why she'd chosen one of the most painful. She would have to be more careful around Sunny from now on. The last thing Holly wanted was for anyone to think she needed her pity.

Sunny didn't know what to say. "I'm sorry."

"That I told you?" Holly lifted an eyebrow.

Sunny shook her head. "No, I'm glad you told me. I'm sorry your mother is an idiot."

"*Was* an idiot," Holly corrected. "We're closer now." *Change the subject, Holly.* "Anyway, your side of the room is cleaner than it was when you left." Holly rolled her shoulders to relieve some of the tension that was building there. "So I'm going to sleep. 'Night."

"Good night, Rose." Sunny climbed into bed, exhausted in every possible way. *Oh God, please help her. She's hurting so badly.*

chapter seven

The next day, Sunny got up at around seven-thirty and was already down in the cafeteria by the time Holly stumbled out of bed. It took her about five minutes to get ready, three of which were spent trying to locate her missing left shoe. It was unfortunately the other half of her only pair. *I really need to go shopping.* Holly shuddered at the thought.

She used to be a pro shopper. Holly supposed that's what came from being a "spoiled," little rich kid, yet now she hated malls because the mall was the one place where she felt self-conscious about her looks. How could she not when everyone went there to find that special outfit that made him or her look like the cover of "In Style"? She, on the other hand, looked for what make her look the worst.

By the time Holly got down to the cafeteria, all the Rice Krispies were gone. Holly glared around the room looking for the culprits. Instead, she caught sight of her roommate. Sunny was hanging out with a perky, little redhead. Holly felt a small tinge of envy but quickly squashed it. *Give it a rest, Holly. She doesn't want to be your friend.*

Sunny caught Holly staring at her, but Holly quickly looked in the opposite direction. *I wonder why she's so scared of me?* Sunny thought. At five-foot three, she couldn't imagine anyone being intimidated by her. Not even her little brother took her seriously anymore.

"Who's that?" Jasmine, the redhead with Sunny, asked.

"Huh?" Sunny was pulled out of her thoughts. "Who's who?"

Jasmine pointed with her celery stick at Holly. "Raggedy Anne over there."

Sunny glared across the table. She didn't know why, but she felt a sudden urge to protect her roommate. Jasmine caught the drift.

"Sorry," Jasmine flicked her hand indicating she obviously wasn't, "but she doesn't dress very well. So who is she?" she asked again and leaned toward Sunny.

"That's Rose Johnson." She paused and looked over at Holly who was currently harassing the lunch lady. Sunny smiled and added, "She's my roommate."

"Oh," the girl said. Her face was starting to match her hair. Sunny figured Jasmine assumed she and Holly were roommates because they'd been friends before college or that they were just friends period. Sunny couldn't help but smile at the irony of it all and then couldn't resist waving her new "best friend" over to her table.

"So you're the one who stole the Rice Krispies." That was the first thing that came out of Holly's mouth. This was aimed at Jasmine who was now quickly changing from red to white. Sunny had to hand it to Holly. She was very good at intimidating people. Sunny figured Jasmine was already imagining Holly sneaking into her room in the middle of the night and cutting her into little, bite-sized pieces. Knowing full well that laughter would get her roommate's glare shinning on her, Sunny bit her lip and decided it was much safer to stare at the ground.

Something looked very…familiar. "Hey! Aren't those my tennis shoes?"

"Yep," was all that Holly said as she grudgingly chewed on Corn Flakes.

Humph. The chick was not going to filch her most comfortable shoes without a fight. "What was wrong with your shoes?"

Holly tilted her head slightly to the side. "I looked everywhere for my left sneaker, but then I remembered it was thrown out the window yesterday." When Sunny said nothing, Holly shrugged and turned her attention to making Jasmine's life miserable. The redhead was too easy a target, but she was bored and had no other candidates at the moment.

Jasmine made a big deal out of how she was going to be late for her class, which, Sunny noted silently, wouldn't start for another forty-five minutes.

As Jasmine hurried off, Sunny finally looked at Holly. "Try not to do that."

"Do what?" Holly asked innocently.

"Send any of our dorm mates into cardiac arrest." Sunny smirked, "I hear that kind of thing could go onto your permanent record."

"Hmm…Do you think that would appear before or after attempted manslaughter?"

When Sunny just stared wide-eyed at Holly, she burst out laughing. "I'm just kidding!"

Sunny laughed, "Okay, good, because I was about to call off all bets on this little tug-of-war between the two of us over our dorm room."

Holly snapped her fingers. "Shoot! I never thought of that angle." She sent Sunny a dangerous look. "You know…I'm wanted for first-degree murder in nine states. Texas was the only place they'd let a juvenile delinquent like me go to college."

Sunny sent her a hard look and attempted not to smile. "Nice try, but don't give up your day job as a linguist. Acting's not your thing."

"Actually, my mo . . ." Holly suddenly got quiet.

"What?" Sunny asked curiously. Holly seemed as if she was just becoming comfortable around her.

Holly realized how close she'd come to repeating some of the same information to Sunny that she had a year ago. If she wasn't careful, it would only be a matter of time until Sunny found out the truth. Holly didn't want anyone, especially her roommate, to know who she used to be. She detested Hollywood Rose Johnson, daughter of Steven Edward Johnson III. She pushed away from the table so suddenly that Sunny jumped. "I have to go."

"Rose, what's wrong?" When Sunny said her name, she looked like Sunny had slapped her.

For an instant, the shield that usually guarded Holly's eyes was gone, and in that moment, Sunny could have sworn that she saw fear. "I just have to go." Not leaving time for a response, Holly ran out of the cafeteria.

Sunny stared after her, wondering if she would ever be able to understand her roommate. What was so odd was that half the time, Sunny felt as if she'd known her for years, but then a wall would suddenly spring up between the two of them leaving Sunny feeling confused and hurt. *God, what were you thinking when you made the two of us roommates?*

Holly detested English class. That was odd considering she was a linguistics major, but Holly would have been the first to say linguistics was all about the components of a language and how they worked. It was not about how those components went together for another viewer's entertainment. In other words, Holly couldn't write to save her life. Once again, her photographic memory was of no use. *Why did I agree to take the honors class? What honor is there in failing?* Holly's thoughts were interrupted by a loud bang. She turned around with the rest of class and recognized the guy who had been with Sunny the other day in the café.

"You know," whispered the girl behind her who had glasses and curly brown hair, "that's the second time he's done that. He did the exact same thing in my biology class yesterday. Do you think he just does it for attention?"

"Probably," another girl said with a superior tone, "you know how guys are."

Holly looked up at Josh. She found it hard to believe he'd brought attention to himself on purpose. He was turning bright pink. Holly even started to feel sorry for him but then caught herself. She had bigger problems. He was heading toward the seat next to her, and Josh didn't look very happy to see her either. He kept on eyeing her backpack suspiciously. When Holly realized why, she had to stifle a laugh.

Class went downhill from there. It turned out Josh was left handed, which meant that every time Holly and he tried to take notes, they bumped elbows. After fifteen minutes of the war for space, Holly had had enough. "You know," Holly hissed, "there are some left-handed desks in the back."

Josh didn't look up from his notes. "I tried to get the closest seat possible to the front."

"Oh really," Holly said, "and here I thought you wanted to sit next to me." Josh smirked. *Man, he's cute.* When Holly thought about it, he didn't seem so dangerous. Besides, he wasn't the one who had invaded her dorm room. There was no reason she couldn't at least be civil to him. Unfortunately, she didn't have much practice being civil; so for the moment, sarcasm would have to do. "Why did you want to be so close? Do you like being spit on by the professor or something?"

"Not this early in the morning. Actually," Josh finally looked at her, "since you're so nosey, I'll tell you. I don't have my contacts in. So I can't see unless I'm close up."

"There's nothing to see. The professor's just lecturing. Don't tell me you're deaf and need to read her lips."

Well, she had him there. Why had he sat down next to her? He'd analyze that later. "How was I supposed to know she wasn't going to use overheads or PowerPoint or something else like that?"

"Nice recovery," Holly said. The brunette with the glasses shushed them. Holly turned around and glared, which had the girl slightly recoiling back into her seat.

Josh leaned close to Holly and whispered quietly, "You know, that girl was in my biology class. She shushed me then too. Do you think she's looking for attention or something?" *That's funny, she asked the same thing about you.* Holly looked at Josh and smirked, "Maybe you just talk a lot."

Josh grunted some unintelligible comeback and didn't say anything else for the rest of the period.

UT provided a plethora of brain food for its students. At the moment, Holly was enjoying some of its finest cuisine…Dairy Queen. Holly was one of those people who always ordered the same meal in every restaurant, which meant that if she wanted a hamburger, she went one place. If she wanted a steak, she went to another place. At Diary Queen, it was a country basket, four-piece with a coke, straight up.

Holly watched some college girls walk by and look longingly at her food. In the end, they settled for a salad. Just like anyone blessed with a high metabolism, Holly didn't understand why someone would put themselves through the torture of lettuce when they could be eating fried grease. She shrugged and continued eating. When Holly finished, she crumpled her trash into a ball, aimed for the trash, shot, and missed. Grumbling, Holly threw it away like a normal person and then headed for the Co-Op. She needed to pick up books for a few of her classes.

The Co-Op was right across the street from UT, which meant it was very close, but there was one minor problem—the street. Neither car nor cyclist gave a hoot about the well-being of a pedestrian. Holly surmised that the only reason they ever stopped was that they didn't want to get a dent in their beautiful sports cars.

Holly safely made it to the store, and once inside she found herself immersed in UT merchandise. There was even a UT Monopoly game. Holly grimaced when she looked at the clothes. She might dress badly, but there were some lines even she wouldn't cross. In her opinion, the only bad thing about UT was the school color, burnt orange. Holly, who could make brown look good, didn't dare wear that color.

Holly looked at the time and then reminded herself why she'd come and headed down to the basement where all the books were kept. Downstairs there was a wide array of art and school supplies. Holly would be the first to admit she was a horrible artist, but she liked looking at the collection of mediums, tools, and surfaces anyway. She would try to imagine what could be done with it all and...*I've gotten off track again.* Holly forced herself away from the oil paints and headed into the connecting room. Had she been blind, Holly still could have found her way there. The room smelled of beat-up, dog-eared books and of ones that were still tightly locked in their in shrink-wrap. Looking at her watch again, she forced herself to grab the books she needed and head back upstairs to the cash registrar before she was late to her next class. When Holly got upstairs, she was once again hit with burnt orange. It was enough to give someone muscle spasms.

Holly's total was a little under three hundred dollars, and she'd only bought books for two of her classes. *The books almost cost as much as the classes. Then again, they claim to teach students through osmosis. That would be nice.* Holly was happily a part of the first generation of students who, if she wanted to, could pop a CD-ROM into her laptop and have the textbook read to her. Holly smiled. *How did people survive before computers?*

Holly was walking to her first linguistics class when someone came up from behind and placed a hand on her shoulder. Not being used to, or receptive of, human contact, Holly nearly jumped out of her skin. She was ready to verbally thrash the hapless soul, who had apparently mistaken her for someone else, when she came face to face with Sunny. Holly thought she would have had better chances with a stranger.

Sunny had an odd look on her face. "Rose, couldn't you hear me calling you?"

Holly almost glanced over her shoulder to see who Sunny was talking to when she realized Sunny was talking to her. Holly suddenly became confused. *Why is she calling me…? Oh, shoot! That's me.* Holly was caught with her guard down. She had never been a good liar, which made pretending to go by a different name exhausting. "Sorry, I was daydreaming."

Sunny raised one eyebrow. "You were daydreaming?" She laughed as if Holly had just told her a joke. Holly wasn't quite sure how to respond. "So what class are you going to?"

"Linguistics."

"Ah, yes, the scientific study of language and its structure."

Holly smiled, "Yep, and what are you doing here? Don't tell me you've decided to major in linguistics too."

"Yes," Sunny said with a dry tone, "you've inspired me greatly. What can you do with a linguistics major anyway?"

"Confuse people," Holly told her with a grin. When Sunny just laughed, Holly continued. "Actually, there's a demand for linguists right now."

Sunny had a look of bewilderment on her face. "Why?"

"Have you ever heard of GUI?"

"Sounds gross."

Holly rolled her eyes. "Not gooey, you dope. Graphical User Interface."

"Oh right, why didn't I think of that?"

Holly took a deep breath, as if she were about to explain nuclear physics to a two-year-old. "Do you remember back when you had to type commands into the computer? There weren't any handy little save buttons or a trashcan you could drag a document into to delete it."

"Vaguely," Sunny said, wondering all the while what Holly was getting at.

"Okay, well that was DOS. Today we use GUI, which has nice little graphics. For instance, if you want to put something into a folder on the computer, you drag the file over to an icon that looks like a folder."

Sunny shrugged, "So we used DOS, and now we use GUI. What does that have to do with linguistics?"

Holly sent her a look of exasperation that said, "Let me finish. The newest technology now is Voice, which is where people just talk to their computer instead of type. There's already some software out there, but it's clunky and not worth the effort. So computer companies are hiring linguists to help improve Voice technology. Get it?"

Sunny glared at her. She could assimilate facts as well as Holly could, just not as fast. "You were right the first time. People take linguistics to confuse people."

Holly smirked. "No, that's just a perk. So why are you here?"

Sunny glanced at the piece of paper in her hand. "Well, I think my sign language course is in this building." She turned her paper sideways for inspection. "Unless, of course, I have this thing upside down; so, in that case, I'm not going to class at all today."

Holly smirked and asked, "What do you have after that?"

"Psychology."

Holly's lip curled. "Good luck in that class. I'm not taking it this semester, which means I have four months to find a way to weasel my way out of it."

Sunny laughed, "Maybe I shouldn't tell you this, but I'm majoring in psychology."

A look of horror came across Holly's face. "Psychology?" She could barely make out the word.

"Yes, psychology. You know, it's the scientific study of the human mind and its functions, especially those affecting behavior in a given context." Sunny smiled victoriously, "That's on page 1096 of *The Oxford American College Dictionary.*"

For a moment, Holly looked confused, but then she burst out laughing. "Touché."

Sunny smiled and slung her arm around Holly's shoulders as they walked into the building. Holly immediately tensed, but then, to the surprise of them both, she relaxed and put her arm around Sunny.

chapter eight

*S*unny tried to no avail to get Holly to come with her to church. According to Holly, she would rather die than wake up before ten on a Sunday. "Suit yourself." Sunny just shrugged. She was determined not to let her face reveal her disappointment. Her own pride wouldn't allow it. Instead, Sunny did the only thing that she knew to do. She prayed that God would soften her roommate's heart towards her and the Gospel. Sunny knew He was the only one who could conquer the impossible, and Holly was just that—impossible.

Elizabeth hadn't been able to talk her roommate into coming, and Josh and Bret were "no shows" as well. They'd gone to see the Dallas Cowboys play and wouldn't be back in Austin until later that evening. Therefore, it was just the two of them.

Sunny liked the preacher. He spoke in down-to-earth terms, and his sermon was filled with wisdom applicable to her life. That day the pastor urged them to become a light to a world that lived in darkness. She'd heard other pastors say the same, but he made her feel like she could live for God just by living with her eyes fixed on Him. The pastor said that for many people the only time they would see the love of God was through ordinary Christians. Throughout the service, Sunny continued to think about Holly and how exciting it would be if she discovered her Creator. Sunflower White had never boasted about being able to understand the inner workings of the human mind, but she knew Holly didn't think anyone cared about her. Sunny desperately wanted to prove her wrong. Maybe if she showed Holly that she loved her, then Holly would be ready to trust in the God who loved her. Sunny remembered how frozen her roommate was toward her or anyone who attempted to bridge the gap. *God, please help me. I can't do this on my own.*

It was four in the afternoon when Josh saw Sunny walk into the library looking like a general under siege. He was in the library "studying" for Mr. Snooze's biology quiz. "Sun, over here." Josh waved to catch her attention. He was about to yell across the library and ask what was wrong, but he was shushed by the brown-haired girl with glasses.

Bret leaned over and loudly whispered to Josh. "Dude, this is getting creepy. I think she's following us."

Josh nodded his head in agreement. He did not like being shushed at every turn.

When Sunny reached their table, Bret noticed Sunny's stress as well. "What's wrong?"

"I have an English paper due tomorrow, and I haven't even started," Sunny said without even taking the time to look at them. She flopped down into one of the hard, wooden chairs at a table and pulled out her laptop.

"Bummer," Bret said and then got up to get a drink. He wasn't worried about his paper because he was reusing one of his old essays from high school.

When Bret left, Josh lifted a questioning eyebrow at his friend who was impatiently tapping her foot while she waited for her computer to boot up. Thirty seconds was too long. "Since when do you put off your homework until the last day? Aren't you the one who's always lecturing me about that?"

"I know, I know, but, Josh, I'm not used to all this home-work."

"No kidding," the brown-haired girl interjected.

"Oh, hi, Elizabeth," Sunny waved. "I didn't see you when I walked in."

"You know her?" Josh asked surprised.

Sunny sent him a strange look. "Yes, we worked on our calculus homework together, which is one of the reasons why my English paper hasn't been started yet," she added with a mutinous tone.

"I'm working on mine too," Elizabeth told her. "Will you come with me to go look up some information? Maybe it will inspire you," she added with a grin.

"Sure," Sunny set her laptop down next to Elizabeth's books. "Josh, will you watch our stuff?"

Josh looked up from the sports magazine he'd been reading. "Yeah, sure," he said distractedly. He was trying to remember where he'd left his notes. As the two girls walked off, Bret returned. "Hey, Bret, can you watch our stuff? I have to go back to the dorm. I think I left my notes there."

"Okay. Mind if I borrow your magazine?"

"Sure, just don't drool on the pages again."

Bret glared at Josh, "I only did that once."

"Once is enough," Josh said as he walked off.

"I was asleep!" Bret yelled back at him and was surprised when no one told him to be quiet.

It didn't take Josh very long to get back to his dorm. During basketball season, his coach used to make the team jog everywhere they went, and Josh hadn't lost the habit yet. Bret had only jogged whenever Coach was around and found that ritual easy to drop. He was currently working on Josh to do the same.

Two years ago, if anyone had told him he would be best friends with Bret Thatcher, he would have died laughing and told them to get their head examined. Two more unlikely best friends, there would never be. Yet what they had in common overshadowed all their differences. Bret had become Josh's brother in Christ after the basketball finals back in their junior year, and now they were inseparable.

The elevator took too long for him, so Josh jogged up the steps to his floor. It was not that he was in hurry to study; Josh was just impatient about some things by nature, like elevators. He rounded the corner, past the coke machines, and reminded himself to get some caffeine before he left. He'd need it if he were going to study for Mr. Snooze's test.

"Hey!" someone yelled from across the hall. "Tampon! What's your hurry?"

When Josh realized they were talking to him, he felt anger surge through him. He imagined what it would be like to slam his fist into the guy's face. Josh mentally shook himself. *What's wrong with me? The guy is just being stupid. Keep walking.*

"Hey, Tampon! I'm talking to you."

God, please help me. Josh felt peace wash over him. Confidence flooded through his system as he walked into his room and closed the door behind him. *Thanks, God. I can always count on you.* By now, Josh knew he had the power to overcome any desire to do wrong. Others might call him weak, but he knew the truth. The strongest man was the one who won the fight. Whether the guy back there knew it or not, Josh had just won the hardest battle known to man—the battle to control himself.

After they'd gotten what they needed, Sunny and Elizabeth headed back to the tables. "Where's Josh?" Sunny asked Bret. She surveyed the large room but didn't see her friend anywhere.

"He went back to our room to grab something," Bret said and then lazily looked up from Josh's magazine. He did little to hide his displeasure when he saw Elizabeth Warner.

After listening to Elizabeth complain about Josh and Bret for the past fifteen minutes, Sunny was well aware of their mutual distaste. She assumed that the further away they were the better. There was no use in starting a battle of the sexes in the library. "Well, when Josh comes back, tell him I'll see him tomorrow."

"Sure thing. Where are you guys going?"

"Somewhere quieter," Elizabeth told him matter-of-factly.

Bret glared at her but then smiled to himself as she walked off. *Good luck writing your English paper.*

With a deep sigh, Sunny forced herself to open her laptop and start the word processor. She typed her name, but when she looked at the screen, it said Lxfysgtk Viozt. Sunny's eyes narrowed. "What's wrong with my computer?"

Elizabeth glanced at the screen. "What did you type?"

"My name," Sunny said dryly.

"I hate to break it to you, pal, but you need a refresher course in typing."

"Very funny. I'm not that bad." Sunny tried to type her name again, but she got similar results. "There must be something wrong with my computer." She mentally berated herself for cheeping out and not getting a warranty.

"Type something else," Elizabeth suggested.

O'd ugofu zg yqos Tfusoli. "What did you type that time?" Elizabeth leaned over to get a better look at the screen.

"I'm going to fail English," Sunny grumbled.

Elizabeth stifled a laugh. "Has your computer ever done this before?"

"No, it hasn't. She's dead."

"Who, the computer?"

"No, my roommate." Sunny snatched up her laptop. "I'll see you later, Liz."

"Bye!" Elizabeth waved at Sunny's back. "Call me if you need help getting rid of the body."

chapter nine

Sunny stormed into her dorm room and slammed the door behind her. Holly, who was currently struggling with her own paper, slowly looked up. "Rough day?"

"Yeah, you see, I have this paper due tomorrow, and my keyboard is malfunctioning." Sunny sent her a death look, but Holly's eyes were glued to her own screen.

Holly noticed the strain in Sunny's voice, but didn't think much of it. "That figures," Holly said distractedly as she attempted to think of a more eloquent way to word the crummy sentence she was working on. "I love computers, but they always choose the worst times to die on you."

"Actually," Sunny said furiously, "I don't think it was my computer's fault."

Holly looked up from her laptop and tried to figure out why Sunny was looking at her so strangely. "Are you hinting at something?"

"I wouldn't think I'd have to." Holly barely had enough time to retract her hands from her computer as Sunny snapped the top down. "When did you do it, Rose?"

Sunny was acting so out of character that, though Holly should have been on guard, she was much more curious about her roommate's strange behavior than her own well-being. "When did I do what?"

Sunny's face got redder. "Don't play dumb. You're not very good at it."

"Thanks, I think, but I really have no clue what you're talking about."

This time Sunny yelled at her, "As if messing with my clothes and books wasn't enough, now you've screwed with my computer. Did anyone ever teach you to respect other people's property?"

"Actually, no, they didn't, but I didn't touch your computer. Just because it isn't working doesn't mean I had anything to do with it." Holly was beginning to get uncomfortable. Other people had looked at her with that same look of distaste, but for some reason she had been stupid enough to believe Sunny was different.

"I suppose the keys just magically rearranged themselves." Sunny could feel herself getting worked up. It infuriated her that Holly looked hurt, as if she hadn't done anything. *How could she do this to me after we were just starting to become friends?* Sunny thought. *Maybe some people never change.*

"What's wrong with the keys?"

"You have an eidetic memory, remember?" Sunny could hear the sardonic tone in her voice, but she didn't care.

"Just give me your computer," Holly said through gritted teeth. *I don't have time for this.*

"Go ahead." Sunny shoved it into Holly's lap. "Type your name."

Holly typed "Igssnvggr Pgiflgf." Then she typed some more. After a minute of messing with the computer, Holly looked up at Sunny. "Someone's playing a practical joke on you, but they didn't do a very good job of it. They put the letters in the order of the alphabet from left to right, top to bottom. Look." Holly typed the keys for the letters QWE. ABC appeared on the screen.

Sunny leaned forward until her eyes were only a few inches from Holly's. "You messed it up; you fix it." She grabbed Holly's laptop before Holly could stop her.

"Hey!"

Sunny didn't even look back as she walked out the door. "I'll be on the first floor of the library."

Holly flinched as the door slammed. She forced herself not to cry. It was her own fault. Hadn't she known from the beginning she would get hurt if she let Sunny into her life? Holly's face turned into a scowl. She hadn't allowed Sunny into her life. The girl had barged in, effortlessly scaling all the walls that Holly herself had built for protection. Then in the same way, Sunny had just walked out and slammed the door behind her. Sunflower White was just like everyone else.

Holly stormed into the library. It hadn't taken her long to fix Sunny's computer, but it had been long enough for her temper to flare up to its full glory. Holly spotted Sunny and another girl sitting at a table near the back and headed toward them. Elizabeth was the first to see her storming towards their table and nudged Sunny who was hunched over some papers. Holly dropped Sunny's laptop onto the table with a loud bang.

Sunny's hand snapped up. "Hey! If that's broken, you're paying for it."

"I think I can afford it. Get up," Holly's voice was like ice.

"What?"

"I said get up!" Holly yelled. Even Elizabeth wasn't brave enough to shush her. Everyone in the library watched in silence, everyone except Sunflower White.

Sunny pushed away from the table and sent the chair sprawling.

Her control snapped. "You want a fight? Is that what you want?" Sunny yelled. "Well, now you have one. What is your problem?"

"My problem is you." Holly poked Sunny with her finger. Sunny returned Holly's look glare for glare. "You stormed into our room, accusing me of something I didn't do, and then made me fix your stupid computer! I don't have anymore time than you do, Sunflower, but I would have helped you anyway. You could have asked if I'd done something to your computer. I'm not a liar, but you didn't even give me a chance!" Holly couldn't believe she'd said the last part because it revealed for the entire world to see how desperately she wanted that chance.

Sunny couldn't believe Holly was making her look like the one who had started it all. "Oh, now we're talking about chances!" Sunny yelled. Holly couldn't hear the hurt in Sunny's voice, but it was there never the less. "You made up your mind about me before we ever met. You were determined from the beginning to make me the bad guy. You trashed my stuff and now you expect me to believe you didn't mess with my computer?"

"Actually, if you care to remember correctly, you're the one who trashed my stuff and . . ."

"Um, excuse me," said a small, squeaky voice. "I'm sorry to interrupt, but I'm going to have to ask the two of you to continue this outside." It was a librarian. Both Holly and Sunny turned and glared at her. The little librarian gulped, but behind her was a security guard.

"That's not necessary," Holly said calmly. "I just had to drop something off. I'm sorry for the disturbance." Holly picked up her own laptop and gracefully walked off.

"So" Elizabeth said after everything had calmed down, "that's your roommate." Sunny grunted in response. She was thinking about the last thing Holly had said.

'I'm sorry for the disturbance?' She sounded like she just stepped out of finishing school. Sunny, who was still trying to douse her own flames, found it hard to believe that someone who had just been furious could quench her anger so easily. *What does it take to*

gain that kind of control? Sunny tried to shake her thoughts. It was now six o'clock and she still had to write her paper. Sunny looked at the screen. At the top it said "Igssnvggr Pgiflgf." She narrowed her eyes at the screen. Something was wrong.

"Elizabeth?"

"Yes?"

"Have you ever seen the name Rose spelled with nine letters?"

Elizabeth looked at her a bit strangely. "No, I haven't. Why?"

Sunny was too busy translating the name to answer her. *Hollywood Johnson.* Shock hit Sunny like lightning. *It can't be! That girl was so cool and…beautiful.* The more Sunny thought about it, the more she realized that Rose was Holly from the airport. *Why would she keep that from me?* It didn't take Sunny long to answer her own question. She looked at her keyboard again. Suddenly, her English paper did not seem so important anymore. *Some godly example I've made.*

Sunny finished her paper at midnight. It was as good as it was going to get. She said good night to Elizabeth and walked over to Josh's table. Bret was snoring so loudly Sunny was surprised she hadn't heard him from across the library. He was using a stack of notes and magazines for a pillow. Josh looked like he was about to nod off as well, but he managed raise his head when she tapped him on the shoulder.

"Hey, Sun. Finished?" He yawned and rubbed his eyes.

"Yes, can I talk to you about something?"

"I'll walk you back to your dorm." Josh reached for his magazine. "Bret!" He yanked the magazine out from underneath Bret's head.

Bret woke up with a start and let out a feminine squeak. "Help!" He yelled out and then looked around. Once he realized he was no longer falling off Mount Everest, he turned a beautiful shade of red.

"Yuck!" Josh had a look of disgust on his face. "You slobbered all over my magazine again." Josh wiped the cover on Bret's shirt.

"Hey!"

"You're lucky that I don't hit you over the head with it," Josh continued to glare at his friend and wondered if there was such a thing as disinfectant for periodicals. "I'm walking Sun back to her dorm. I assume you can find your way back to ours without hurting yourself."

Bret mumbled some unintelligible curse at Josh as Sunny and he walked out. When they got outside, Josh took a sideways glance at his friend. He decided to wait and let her start talking. For some reason that was beyond him, girls usually solved their own problems by simply talking about them. That was perfectly fine with him. He didn't have to do anything and then was praised for being a good listener.

"I think I really screwed up with Rose, I mean Holly, tonight."

Uh oh. She was already confusing him. "Who's Holly?"

"It's Rose's real name." Josh looked even more confused. "It's a long story, one that I'm not even sure I completely understand yet."

"Well," Josh said, "keep me informed on the whole alias ordeal. What did you do to Rose/Holly?"

"I didn't trust her."

"I'm not following you."

"When I got around to typing my paper tonight, I found out someone had messed with my keyboard. I assumed she'd done it, considering she's been trying to make my life miserable since the moment I arrived."

"That sounds plausible, except that I thought the two of you were getting along now."

Sunny shook her head. "I thought we were too. That's why I got so upset tonight."

Warning flags went up in Josh's head. He'd seen Sunny angry. It didn't happen very often, and for good a reason. When she got mad, she made the Incredible Hulk look like a two-year-old throwing a tantrum. "Did you deck her?"

Sunny looked startled and then annoyed. "Seriously Josh, sometimes you really don't understand girls at all. When was the last time I actually hit someone, other than one of my brothers?"

"Me, back in third grade."

Sunny growled at him. "You're never going to let me live that down, are you?"

Josh smiled. "Maybe when you're eighty." Sunny didn't laugh.

"Okay, okay," Josh said sincerely, "I won't joke around anymore. What did you do?"

Sunny sighed. "Basically, I stormed our room, and without giving her a chance to defend herself, I forced her to fix my computer."

Josh was silent.

"Well?" Sunny jabbed him before he could enter into his pensive mood. There was no telling when he would come out of it.

"Sunny, does it really matter if she was the one who messed up your computer or not?" Sunny started to defend herself. "Hold on," Josh held up his hand, "I know you want to be her friend and that it hurts your feelings that she would break your trust like this, but in a way, what you did sort of broke her trust too. Didn't it?"

"Thanks," Sunny grumbled, "as if I didn't feel bad enough already."

Josh shrugged and smiled. "What are friends for?"

"You really aren't as cute as you think you are, you know."

"The lighting isn't good this time of night."

Sunny laughed. "Neither are your jokes."

Now it was Josh's turn to laugh, but he quickly stifled it when he saw Sunny's mood somber again. "Sunny, don't worry about this thing with your roommate. Just pray to God to soften her heart toward you and that you can have discernment in this whole thing. Let the girl know you're sorry for jumping her case, and if she did mess with your computer then that's done with. You still want to be friends with her, don't you?"

Sunny slowly smiled. "When did you get so smart?"

"Are you saying I wasn't smart before?"

Sunny laughed. "I don't remember you being this bad at taking complements."

Josh laughed with her, and then they walked in silence the rest of the way to her dorm. After Sunny hugged him goodnight, she slowly made her way to her room. She got to the door, took a deep breath, and quietly stepped in. She'd been prepared for World War III; instead, Holly was asleep at her desk. Gone was the angry girl from the library and in her place was a child who was tired and completely lost. Sunny realized at that moment that this was what God saw. He didn't the clothes or the haircut. He saw her for who she was and loved her for it. A lump rose in Sunny's throat. How could she have been so blind? *Let Me love her through you,* Sunny heard God say. Speechless, she nodded her head.

Sunny reached out and gently woke Holly up. Then she helped her to bed. Holly was awake enough to say thanks. After Sunny turned out the light, Holly mumbled something to her. "Sunny, I didn't hurt your computer."

Sunny searched her own heart, only to find that she held no resentment towards Holly at all. "I believe you. Thank you for fixing it for me." Sunny paused for a moment. "I know you didn't have to."

"What are friends for?"

Sunny's eyes welled up. "Good night, Hollywood."

The silence lasted so long Sunny thought Holly was asleep. After a minute, though, Holly spoke, "How did you find out?"

"You've always reminded me of someone; I just couldn't put my finger on it. Today you typed your real name into the computer." Sunny decided to ask the question that had been weighing on her mind. "Holly, why didn't you tell me?"

Once again, Holly took her time answering. "I didn't want you to know who I used to be."

You haven't changed as much as you think. "So why did you try to keep me from learning about you now?"

That was the last question Holly had expected, and truthfully, it stumped her. "I guess I didn't want you to be disappointed. Why aren't you? I mean, why are you still here?"

"Because God created a part of me to be drawn to something in you."

"That doesn't make any sense."

"Does it have to right now?"

"I don't know anymore. I used to think so."

"Well," Sunny yawned, "while you're discovering the secrets of the universe, I'm going to sleep."

Holly smiled, because discovering the secrets of the universe was exactly what she'd been trying to do. "Good night, Sunny."

chapter ten

*T*he next day, Holly woke up to the sound of Sunny's alarm clock. She grumbled and then finally got out of bed. Sunny looked wide-awake. "Why are you so happy? It's seven in the morning." Holly sat on the end of her bed and stared at her closet, trying to muster the energy to find something to wear.

"I'm a morning person," Sunny said cheerfully.

Holly sent her a look of disgust. At least she thought that's what it was. She couldn't be sure.

A perplexed look suddenly crossed Sunny's face. "Holly, what happened to your eyebrow and nose ring?"

Holly shrugged, "They were fake. I hate needles."

"Anything else I should know about?"

"I don't smoke."

Sunny's eyes widened. "What! Why would you pretend to smoke?"

With the fumes of sleep still on her brain, Holly had to concentrate hard to form a coherent sentence. "I thought it would make you want to leave."

Sunny looked shocked. "What did you do? Just light the things on fire and watch them burn?"

Holly willed her face not to blush. "Pretty much."

"That's about the dumbest thing I've ever heard of," Sunny said bluntly. Then she remembered Josh and his glowing ball of fire. "Okay, maybe it's the second dumbest thing I've ever heard of."

"Considering all the headaches it caused me. I think you might be right." Holly held out her hand. "Truce?"

Sunny grinned. "Truce."

In the line for breakfast, Sunny looked over at Holly, only to see her face fixed with a scowl. "What's wrong?"

"It doesn't matter how early I get here. The Rice Krispies are always gone."

"The horror!" Sunny exclaimed.

Holly elbowed her to get the goofy grin off Sunny's face. "I always ate Rice Krispies back home."

Sunny pretended as if she were playing a violin. Holly laughed, but then cut herself off when she saw Jasmine coming. "Be nice," Sunny whispered.

"But she's a ditz," Holly complained. Sunny didn't have time to respond.

"Hi, Sunny!" Jasmine didn't even acknowledge Holly's presence. "Sunny, this is my roommate Elizabeth."

Holly recognized Elizabeth immediately, and if she wasn't mistaken, Sunny knew Elizabeth too. At the moment, the girl looked like she had just been run over by a freight train. Obviously, mornings were bad for her too. Still, she was awake enough to realize she already knew Sunny.

"Oh, hey!" Elizabeth also recognized who Sunny was standing with. Her eyes bulged as she looked suspiciously between the two of them. She was probably checking for weapons of mass destruction. "Are the two of you cool now?"

Sunny was about to answer her when Jasmine cut her off. "Oh, Elizabeth, you know Sunny already?" she seemed disappointed. "Well, that's just perfect then. Sunny do you want to sit with us?" Elizabeth's gloomy face suddenly lit up. Sunny was torn, but then decided to let propriety win this little battle for her.

Sunny smiled at Elizabeth to let her know what she was doing. "Actually, the two of us were going to sit together." Sunny pointed at Holly.

"Oh," Jasmine said, now fighting her own inner war. "Well, you can sit with us too, I guess."

"Thanks," Holly drenched that one word with as much sarcasm as she could and then led the way to an empty table.

For Holly and Sunny, breakfast was torture. Jasmine talked without cease for thirty minutes. *It might not have been that bad,* thought Holly, who wasn't a big talker herself, *if the girl hadn't jabbered about herself the entire time.* She had to hand it to Elizabeth. She must have a lot of patience. Even Sunny, who Holly had thought was the queen of patience, was starting to roll her eyes. Another glance at Elizabeth told Holly it wasn't virtue keeping her from grinding her teeth. It was exhaustion. Holly wasn't that tired, so she decided it was time to stop listening to Jasmine's autobiography.

"So Liz, when was the last time you went to sleep?"

Elizabeth's head snapped up. "Huh? Oh, I'm not too sure I've woken up yet. I'm one of those people who needs lots of sleep, and I haven't been getting much lately."

"How come?" Sunny asked before Jasmine could continue.

"I'm a music major, which means I have absolutely no life or any time to do little things like sleep."

"I didn't know that UT had a good music program," Holly remarked. She really didn't care if UT had a music program at all.

She just thought it was safer for Jasmine's health if Elizabeth kept talking. Holly twirled a butter knife through her fingers just in case.

"Actually, for awhile I wanted to go to South West Texas, but my brother talked me into coming here, and UT *does* have a great music program."

"South West Texas, where's that?"

"Actually, a year ago they changed the name to Texas State University of San Marcos," Elizabeth explained.

Holly was curious now. "Why did they do that?"

"I don't know. I guess because they had a bad reputation for being a party school. So I suppose they thought that if they changed the name, then people would look at them differently."

"Hmm . . ." Sunny said. "That sounds like a girl I know." She shot a look at Holly. Holly tried to kick her under the table but missed.

"Ow! What did you do that for?" Jasmine whined.

"Sorry," Holly said insincerely, "I wasn't aiming for you." Jasmine glared at her, but Holly was too preoccupied to glare back. Holly didn't know how it started, but Sunny and she were having a staring contest. Even though Holly knew she was acting half her age, she wasn't about to lose.

After about a minute of being ignored by living statues, Jasmine got up and left. "You guys are weird." That did it for Sunny. Later, thanks to her photographic memory, Holly would remember everything in crystal clear detail. Sunny hadn't laughed; she spewed. As it turned out, Sunny had water in her mouth, water that went all over Holly and Elizabeth, primarily Holly.

"Ew!" both girls shrieked. Water got into Elizabeth's eye, so she hurried to the bathroom to fix her contact. Holly picked up her own glass of water and threw what was left on Sunny. Sunny retaliated, or at least she tried to. Anticipating her, Holly ducked under the table. The whole thing was like something out of The Three Stooges, minus a stooge.

Unfortunately, the fun was short-lived. Someone from another table bellowed. Holly got out from underneath the table and looked up. Holly was a bit taller than average, but the Amazon that Holly was currently cowering beneath had to have been over six-three. Holly quickly scrambled over to Sunny who was now standing and staring wide-eyed at Godzilla girl. She had water on her and did not look happy about it.

"Couldn't you have picked a smaller person to drench?" Holly whispered to Sunny who had turned sheet white.

"I was aiming for you," she whispered back, and then to the other girl said, "I am so sorry. I . . ."

"Not as sorry as you're going to be when I'm done with you." Godzilla then proceeded to call Sunny a series of names that even Holly, who had traveled the streets of L.A., had never heard.

Sunny turned whiter by the second. Holly decided to step in. "I'm sorry to interrupt, but this really was all just a misunderstanding. There's no need to . . ."

"I'll deal with you next."

Under her breath Holly whispered to Sunny, "Okay, on the count of three, run for the door: Three!"

They bolted to the nearest exit. Holly turned around to see that the girl hadn't followed them outside.

Sunny turned and hugged Holly, "We made it! I thought she was going to eat us for breakfast."

"Correction, I kept you from being eaten for breakfast. The security guards would have been there in time to save me from becoming her second course."

Sunny just shook her head. "Whatever. Do you think she'll come after us?"

"Doubtful. It's a big campus, and I'm sure she has better things to do."

"She didn't seem preoccupied a few minutes ago."

"Yeah, but that's just because she was angry. Once she thinks about it, she'll realize that unless you're the Wicked Witch of the West, water doesn't hurt. On the other hand, probation would definitely leave a scar on whatever career she's pursuing."

"True, but are you sure she'll come to that conclusion?"

"Just don't find yourself in a dark alley with her, and you'll be fine."

Sunny smiled at Holly. "Thank you."

Holly started to get uncomfortable. She was beginning to care about Sunny and that terrified her. The last time she'd cared about someone, they ended up dead. "It's not a big deal. I've gotten out of bigger messes with scarier people before."

"Who?"

"My dad."

"Do you want to talk about it?"

Yes. "No, not really." *Change the subject.* Holly looked around for inspiration. She saw it heading her way. "Don't you know those two?" Holly pointed off towards Josh and Bret. They were both walking towards them. Josh looked angry, and Bret looked like a kid who'd just gotten caught skipping school.

When Josh spoke, he did little to hide the irritation in his voice. "We came by before class because Bret has something to say."

Bret glared at Josh. "Thanks, Mom," he mumbled, "I think I can handle this on my own." When Josh didn't move, Bret tried a more direct route. "Scram."

"I'll be over there." Josh pointed to a tree only ten feet away.

"What do you think I'm going to do? Hurt them?" Sunny and Holly were immensely enjoying this macho battle. It wasn't what they said that made it so amusing. It was the way they both kept trying to stand taller than the other one.

"No, actually," Josh said, "if anyone needs protection, it will be you." With that, Josh walked off.

Bret started tracing lines in the dirt with his tennis shoe.

After about a minute of this, Sunny got impatient. "Well, what's the problem?"

"I really don't like Elizabeth."

"I'm sorry," Sunny said dryly. "Is there a reason why Josh dragged you all the way over here to say that?"

"Sort of." He started to play with the dirt again.

Holly rolled her eyes. "Spill, we have to get to class."

Bret looked at Sunny. "I messed up your keyboard."

"What?" Sunny and Holly said simultaneously.

"Why?" Sunny's fist clenched. She was ready to throttle him.

"I thought it was Elizabeth's computer, and she's been so annoying. I mean I can't even talk without her . . ."

"I really don't care. Do you have any idea how huge of a mess you made with your little practical joke?"

"I, um, I'm sorry."

"You're sorry! That won't change . . ."

Holly, not wanting to witness another fight, cleared her throat. Bret and Sunny turned and looked at her. "Once again, we really need to get to class. So let's discuss this over lunch, your treat." Holly pointed at Bret.

Bret didn't know if he wanted to slug her or kiss her. On one hand, she was making him pay for lunch, but on the other hand, the girl just saved him from an early death by exposure to Sun. *That was kind of funny.*

Holly waved her hand in front of his face when he started smiling to himself. *We've lost him.* "So do we have a deal?"

Bret put on his business face. "Are we talking lunch at Subway?"

"Nope, we're talking lunch at Jaime's Spanish Village."

"Where?" Sunny asked.

"I'll show you guys."

"How come I have to pay for you too?" Bret complained.

"Because it's the price I charge for fixing her computer."

Once Bret realized he was fighting a losing battle, he walked off mumbling something about how no one knew how to take a joke anymore.

Sunny looked guiltily at Holly, "I'm . . ."

Holly held up her hand and shook her head. "Don't apologize. I would have thought the same thing."

Sunny smiled with a look of relief on her face. "So is Jamie's Mexican Village expensive?"

"No," Holly told her with a mischievous grin, "but he doesn't know that." Holly pulled out her cell phone and called the restaurant.

chapter eleven

s it turned out, Elizabeth and Josh came too. All four of them claimed to be victims of "The Great Keyboard Assault." Extremely outnumbered, Bret agreed to pay for them.

None of them, except Holly, had ever been to Jamie's Mexican Village. Before they arrived, Sunny asked Holly what the place was like. Even if Holly been a good with words, she still would have had difficulty describing the restaurant simply because there was no other place like it. When you walked in, you felt like you'd entered a cave. There was no way of telling how big the place was until you searched every nook and cranny. Josh, who was claustrophobic, had some minor problems when he walked in. The ceiling slanted, giving him the illusion it wouldn't stay up for much longer. He didn't complain, though. Sunny and Bret knew he was a baby when it came to closed-in places, but Holly didn't have to know.

Bret wasn't complaining either. The place looked fun, not expensive. His good humor left him the moment he looked at the menu. "Twenty dollars for bean and cheese nachos!"

"Yes," Holly grinned, "what did you expect in a nice place like this?" Bret looked around. He didn't see any waiters in tuxes.

"I think we'll have two of those to begin with," Sunny said to the waiter. He nodded and walked off. By the time they had their drinks and nachos, Bret looked sick. He groaned every time someone placed an order. None of the main courses were under thirty dollars.

When the food came, Holly started to take a bite when Josh said, "Let's pray. I'm starving."

Everyone at the table bowed their heads. Holly looked at Sunny who had her eyes closed. *This is weird. Oh well, if they want to pray, they can. It's a free country.* Josh prayed. "Dear God, thank you turning what started out as a bad joke into a time we could all be together and have fun. Please bless this food. Oh yeah, and if you don't mind, please help us pass all of our classes."

Sunny chuckled, "Amen." Everyone looked up, except for Holly who'd been watching Josh pray. *He sounded like he was talking to someone right here.* Bret broke Holly's train of thought.

"You guys do realize I'm going to have to file for bankruptcy and drop out of college."

Sunny looked at him unsympathetically. "I guess that means no one will be around to mess up my keyboard."

"That's good," Holly told her, "because I don't have time to fix it again."

If possible, Bret now looked more pathetic. "Guys, I said I was sorry. I didn't mean to hurt your computer."

"No, you meant to hurt mine," Elizabeth pointed out.

Bret remembered she was there and then turned red. "You guys told her?"

"I was right behind them when you came clean. I'd just come out of the cafeteria."

Bret stared at the table. Surprisingly, Elizabeth was the one who bailed him out. "Well, it was a kind of funny prank." Everyone except Bret looked at her as if she'd lost her mind. "I mean, it wasn't very nice, and if it had been my computer, you'd be dead right now. Still, you should have seen these two." Elizabeth pointed at Sunny and Holly. "I thought they were going to start throwing punches in the library." Holly chuckled because she had been ready to sock Sunny. Elizabeth went on, "I think the best part was when that poor little librarian walked up. When the two of you glared at her, she looked like she was going to collapse in horror." Everyone laughed, and Bret sent Elizabeth a look of gratitude.

Josh couldn't stop staring at Holly. She'd caught him looking at her about five times already. *This is getting embarrassing.* He couldn't help it. It was the first time he'd ever seen her laugh. Her entire face seemed to light up. Josh mentally shook himself. What was wrong with him?

Holly glared at Josh again. *Is he staring at me? No, he can't be. He just has to look at me sometimes because I'm right across the table.* Holly looked up, and Josh looked away fast. *See, he doesn't even want to make eye contact with you.* For the first time in over a year, Holly wished she looked good. She'd never been able to pull off looking ugly, but she definitely wasn't a knockout anymore. No one could be with the clothes she was wearing.

Sunny had a clearer perspective than Josh or Holly on the little dilemma. *This is so stupid.* "Hey guys, do the four of you want to see a movie this weekend?" Sunny saw Bret pale, and she smiled. "We'll go Dutch."

"I'm in then," Bret said. He turned to Elizabeth and said, "Are you coming? I promise not to touch your computer."

"That's a good thing," Sunny mumbled, "considering it's my stuff that gets messed up."

"You're just lucky to have friends who meddle with your things."

"Yes," Sunny said dryly to Bret and then turned to Holly. "By the way, when am I going to get my tennis shoes back?"

"Whenever I go shopping."

"And that would be when?"

Josh cut off whatever smart retort Holly was going to say. "What movie do you guys want to see?"

"There's a movie that just came out that I want to go to," Elizabeth told him.

Josh sent a look at Bret, "I'm thinking of a two-word expression that rhymes. Its purpose is to turn all males into saps."

"Chick flick," Bret said.

"Bingo!"

"Actually," Elizabeth said, annoyed, "it's a drama about a boy who grew up on the streets, and then his deadbeat parents are killed. He goes around from home to home for a while and then this woman takes him in as her own son."

"Well," Josh said, "now that we know the whole plot, we can pick another one."

"No," Sunny cut in, "that one sounds good." She looked at Holly and Elizabeth. "How about we agree to seeing this one, and then you guys can choose the next."

Josh nodded, "Deal."

"Who's in it?" Bret asked.

"I can't remember," Elizabeth tried to think. "I've never seen the boy before, but the woman is famous. She was in . . ." As Elizabeth trailed off, Holly thought to herself. *Please don't say 'Turning Tide.' Please don't say...*

"*Turning Tide,*" Elizabeth announced. No one noticed Holly's face fall. "You know, that old movie that came out right before we were born. She's been in a lot of other stuff, but that was the movie that made her famous."

"You're talking about Anne Tricony," Holly said dryly.

"Oh. yeah!" Bret looked so happy that Holly wanted to slap him.

"So do all of you want to go?" Sunny asked them.

Everyone said yes, except Holly. Sunny stared at her expectantly. *It's not what you think,* Holly wanted to tell her. *I already saw the movie at the premier, and frankly, I don't want to see her acting like a mother, when she's not that good at it in real life.* Holly knew that wasn't completely fair. Anne had been trying to make it up to her daughter for the past year, but Holly didn't know if she could ever forgive Anne for ignoring her for the first sixteen years of her life. Holly looked at Sunny. *She really wants me to go.* Holly thought about it and decided making Sunny happy this once was worth suffering through the bogus movie for a second time. "I'll go." Holly looked at Sunny who beamed at her. It was strange, but that smile almost made up for having to watch her mother at the movies again.

Josh was trying to analyze Holly's strange expression. It was almost as if Holly were afraid to go to the movies. *Does she just not want to be around me?* Josh shook himself. *Stop that.* To get his mind off Holly, particularly her face, Josh said, "Well, it looks like everyone's done, and I have go." Bret glared at the bill, which was one hundred and eighty dollars.

Bret trudged over to the cash register. A short little old lady rang up the total for him. "That will be fifty-five dollars and thirty-five cents," she told him.

"What?" Bret exclaimed. The old Hispanic woman jumped. "But," Bret continued as his friends gathered around him, trying not to laugh, "I thought it was a hundred and eighty dollars."

The woman stared at him strangely and then looked at the bill, not to check the price but to see how many drinks he'd had. "Well, if you want to pay that much, sir, you're welcome to." Bret looked around the room. Sunny was the first to crack.

"Gotcha!" Josh said.

For a moment, Bret just stood there gaping at them. "You," he said pointing his finger at Josh.

"No, actually it was Holly's idea," Josh said. Bret turned and stared at Holly who looked up at him innocently.

Bret gave her a dirty look. "What did I ever do to you?" Holly opened up her mouth, and Bret cut her off. "Don't answer that."

Holly felt as if the rest of the week went by too slowly to be exciting and too fast to get her work done. As much as she hated to admit it, the movies hadn't been that bad. She couldn't say she actually enjoyed the movie, but she had spent her Saturday nights in worse circumstances. Ever since she was ten, not one week had gone by that her father hadn't forced her to go to some party or function. She had found it easier to be the perfect, dutiful daughter for six painfully long years than to fight against him. Holly always told herself Natasha's death had liberated her from her father's grip, but then why did she still feel trapped? Why did she always feel like the world was closing in on her? It seemed as if the harder she pushed, the closer she came to suffocating. Holly knew there was an answer to her problems. She just didn't know what that answer was.

Thinking of these things, Holly sat on her bed and stared at her computer screen. Computers had always been a hobby for her. They were a mystery, a challenge, which fascinated her to no end, but tonight it was just a chunk of plastic. She hated being depressed, especially when there wasn't a logical reason to be depressed. She wanted to be able to blame something, anything. It irritated her that her emotions and feelings were dictated by something other than circumstance. That irritation led her in a full circle back to wanting to nail something for her misery. Holly looked around the room. Unfortunately, Sunny was out with Josh. *Big surprise there.* Holly refused to be chastised by the little voice inside her head that reminded her she could still be out with them. Why had she made herself leave?

Not wanting to think about her own stupidity any longer, Holly switched gears and turned off her laptop. There was no need to run down the battery power, and she was too lethargic to get up and plug it in. Holly reached over and set her PC on her desk and then flopped back onto her bed. She really was tired but sleep wouldn't come. Her mind kept racing. *Why did my life turn out like this?* Holly's thoughts raced back to the movie. She'd left at the ending, claiming she had to study for a test. She hadn't been able to bear it any longer. Fiction or non-fiction, how could she watch Anne pretend to be the mother that Holly had so desperately wanted her to be? Holly thought Anne deserved an Academy award for her performance. She remembered how Anne's character had held the little boy in her arms. She had told him she would always be there for him and never leave him. *Maybe I'm just unlovable.* Hundreds of thoughts poured through her mind. Memories of her mother, her father, Natasha, and Torie flooded through gates she'd worked so hard to keep shut. The only one who'd ever seemed to care was Natasha, but then again, Natasha had been paid to care about her. Hopelessly trying to make sense of it all, Holly sobbed into her pillow and wished she'd never been born. She knew it was stupid to throw a pity party, but she had never been able to get past the fact that no one loved her and no one cared.

"Do you like Holly?"

Josh glanced sideways and saw Sunny smirking at him. He cautiously answered, "That depends on your definition of 'like.'"

"You know what I mean."

"I think you're trying to play matchmaker again."

"You didn't answer the question," Sunny pointed out.

"I can't."

"Why not?"

"Because I don't know. I won't lie, I am little bit attracted to her, when she's not throwing tampons on me." Sunny laughed and Josh continued, "But, Sunny, you know what the Bible says about Christians marrying non-Christians."

Sunny just looked at him. "Josh," she said in an exasperated tone, "I'm not talking about marrying her. I'm not even talking about dating her. I just asked if you like Holly."

"And I'm trying my best to tell you I don't want to like her."

"What? That's dumb."

Josh glared at Sunny. He hated being called dumb, and Sunny

knew it. "As always, I admire your bluntness. Seriously, though, I think she might be someone sent to make me mess up in my walk with God. You know, like a temptation or something."

Sunny stared at him for a long time. "I don't think I've ever been ashamed of being your friend, until now."

"Sun . . ."

"No, you listen this time. Has the thought ever occurred to you that Holly might be someone sent to help us? I know she's not a Christian, but that doesn't change the fact I want to be friends with her. She's lost, and we're the only ones who can help her find her way."

Josh rolled his eyes. He wasn't in the mood to be preached at. A small voice in the back of his mind told him that wasn't what Sunny was trying to do. Thankfully, the voice was easily ignored. "What is she? A mission field?"

"She's a human being. Still, I don't become friends with people to convert them." Sunny sent Josh a scathing look, "I became her friend because I like her. If you like her, then you should do the same."

Josh refused to let guilt creep in. Instead, he decided to divert the attention in another direction. "That's sounds great, Sunny, but I can't tell anymore if you want to help her find her way to God, or if you just like being around her as a friend. Sooner or later you're going to have to share your faith with her, and there's no promise she's going to be happy about it. What happens then to the friendship you've worked so hard to create? The only people who are safe to be friends with are other Christians."

"You know, Josh, that's the kind of attitude that makes non-Christians despise us."

"Sunny, listen to me, the Bible warns us that we become like the people we hang around with."

"Then I suppose I won't be hanging around you much longer. I couldn't bear it if I turned into the spiritual snob you're sounding like right now. Good night, Josh." Sunny started to walk off before he could see she was on the verge of tears.

"Who are you to tell me about my walk with God?" Josh shouted at her.

Sunny slowly turned back and tried to erase the hurt from her face. "I used to be your best friend, but I'm not asking you to listen to me, Josh. I'm asking you to stop listening to yourself and what you think is right and to start listening to God." Josh started to say something but then stormed off. Sunny watched him go and then slowly walked up to her room. She couldn't shake the feeling that some of what Josh had said was true.

Before she opened up the door, Sunny heard Holly crying. Every fiber in her being wanted to be anywhere but where she was. She'd had enough for one day. *God, what do You want me to do? Should I go in or leave her alone?* Instantly, Sunny felt peace for the situation, and compassion for Holly washed over her. Sunny understood what God was telling her, so she walked in and over to Holly. "What's wrong, honey?" Sunny touched Holly's shoulder. Holly didn't try to back away, but she kept her back to Sunny. Sunny kept standing where she was until Holly looked up at her.

"You don't have to do this." Holly tried to wipe away the tears from her eyes, but they kept on filling.

Sunny smiled, "What are friends for, right?"

"I haven't been a very good friend to you."

"Here's a hint—I have a short fuse and an equally short memory. All of that is behind us now. So what's wrong?"

"It's stupid," Holly tried to regain control over her voice.

"Believe me. It couldn't be any dumber than the conversation I just had with Josh."

"Are the two of you still going out?"

Sunny eyes bulged. "Are you insane?" Sunny saw the look that passed over Holly's face and instantly regretted what she'd said. "I'm sorry, but did you really think we were going out?"

"Obviously," Holly mumbled, not knowing whether she should be relieved or embarrassed.

"Sorry, I just can't imagine going out with a guy who I've thought of as my brother for my entire life. Still, we do hang out a lot, so I can see where you got the idea. Just know that neither of us have feelings like that for each other." Sunny shuddered at the thought. "Anyway, I'm sure you weren't up here crying about my nonexistent love life. What's going on with you?"

"Remember how I told you a long time ago that my mother is an actress?"

"Oh, yeah, that's where you got your name from, right?"

"Yes," Holly said. "Do you remember me telling you that when I was little my mother didn't want to have anything to do with me?" Holly watched Sunny's face. She didn't look uncomfortable, just a little angry.

"Yes, I remember."

"Sunny, my mother is Anne Tricony, the actress in the movie tonight."

Sunny stared at her in shock, "Anne Tricony—the Anne Tricony?" Sunny looked at Holly's face. She did look like her, except for Holly's eyes, which were blue instead of green. Sunny started to put the pieces together. Here was Holly who had to watch her mother, who'd never cared for her, pretend to love and care for some little boy. Sunny tried to imagine what that must be like. She couldn't, but she could understand why Holly was crying. She would have too. Sunny didn't know what to say, but luckily, some things in life were better said without words. She reached over and hugged Holly. That was about all the Holly could take. She didn't care anymore if Sunny saw how vulnerable she was. Holly sobbed onto her shoulder, and Sunny rocked back and forth, as her own mother had done when she was little and had woken from a bad dream. *What would it have been like if my mother hadn't been there? How selfish does someone have to be not love her own child?* Sunny shuddered. *O God, does she think this is her fault?* Sunny resolved to call her parents that night and to tell them thank you and how much she loved them. Right now, she would thank God. He was the One who gave her such wonderful parents, and He was also the One who wanted to fill the void in Holly's life. If only she could prove it to her.

chapter twelve

Neither Holly nor Sunny talked about what happened that night. They didn't have to. Holly noticed Sunny stopped spending time with Josh, and even though she was closer to Sunny than she'd ever been to anyone, she didn't feel right asking what was wrong. She didn't want to intrude on their relationship. Holly had finally given up pretending she didn't like Josh, but since he made it clear he didn't like her, she knew nothing would ever come of it. Holly started to become friends with Elizabeth as well. Jasmine, to everyone's delight, found her own group of friends.

Bret, unlike Holly, felt perfectly comfortable confronting his best friend, especially since Josh had been moping around like Eeyore for the past few weeks.

"Let's go shoot some hoops," Bret said one day while Josh was lying on his bed staring at the ceiling.

"Are you begging for a beating?"

"Funny," Bret said dryly, "it's not my fault God made me three inches shorter than you."

"Whatever," Josh rolled over onto his side to face the wall.

Bret turned on the light. "Get up, you lazy bum. When was the last time you worked out?"

Josh flexed, "Yesterday."

"Lifting doesn't count. Come on, before you get old and fat."

Josh threw a pillow at him and then regretted it because it was his only one. He grumbled and rolled off the bed. "Fine, I'll go."

By the time they got to the gym, Josh was already feeling better. It had been good for him to get out of bed for something other than class. Bret snatched the first ball he saw and headed for one of the baskets.

"Losers can have the ball first," Bret passed the ball to Josh. Irritated, Josh faked to the left and shot up. He hissed when he air balled it from five feet away. For him, the game went downhill from there. Bret beat him without even trying. It took all of Josh's hard-earned self-control not to throw a tantrum.

Bret stopped dribbling. "Okay, what's going on?"

"Nothing," Josh said a little too forcefully.

"Man, Josh, tell me what's wrong. Is this about Sunny?"

"I said nothing's wrong. Now back off!" Josh shoved Bret away from him and stormed off. Bret stared after him shaking his head. He left the ball where it was and went outside. He didn't feel like going back to the dorm only to face Mr. Gloom, so he just sat under some shade and rested his head on a tree. He was about to fall asleep when someone called his name.

"Hey, Bret."

He lazily opened one eye. "Oh, hey, Holly. How's it going?"

"Aside from my evil linguistics homework, everything's going great. How about you?"

"I'm fine," he mumbled.

Holly laughed. "That sounded believable. Do you want to talk about it?"

"Sure," Bret said and then moved over so Holly could sit down. "Did you know that Josh and Sunny had a fight?"

"Yeah, I figured as much. A few weeks back, Sunny stopped hanging out with the two of you."

"Do you know what they fought about?"

"Not a clue. Do you know?"

"Not really, I just remember one night Josh came into the dorm in a huff and said Sunny was judgmental and interfering."

Holly thought of all the times that Sunny had had every right to judge her and hadn't. "That doesn't sound like her at all."

"No kidding. She's just honest, very honest, if you catch my drift. If you're doing something she thinks is wrong, she'll tell you. She's cool that way, but sometimes we don't want to hear it. That's what I think happened with Josh that night. Sunny told him something he didn't want to hear."

"Have they ever gotten into a fight like this before?"

Bret shook his head, "They've been in fights, but I've never seen it last longer than a day. Unfortunately, they're both too stubborn to say 'sorry' until the other one does. I know Josh doesn't seem like it, but don't let him fool you." Bret remembered the basketball game. "Speaking of him, Josh isn't doing too well. How's Sunny?"

Holly bit her bottom lip. Should she talk about Sunny to Bret? Would that betray her friends trust? "Well, I still don't know her nearly as well as you know Josh, but she does seem sad, I guess. She tries to hide it, though."

"See what I mean?" Bret threw up his hands. "They're stubborn. The two of us let the whole world know when we're upset. They, on the other hand, don't want to 'bother' anyone with their problems and in the end drive us absolutely insane!"

Holly laughed. *Now this guy would do great in L.A.* "So do you have any ideas how we can help?" she asked. Bret smiled mischievously, and Holly returned the grin.

"Have you ever been to San Antonio?"

"San Antonio? Holly, can't we hang out someplace closer to school?" It was Tuesday night and the last thing Sunny wanted to do that weekend was go out of town. At the moment, she was struggling through her calculus homework, big surprise there. That one class took up half her study time. Why did God create calculus? He probably did it just to test her patience.

Holly cleared her throat to get Sunny to snap out of whatever she was thinking about. From the look on her face, it must have been painful. "Yes, San Antonio. I hear it's a lot of fun."

"So is Austin," Sunny said distractedly. *Why isn't this problem coming out the right way? I'm doing exactly what the book says to do. At least, I think I'm doing what the book says.*

"I'll make you a deal. You've been bugging me to come with you to church for weeks now. So if you come with me on Friday to San Antonio, then I'll go with you to church on Sunday."

Darn! Why did she have to drag God into it? "Fine, you have a deal." Sunny thought briefly about how tricky God was sometimes. The question was, who was He getting the best of…Holly or her?

"Good," Holly smiled and then thought about having to go to church. When was the last time she'd gone? Had she been eight? Holly glanced over at Sunny who was currently punching her calculator. "What did that thing ever do to you?"

"It won't give me the right answer," Sunny clenched her jaw.

"How uncooperative of it," Holly mumbled to herself. If Sunny had heard Holly, then she was doing an excellent job ignoring her. Sunny kept switching back and forth between glaring at her book and her calculator. Holly finally couldn't take it any longer. "Let me see your book."

"No, I can figure it out on my own." After a brief tug of war, Holly let go. *Fine, be frustrated.*

Fifteen minutes later, Sunny walked over to Holly and shoved the math book under her nose. "All right, you figure it out. Just don't make me feel dumb like you did last time."

"I still can't believe you didn't know what Crammer's rule was. Didn't you take algebra?"

"Yes, I studied before the test and then happily forgot the information as quickly as I could."

Holly looked shocked. "You studied for a math test?"

"Shut up and figure out the answer."

"It's a proof. You already have the answer."

"I know that." Sunny glared at her. "I told you not to make me feel stupid."

"I'm sorry, but I'm not trying to."

"Oh, so it just comes naturally?"

"Yes. I mean, no." Now Holly was frustrated, and it wasn't because of the math problem. "Just let me figure this out." Holly looked at Sunny's work. "This is right."

"No, it's not."

"Yes, it is."

"If it were right," Sunny said irritably, "then it would match up with that answer," Sunny jabbed the page, "but I keep getting a really small number."

"Show me what you're doing on your calculator."

"I know how to use a calculator."

Holly was losing her patience. "Show me what you're doing, or I'll hit you over the head with the math book."

Since it sounded like Holly was serious, Sunny worked the problem for her. She got the same answer she'd been getting all along. Holly took the calculator from her and hit the "mode" button.

"You're working in degrees. You should be working in radians."

Sunny glared at her. Holly held up her hands in surrender, "Sorry!"

Sunny continued to glare at her. "You're lucky you're good at math. The rest of us actually have to struggle."

"Um, Sunny, it doesn't take a genius to figure out how to use a calculator."

Tired of glaring at Holly, Sunny slumped down and started to work on the rest of her homework. Seeing Sunny work on her homework made Holly feel guilty about her own. Grumbling to herself, Holly turned on her laptop and started yet another English paper. When she couldn't think of anything to type, Holly drummed her fingers on the keys just lightly enough so that nothing appeared on the screen. After about a minute of this, Sunny threw down her pencil. "Holly, stop!"

"What?" *Okay, she's getting annoying.*

"That thing you're doing on the keyboard."

"Oh, you mean this." Holly drummed on the keyboard again, this time louder.

"Stop it."

"Don't be such a baby, Sunflower."

"Don't call me that."

"Okay, Sunflower."

Sunny picked up her pillow and threw it at her. It hit Holly square on the head. Holly grabbed her own and retaliated. What had started out as a late night joke turned into an all-out war.

"Truce!" Holly yelled out, waving the white cover of her pillow like a flag. The two girls looked around, surveying the damage. Holly saw something on the floor with its batteries rolling next to it.

"Darn. That was my alarm clock." Sunny reached down to pick it up.

"Will it still work? Mine won't help us very much."

"I know," Sunny said dryly. "I can't think of any machine that could take that kind of abuse and live to tell the tale."

"It woke me up."

"Holly, it was an alarm clock. It's supposed to wake you up."

"Not on Saturdays," Holly pointed out.

"How was the machine supposed to know that? You should have turned it off the night before."

"Some friend you are," Holly said.

"Huh?"

"You're taking its side."

Sunny laughed. "I can't believe we're having this conversation."

"You started it, Sunflower."

"Oh, so we're back to name calling, Hollywood?"

Holly grimaced. She really did detest that name. "Why did our parents do that to us?"

Sunny made a face. "They wanted us to be miserable for the rest of our lives."

"No kidding. I don't even like Hollywood, the place I mean."

"Get this," Sunny said, "I'm allergic to sunflowers."

Holly looked at her in disbelief. "You're kidding."

"Nope, I'm not. I'm allergic to about everything with pollen in it, but it worked out better in the long run. Do you know how many pictures there would be of me sitting in sunflowers? My parents are corny like that."

"My mother is too, in her own way. She dreamed I would become an actress and be just like her."

Sunny snickered. "I can just see the headlines now: 'Star Hollywood Johnson Takes Hollywood by Storm.' "

"Something like that," Holly grumbled.

chapter thirteen

"Okay," Holly stretched as she quizzed Sunny, "here's an easy one. Who is the Father of Genetics?"

"Um, John Medal."

"Johann Mendel," Holly corrected with a sigh.

"Close enough."

"Yeah, right," Holly rolled her eyes, "Describe the Law of Segregation."

"Hmm…," Sunny said, "prejudice is wrong, and it shouldn't happen."

Holly made a face. It was around five o'clock Thursday evening, and they had a biology test the next day. It was October, which meant the Texas summer was taking its last stand. In celebration of the weather, Sunny had suggested they work outside. Holly, who hadn't wanted to look at their messy dorm room one moment longer, had agreed. Now she wondered if agreeing had been such a smart idea after all.

"Sunny, I thought you said you studied."

"Of course I studied. How would I have known any of the other questions on DNA and genetics?"

"By reading the book," Holly offered.

"Some of us," Sunny crossed her arms over her chest, "can't remember, verbatim, everything we read."

Holly put her hand over her head and said in a pained voice, "It's a huge burden, I know, but someone must carry it."

Sunny poked her, and Holly squeaked, "All right, Hollywood. What is the Law of Segregation?"

Holly poked Sunny back. "Since you're dying to know, the Law of Segregation states that each inherited trait is defined by a gene pair. Parental genes are randomly separated to the sex cells so that sex cells contain only one gene of the pair. Offspring therefore inherit one genetic allele from each parent when sex cells unite in fertilization."

"Why didn't I think of that?" Sunny sent a look at Holly that conveyed she was not amused.

Holly opened her mouth to come back with something but all that came out was a groan. "Oh no."

"What?" Sunny asked and looked over her shoulder. There were a fair amount of people outside, but one person caught her eye. He looked like a Pillsbury Doughboy with glasses and a bad haircut. His shirt was partially hanging out, and his shorts were too short. It didn't look like he was setting a fashion statement; he probably just hadn't bought any new clothes in the past five years. The boy seemed to be heading in their direction, though rather slowly considering the massive amount of books and who knows what else that he was carrying. *Ever heard of a backpack?* A side glimpse revealed he was wearing a one, but it looked empty.

He wasn't watching where he was going, but luckily, others were. They didn't look like they wanted to be trampled so late in the day. Sunny flinched when he almost ran into a pole. *The guy needs a stronger prescription.* Sunny looked at her friend who was also watching the horrifying scene. "Holly, do you know him?"

Holly didn't miss a beat, "That would be Dilbert."

"Dilbert?" Sunny smothered a laugh, because the kid looked like a Dilbert. "Does he go by Dil?"

"No, he doesn't like to be called that." Holly flinched. "He's very proud of his name."

"Good for him. He's not very good at walking, is he?"

Holly chuckled. "No, but he could probably tell you how far it is from the library to his dorm in millimeters. By the way, when he does finally get here," Holly grimaced when he ran into a kid on a bike, "don't mention anything about languages, and whatever you do, don't ask him about his major."

"Right," Sunny said slowly and gave Holly a weird look. She was about to ask Holly to explain but...

"Hello, Holly Rose Johnson. How are you today? Actually, it is evening, but the word 'today' is a general term, is it not? It is much like the word . . ." Holly could see he was entering what she liked to call The Dilbert Zone, so she cut him off.

"Dilbert," Holly said forcefully, "this is my friend, Sunny. Sunny, this is Dilbert."

Dilbert cleared his throat, and Holly rolled her eyes. "I'm sorry," Holly's words dripped with sarcasm. "This is Dilbert Bryant MacDonald. He believes in calling people by both their first and last names, and occasionally by their middle names if people are dumb enough to give them to him." Dilbert didn't catch the last part. He was too busy staring at Sunny. An odd look passed over his face; it was almost as if... *Uh, oh.*

Dilbert's lips turned up in what must have been a smile. Holly couldn't be sure, considering she'd never seen him look anything but bored.

"What is your surname?"

"White," Sunny said hesitantly and looked at Dilbert as if he'd just sprouted wings.

"Why did your parents name you Sunny? Were you like the sun to them?" Sunny was about to laugh at the guy's attempt to make fun of her name when she looked at his face. He was seriously trying to compliment her. *That's about the worst come-on I've ever heard. Even Bret can think up better lines.*

"Actually," Sunny didn't see Holly's warning signals, "my real name is Sunflower, Sunny is just . . ."

"Oh you poor thing."

Sunny lost her train of thought. "Huh?" *My name's not that bad.*

"You have fallen prey to the very thing that has plagued my life. People have attempted to shorten your name, thereby cheating you of your first earthly possession."

Is this guy for real? "Actually, it was my idea when I was about five." That was the last straw for Holly. She cupped her hands over her face to hide her laughter, but her snort gave her away.

Dilbert did a remarkable job of ignoring her. "I see. Do not blame yourself, Sunflower White. The pressures of this world are too much for such a young child to bear, but I would be more than happy to aid you in reclaiming your birthright." That got another snort out of Holly.

"Um, thanks," Sunny looked around trying to locate the candid camera.

"It is my pleasure, Sunflower White." Sunny looked over at Holly who was doubled over. *It would serve you right if I told him your name, but that would be cruel and very unusual punishment.* Dilbert kept staring at her. Sunny looked at Holly again, but she just kept laughing. *You're a big help.*

Sunny looked back at Dilbert and attempted to start a normal conversation. "So what year is this for you at UT?" Sunny thought it was a simple question, but, as it turned out, everything had a long story behind it when Dilbert did the telling. In the end, Sunny still didn't know what year he was in. Supposedly, this was his first year of college, but he had so many credits behind him that he was somewhere between his sophomore and junior year. Still, according to him and all of his glowing achievements, he should be a senior. *Maybe if I just stare at the ground, he'll get the picture and leave. Are those Velcro shoes? I didn't know they came in adult sizes. It's a good thing they do. The guy probably never learned to tie his shoes.* When Sunny finally looked up, she smiled with relief because Elizabeth was heading her way.

"Hey! I was just by y'alls' room."

Elizabeth's Texas accent sent Dilbert into another tangent. "It is interesting how cultures misshape words that they are too lazy to pronounce. I believe that children in our school systems should be taught to speak correctly. It is the French who believe that they can slur their words together, not the English." Dilbert looked at Elizabeth as if she were something nasty he had just stepped on. "We regard proper diction as a sign that one has been educated."

Elizabeth looked around, "Oh darn, and here I thought I was in America. I can't imagine how I ended up in England." Holly started laughing again. "So Sunny, how's the biology exam coming?"

"Her name is Sunflower White," Dilbert said irritably.

"Really?" Elizabeth feigned surprise. "So that's why our calculus teacher always calls you that when he says role. I never would have guessed. So" Elizabeth turned to Dilbert, "I'm assuming your expertise is not Ebonics. What are you majoring in?"

Ignoring Holly's groan, Dilbert took a deep breath…

Twenty minutes later, Holly butted in. "That's fascinating, Dilbert. In fact, it sounds a lot like what I'm studying. I'm majoring in linguistics."

Dilbert looked extremely annoyed with Holly. "We are majoring in the exact same field."

Holly looked up and smiled. "You mean, we are majoring in the same field," she corrected. "The words 'exact' and 'same' are synonyms; therefore, if they are used together, they form a double modifier. You should be ashamed at the way that you are butchering the English language."

Dilbert looked at Holly in shock, but his surprise quickly turned into fury. He picked up his books and stomped off.

"I have absolutely no clue what a double modifier is," Elizabeth said, "but I'm happy you do. The look on his face was classic. By the way, do you have any clue what he was talking about?"

"Vaguely," Holly said. "Fortunately, though, I tuned him out after the first minute. People like that get on my nerves. The whole purpose of language is to communicate with others, not to confuse them."

"I think he was trying to impress her," Elizabeth elbowed Sunny. "Oh, pardon me, I meant to say that I think he was trying to impress Sunflower White." Elizabeth wiggled her eyebrows.

Sunny made a face. "By the way, Liz, do you know what the Law of Segregation is?"

"No clue."

"See," Sunny grinned at Holly.

Holly shook her head. "You two are hopeless."

"You're probably right about that." Sunny turned her attention back to Elizabeth. "So Liz, how was the movie with your grandmother?"

Elizabeth groaned and slumped down next to Holly.

"That fun, huh?"

"Oh yeah, the best part was when one of the main characters drank too much, and I whispered to myself, 'he looks sick.' My grandmother, who's going deaf whether she wants to believe it or not, thought that I was talking to her. So she asked me what I'd said. I told her never mind, and then she said, 'I hate it when you say that, Lizzy.' She didn't realize how loudly she's was talking, and the people behind us were getting annoyed. So I repeated a little louder, 'He looks sick.' Then my grandmother yelled out, 'Did you say he looks sexy?' That got everyone on our entire row looking at us. To avoid further embarrassment, I yelled, 'No! He looks sick, s-i-c-k.' Then she had the audacity to look annoyed and say, 'You don't have to yell.' "

"That's not too bad." Sunny tried not to laugh.

"The theater was full, and the movie was quiet. Trust me. It was bad."

Holly tried to imagine Torie in a movie theater with Holly next to her, but she didn't have a good enough imagination. Besides, Torie would never set foot inside a public place like that. If she wanted to see a movie, then she would fly to L.A. and go to the premier.

"Well," Elizabeth yawned, "I'm going. I'll talk to y'all–I mean—'you girls' later."

After another hour of what felt like torture to Holly, Sunny figured she was as ready as she was going to be. "So" Sunny said as they walked up to their room, "how do you think I'll do?"

"You believe in miracles, right?"

Sunny laughed and slung her arm around her friend as they walked into the dorm.

chapter fourteen

It was three o'clock on Friday afternoon, and Sunny was on a mission, a mission to find her hairbrush. After fifteen minutes of futile searching, she gave up, and attempted to slide out from underneath her bed. Unfortunately, she ran into a problem. "Ouch!" Actually, she ran into the baseboard of her bed. Sunny finally managed to wriggle her way out without any further mishaps. She was now on a new hunt; this time for aspirin.

Holly walked in whistling to herself. "Hey, Sun, are you almost ready?"

"Yeah, but we're going to have to stop on the way out of town."

"Okay, I was planning to stop anyway. What do you need?"

"A new hairbrush."

"What's wrong with your old one?"

"It seems to have run away," Sunny rubbed her head. She found the aspirin bottle but couldn't get it opened. She turned to Holly for help, but she was preoccupied with Sunny's backpack. "Hey, Holly, what are you doing?"

Holly turned Sunny's backpack upside down, letting everything fall out onto the bed. Sure enough, out fell Sunny's hairbrush. "You know," Sunny put her hands on her hips. "I can't decide if you're useful or just plain annoying."

Holly smirked and started throwing random objects into her own duffle bag. "How did you find stuff without me around anyway?"

Sunny shrugged and popped a couple aspirin into her mouth. "I didn't. By the way, what do you need to pick up?"

"Just some clothes from the cleaners."

Sunny sighed, "Holly, are you ever going to learn how to clean your clothes?"

"Not if I can help it."

"Hmm…By the way, why are w e going to San Antonio again?"

Holly just grinned at Sunny. She slid her index finger and thumb across her mouth as if to say, *My lips are sealed.*

"What's the big deal? Why won't you tell me?"

Holly smiled innocently. *Because you wouldn't come if I did.*

While Holly was inside the laundromat, Sunny walked next store to get a drink at the Diamond Shamrock. She made her way to the back of the store where the soft drink machines were. Sunny glanced at the sixty-four ounce cups and briefly wondered who could drink that much. *Probably truckers who need a lot of caffeine to stay awake.* After Sunny filled up her drink, she turned to grab a lid. There was a barrier in her way, a human barrier. "Oh shoot!" Half her diet coke spilled onto the shirt of a guy who, unbeknownst to Sunny, had been waiting patiently for her to leave so that he could get a drink. Sunny felt herself turn bright red. "I didn't see you there."

"Obviously," Sunny flinched at his tone. When she finally mustered the nerve to look at the guy's face, she was relieved to see he was grinning. "It's okay, I never really liked this shirt anyway. My mom gave it to me. So I put it on about once every year so that I can say I've been wearing it when she asks me." The guy seemed to realize he was rambling and suddenly cut himself off.

Sunny looked at him again and wished he hadn't stopped talking. He was built like an athlete, but he wasn't big like a football or hockey player. No, the guy seemed more like a runner or swimmer. He had sun-bleached hair that just touched the top of his ears. Sunny had to fight the impulse not to brush it out of his face. *Okay, stop drooling and say something.* "Do you go to school here in Austin?"

"No, I'm out of college."

"Oh, okay." *Now what do I do?* She looked around the store for inspiration, anything to break the awkward silence. Sunny looked at her cup. "Do you mind if I refill my drink? I promise not to throw it on you this time."

The guy seemed to think about it for a minute. He must have decided it was worth the risk because he graciously smiled and stepped out of the way. Sunny refilled her drink and successfully put a lid on it. She backed away and tried to think of what to do. When he turned his back to her and headed towards the coke machine, she took that as a 'goodbye' and walked off, but not without noticing him reach for a sixty-four ounce cup.

"So" the guy said after he'd filled his cup, "I was wondering if you want to grab a bite to eat with me sometime?" Mark waited a few seconds before turning around. His heart was beating like crazy. She was the one. He'd known from the second he'd seen her walk out of the laundromat. He'd been filling up his car when he felt the urge to look up. Leaving the pump in gas tank, he had followed her inside the station.

When Sunny didn't answer him, Mark slowly turned from the

machine to face her, but she was gone. *Stupid! How could you let her get away?* Mark started to run out of the store, but someone grabbed him by the neck of his shirt and pulled him back. "What the…?"

"I don't think so, buddy. You're not leaving here until you pay for your drink."

Mark thought briefly about just dropping the drink and running, but the man who currently had his fist clenched around his coke-drenched shirt was at least three inches taller than him. Mark was a black belt in karate, but he didn't want to find out the hard way if this guy had one too. Mark reached into his pocket and yanked out two crumples dollar bills. "Keep the change," he said as he ran out of store. Once outside, Mark looked around. She was gone. *God! How could you do this to me?* Mark felt God's answer immediately. "Well, what if I don't want to wait any longer?" A few people looked at him curiously. They probably thought he was talking to himself. One woman hurried her little girl into the store and sent him a dirty look. Frustrated and annoyed, Mark got into his car and drove off.

"So tell me about this guy. Was he cute?"

Sunny shot a look at Holly. "Since when did you start noticing if guys were cute?"

"I've always noticed," Holly thought of Josh, "but I've never seen you look this flustered before. You definitely didn't have that look on your face when you threw your water on Godzilla girl."

"It's not nice to call her that," Sunny pointed out.

"You've called her that before too, you hypocrite, and don't change the subject."

Sunny bit her bottom lip. "Okay, yes, he was really cute. He had these gorgeous chocolate brown eyes."

Holly started humming the *Wedding March,* and Sunny poked her. "Why didn't you get his number?" Holly asked.

"Because I don't ask guys for their numbers. Besides, the guy is at least five years older than me."

"I'm not seeing the problem."

"That's the beauty of it. You don't have to."

"Ouch, that hurt," Holly kept on grinning.

Sunny scowled at her. The drive to San Antonio was going to be torture, and to make matters worse, Holly was sure to enjoy every minute of it. "I didn't realize you were so interested in my love life."

"I didn't realize you'd be this touchy about it," Holly told her. "If I had known, then I would have teased you sooner."

"What a great friend I have."

"I'll let you choose the radio station," Holly said amicably.

Momentarily appeased, Sunny messed with the dial until she landed on a station she seemed to like. The music that came through the speakers was foreign to Holly. *"I'm gonna do this with my eyes closed. Chains around my hands, chains around my feet, can't tie me down, oh no. I still stand, because You stand by me. How can I fall, when the God of it all, holds me close to Him? What do I need to see but Your loving arms around me?"* Holly looked over at Sunny who was mouthing the words.

"I've never heard this song before. Who's singing?"

"Oh, that's Emily Trace. She's becoming really famous in Christian music. Get this, she's only fifteen years old. Does she sound like she's that young to you?"

Holly shook her head and kept listening to the music. It was a good tune, and the singer had a great voice. "This doesn't sound like Gospel music."

Sunny made a face. "There's nothing wrong with Gospel tunes, but don't insult this song. This is contemporary Christian music. It's like the rock and pop of the Christian world."

"I didn't know rock or pop was allowed for someone like you."

Sunny laughed, "Well, my grandparents still shake their heads whenever they hear me listening to it, but they'll come around eventually. That generation is just afraid of change. My great-grand-mother still refuses to believe that a man landed on the moon. She says it was just a clever hoax to make the Russians mad."

"You're kidding."

Sunny sighed. "I wish I was."

Holly laughed. Sunny's great-grandmother sounded about as delusional as Torie. "My grandmother wouldn't know how to work a computer if it weren't for e-mail. All her friends started using it, so she hired someone to teach her how to work the 'evil machine.' " Holly smiled to herself. She'd had so much fun pulling pranks on Torie. Her favorite one was the time she pretended to be Mrs. Boggs. When Holly was fourteen, she'd overheard her grandmoth-er speaking badly about the poor woman while Mrs. Boggs was out of the room. The next day, Holly had sent Torie an e-mail saying 'she,' a.k.a. Mrs. Boggs, had heard the entire conversation. Torie had, of course, gone over to Mrs. Boggs' home right away to try to worm her way out of the predicament she'd put herself in. Holly would have given anything to have seen how that conversation had played out. While her grandmother was gone, Holly had sent her grandmother another e-mail telling Torie she should learn to keep her mouth shut. Her grandmother had been in a sour mood for the next week and had never trusted e-mails since.

"Holly?"

"Huh?"

"What are you smiling about?"

Holly told her the story. Sunny tried really hard not to laugh, but she couldn't help it. "That wasn't very nice," she said with a grin.

"You haven't met my grandmother; she's not very nice." Holly opened her mouth to say something else but then stopped. The radio was playing another song. "*You can call me what you like. I don't care what you say. My God loves me, and so all I can do is keep on loving you. You push me down. I don't care what you do. My God loves me, and so all I can do is love you.*"

Sunny smirked at Holly, "See, the song agrees with me."

Holly stared suspiciously at the radio. "Well, that's ironic."

"No, that's Christian music. It has a way of playing the song you need to hear when you need to hear it."

"You can't really believe that, Sunny."

"Holly, look around you. I believe everything you see, hear, taste, touch, and smell was created by God. Not only do I believe that He created it all, I believe He did it simply by speaking, and nothing became everything."

"Well," Holly looked at Sunny as if she were nuts, "I guess if you believe that, then believing the radio is magical isn't a big step for you is it?"

Sunny ignored her and listened to the radio in silence. She almost groaned aloud when she heard the next song on the radio. *"Inside I call out Your name, but what good is that when I don't speak of You to the world?"* It was like being woken up with cold water thrown on your face. Today was the first time she had ever shared any part of her faith with Holly in a long time. Why hadn't she? Sunny knew the answer to that question. *Oh, God, I am so sorry. I've been so caught up in trying to be Holly's friend that I haven't talked to her about You. Maybe Josh was right. Maybe I want to be her friend more than I want her to know You. What if we died right now? What excuse would I have for not sharing the most important Person in my life with her?* Sunny shook her head in disgust. *I guess I've been afraid that if I talked to her about You, then she would close up and not want to be my friend. I'm sorry I've tried to take this relationship away from You.* Sunny felt a weight lifted off of her shoulders, a weight she hadn't realized she'd been carrying. Sunny looked over at Holly who was glaring at the radio again. She almost laughed aloud when she heard what was playing now.

"You can say what you want. You can cover your ears and scream. That won't change my God because my God doesn't exist to please man. You can cover your eyes. That won't keep the sun from rising. If you tell the sun it doesn't exist, it will laugh in your face and burn you anyway. Oh my God is an awesome God."

Holly caught Sunny looking at her. She scowled when Sunny

raised her eyebrow as if to say, *I told you so.* Sunny didn't say that, but what she did say irritated Holly, nonetheless. "Yep, you're right. It's just coincidence." If she hadn't been driving, Holly would have slugged her.

chapter fifteen

"How exactly are we paying for this?" Sunny stared at their enormous suite, which was located in a hotel in downtown San Antonio. Holly looked at her and laughed. "I think I can afford it."

"I feel bad about you paying for all this."

"Don't. Besides, I'm not paying for it."

"You're not?"

"No, my dad owns these hotels. We get in free."

"Your dad owns it?"

Holly shrugged. "Someone has to."

Sunny looked like she was about to ask something, but then she stopped herself.

"What?" Holly asked as she tipped the bellhop.

"I don't want to be rude, but is your dad rich?"

"He's not Bill Gates, but he does pretty well. My dad and I aren't close, so I really don't keep track of how much money he has." Sunny could tell by the tone in Holly's voice that she really didn't care. Money meant little to her.

"Let me get this straight. Your mom is a movie star and your dad is a hotel tycoon."

"You got it. You're not going to get weird about this, are you?"

"No, actually I'm going to just stop feeling bad whenever you offer to pay for something."

"That should make dinner easier then. Come on, let's go to the River Walk."

"What's that?"

"It's where we're going. Come on." Holly grabbed Sunny's arm and tugged her off the couch.

Sunny looked longingly at her bed and then followed Holly out the door.

The River Walk was just like it sounded, a river sandwiched by sidewalks. The sidewalks were trimmed with flowers on the ground and colorful lights overhead. Sunny liked it. There were shops, mostly tourist traps, and restaurants that any southern Texas town would be proud of—in other words—Mexican food, hamburgers, and barbeque. On one end of the river stood River Center Mall, another one of San Antonio's more popular attractions. Sunny liked River Center because it held all of the natural beauty of an outdoor mall thanks to its lofty ceilings and glass windows that seemed to stretch for miles. Yet it was still an inside mall, which meant it sported modern luxuries such as escalators and air conditioning.

Ah, the best of both worlds. Sunny thanked Holly for bringing her there. It was nice to get away from school every once in awhile. Her gratitude vanished the moment she saw Bret and Josh heading their way. From the look on Josh's face, it seemed he was surprised as well.

"What is going on?" Sunny whispered to Holly in a tone she

usually saved for Jacob, her younger brother whose sole purpose in life was to annoy her.

"Let's just call it a coincidence." Sunny caught the reference to the car radio but wasn't amused.

"I have another name for it, but I don't think it would be polite for me to say it in public."

Holly ignored her and glanced at Josh. He looked like he was about to strangle Bret. "All right! What game do the two of you think you're playing?"

Holly looked at Josh and did something she hadn't done to anyone in a very long time. She sent him a gorgeous smile. Josh gulped. "Some friends you are," Holly said to Josh and Sunny. "Here the two of us bring you to the most beautiful cities in Texas, and all you do is complain. Typical, isn't it, Bret?"

"I totally agree. In fact, I think we should leave them by themselves. They deserve each other."

Josh opened his mouth to say something, but Bret cut him off, "I'm going to go to the arcade."

"What a coincidence," Holly was truly enjoying the whole scene. "I was just about to go there myself."

Bret took a low bow and then held out his arm for Holly. He somehow managed to make himself look utterly ridiculous and charming at the same time. "It would be an honor, my lady, if you would escort me to the arcade."

Holly hooked her arm through Bret's, and they headed off. Both were completely oblivious to the death looks they were receiving. Well, maybe not completely.

"Josh," Sunny said, "you're turning green. He's not claiming her as his turf; both of them are just trying to get the two of us alone so we can talk."

Josh threw up his hands, "Were you in on this too?"

"No," Sunny let out a long sigh, "it doesn't take very much brain power to figure it out." *Then again, the second Holly shows up, your brain turns to mush.*

Josh ran his hands through his hair. He looked like he was

about to yank it out. Just when Sunny was sure Josh was going to make himself go bald, he sighed and said, "Sunny, I'm sorry about that stuff I said to you. What you're doing is what God would want you to do and . . ."

Sunny cut him off, "Thanks for your confidence, but you weren't too far from the truth." Sunny couldn't believe what she was saying, but she had to get it out. "In the beginning, I tried to be Holly's friend because of God, but then I started to like her, for her. She may not be a Christian, but despite trying to drive me insane, she has a big heart. Josh, we've been best friends our entire lives, and you know I'm more comfortable around guys than girls. But now, with Holly, things are different. Remember when you and Bret became good friends about a year ago? I was so jealous because you had a new best friend." Josh looked guilty and tried to say something. Sunny held up a hand. "No wait. You never made me feel left out, but I realized then, that in a lot of ways, I could never compete. I understood then that you needed a guy friend, and I found out that I wanted a close friend that wasn't a guy. Until Holly, though, there never was anyone I wanted to be that good of friends with."

"Let me guess," Josh smiled, "once you realized Holly could be a great friend, you were afraid that if you were all about God, you'd scare her away."

Sunny smiled at how easily he understood her. "That's about it."

Josh felt a little awkward, but he put his hand on Sunny's shoulder. "This is my fault too, Sunny."

"What did you do? You warned me not to become friends with her."

"I know, but it had nothing to do with God. I used Him as an excuse because I was afraid to be around her." Sunny could see Josh was struggling to find the right words. "I'm drawn to her too, Sunny. Obviously, I like her in some ways you don't," Josh added with a grin. "At least you had good intentions when you tried to be her friend. I stayed away because I was too much of a wimp."

"What do you mean?"

"You're not going to make this easy for me, are you?" Sunny smirked. "I guess not," Josh said and continued. "I'm attracted to her, okay? I admit it. Being her friend is one thing, but being her boyfriend while she's still a non-Christian is a completely different matter. In fact, as far as I'm concerned, she's off-limits."

"Josh, why do you think you have to be her boyf...?"

Josh cut her off. "Because I want to be. This whole thing is difficult because I want to go out with her, but that would be going against what God commands us to do. So I figured I wouldn't torture myself by being near her."

"It looks like we are both in the same predicament, sort of." Sunny winked at Josh. "Both of us want to be close friends with her, but God commands us not to be too close to non-Christians because, in the end, those relationships always have a way of backfiring."

"So what do we do?" Josh asked.

Sunny smiled. "We pray."

Josh and Sunny heard the arcade long before they saw it. As usual, the game room was too dark to see anything but the games themselves. The neon lights threw an ever-real glow on people's faces. Sunny strained her ears to make out the words playing over the loudspeaker, but it was impossible to hear over the bells, sirens, and the clink-clank of tokens hitting metal.

They found the two tricksters playing a heated match of air hockey. Both had a look of determination in their eyes. A few other people stopped to watch as they pounded the poor puck back and forth across the slippery table. *Crack!* Holly hit it with accuracy and strength that could only come from a pro. *Crack!* Bret blocked it, barely. When the puck came back to him this time, he was ready. He aimed for the kill, and it almost went in. Holly sideswiped it, and...

"Ouch!" Josh grabbed his now throbbing left eye. He hadn't seen the puck coming. He'd been too busy watching Holly.

"Oh, shoot, Josh.! I'm so sorry," Holly rushed over to look at Josh's eye. "Let me see."

"No," Josh could hear the whine in his voice, "no, it's fine." He didn't want her to see the tears that were welling up in his eyes. Bret walked over to them.

"Whatever happened to not hurting the spectators?"

"I'm sorry."

Josh could see she was really upset that she'd hurt him. This was an interesting development. "It's okay, but now that I'm injured you have to be nice to me. Are you two ready to go?"

"Sure," Bret headed toward the door, "I would have won anyway."

"That would be a first," Holly smirked, "considering you lost the other four games."

They walked out of the dark arcade. "No way, Bret! You lost? You never lose at air hockey. Way to go, Holly." Sunny gave her a high five.

Bret didn't look very cheerful anymore. "Where did you learn to play like that?"

"If I told you, I'd have to kill you."

"Hmm…Well, I might be dead if we don't eat something soon. Let's go to the food court. I'm starving."

"Bret, we ate an hour ago."

"So?"

Sunny rolled her eyes. "Where are you guys staying?"

"Some fancy hotel near here," Josh said. "I'm still trying to figure out how we're paying for it." The last part was aimed at Bret.

"Let's just say I have connections."

Holly and Sunny started laughing. "Am I missing something here?" Josh looked at them suspiciously. He'd had enough surprises for one day. The last thing he wanted to hear was that they'd sold his liver on the black market.

"Our lips are sealed, Josh. So…Holly, Bret, now that you have the two of us here, what are we going to do?"

"We hadn't planned much for today, but we figured if you were still breathing by tomorrow, we'd go to Fiesta Texas," Bret told them.

"What's Fiesta Texas?"

"It's a theme park owned by Six Flags. You guys will like. . . ." Someone's cell phone cut her off.

"Oh, that's mine," Sunny pulled her cell out and looked at the number.

"Who is it?" Josh asked.

"I don't know. It's blocked." Sunny shrugged and answered it anyway. "Hello? Yes, this is Sunflower White. Who's this? You want to talk to whom? Um, okay." Sunny looked curiously at Holly. "It's for you. Did you give someone my number?"

"No," Holly shook her head and took the phone. "Hello?"

"Hello, Holly, did you miss me?"

Holly felt her blood turn to ice. "How did you get this number?"

"I've missed you every day."

Holly walked away from the group, "Albert, how did you get this number?"

"You didn't think I would stay away forever, did you? I always get what I want, Holly. Did you think you could hide underneath that new look or in that big school of yours? You are my destiny!" There was a slight pause. "By the way, dump your boyfriend. You know who I'm talking about, the one who's wearing the navy blue T-shirt and boring holes through your back as we speak."

Holly looked over her shoulder, and sure enough, Josh was staring at her. "You can't scare me anymore. I'm not a little kid." Holly whispered. She hung up on him and turned to her friends. They were staring at her, waiting to hear an explanation. Josh's phone rang. He kept his eyes on Holly as he pulled out his phone.

"Hello?"

"Give the phone to Holly."

"Not until you tell me who this is."

Albert said mockingly, "This is Joshua Vancouver Timberlaigh. Address 167 Turner Lane, Salem, Oregon. Isn't Holly beautiful? Even in those clothes, she's still twice as pretty as any other girl here. I don't blame you for wanting her, but she's mine."

"Who is this?" Josh demanded as he yelled into the phone.

"Someone way out of your league. Now hand over the phone!"

Holly jerked the cell away from Josh. She hadn't needed to hear what was being said. "Leave my friends alone."

"You shouldn't have hung up on me, Holly. That wasn't a very nice thing to do. Now, unless you want me to walk up right now, you need to promise me something."

"What?" She couldn't believe this was happening.

"My father is hosting a New Year's Eve Party on Friday, December 31. It will be the fête of the season and a great way to start out the New Year. Be there. Au revoir, ma cherie."

Holly hung up and dialed a number on her phone. Of course, he couldn't get her number. Hers was blocked, but her friends' phones weren't. As Holly dialed, she tried not to look at their faces. How much could she tell them? Nothing. "Hello, Robert—no, my line is secure. You did a great job, but it seems the worm has tracked down some of my friend's numbers. Yes, they're right here. Thank you."

chapter sixteen

top pacing." Bret was lying on the end of his bed with his head hanging off the end.

"How can you not be wired after what just happened?"

"We now have phone numbers that even the police would have a hard time getting. Personally, I think it's kind of cool."

"No, it's not!" Josh knew he was sounded like a two-year-old, but he didn't care.

"Josh, it was a stupid prank. Don't worry about it."

"I didn't see Holly laughing."

"I wasn't laughing when you guys pulled that joke on me at the Mexican food restaurant. You, on the other hand, wouldn't stop snickering about it for the rest of the day. It's all in the eye of the beholder, dude."

Josh glared at Bret. He hadn't had his phone violated. Worse, was Holly in some kind of trouble? She had to be. It infuriated him that she'd been so closed-mouthed about the whole thing. All she'd said was the guy was an annoying friend of the family. She could act as cool as she wanted to, but he'd seen her face. She was scared, and he wanted to help her but he couldn't because she wouldn't let him. Josh kicked the leg of his bed. That hadn't been the smartest of moves. He forgot he wasn't wearing shoes.

"That had to hurt."

"Will you shut up?"

Bret scowled and rolled off the bed. "Man, you're really getting on my nerves. I wasn't the one who did that to Holly, and just because she didn't go running to you to save her, doesn't mean you have the right to act like a baby."

"She should trust me."

"Trust you? Who would trust an overbearing jerk?"

Josh shoved Bret backwards into the wall. Warning bells rang in both the guys' heads, but they went unheeded. Bret slammed into Josh, and they both went down. Neither of them knew who struck first, but five minutes later they were both lying on the ground hurting and bleeding. A few minutes later, they heard a knock. Josh grimaced as he hobbled over to open the door.

"We're finally ready for din....Josh, what happened? Bret, are you okay?" Sunny called out to Holly. "Call security, someone's broken into their room!" Holly came running into the room.

"Oh my God!" *Oh no, he's been here.*

Josh saw Holly turn white, "Um, don't call security." Josh sat down in a chair and winced.

"Why not?"

"Because that would be dumb considering we did this to each other," Bret said. He was still lying on the floor. Holly looked at the two of them as if they were nuts. Sunny just rolled her eyes.

"Josh," Sunny crossed her arms, "since it looks like you can walk, go with Holly into the next room. She'll take care of you."

Holly shot Sunny a look, *I will?*

"I can take care of myself," Josh grumbled.

"You think that if it brings you comfort. Now leave before Bret gets up and starts round two." Josh looked at the three of them.

In the end he figured he was safer with Holly than Sunny or Bret. They might gang up on him.

Holly helped Josh into her room. He knew he could have made it on his own, but it felt good to have her arm around his waist. All in all, there were worse ways to spend the evening. "So are you going to play Florence Nightingale?"

"It looks like it—though I don't think I'll be very good at it. Here put this on your head." She'd put ice into a plastic bag and then wrapped it in a washcloth. "How did you get that bump anyway?"

"Bret smashed my head into a wooden bed frame," Josh said lamely and then winced when she tried to wipe some of the blood off his mouth.

"You have such nice friends. Is there any particular reason the two of you decided to beat each other into bloody pulps?"

Josh started to smile, "Ouch! It was going all right for me until I decided to run my face into his fist."

Holly smiled. "It looks like you tried to do that on more than one occasion. So are you going to tell me what the fight was about?"

"Are you going to tell me what the phone calls were about?"

"That depends," Holly said. "Are the two related?"

Josh opened his mouth and then shut it again, "Very sneaky."

Holly laughed until she looked down and saw his sock was covered in blood. "Josh, what happened to your foot?"

"I ran it into the bed. Bret actually had nothing to do with that."

"Do you like pain or something?"

"No, I just try to get it all out of the way at once. OW!" Josh yelped when Holly yanked his sock off. "Be careful!"

"Sorry, I thought you said you like to get it over with."

Josh gritted his teeth against the pain. "Ha, ha."

Holly tried her best to clean him up, but his foot kept bleeding. "I'm going to call the front desk and ask them to bring up a first aid kit. There might even be one up here, but I wouldn't know where to look."

When her back was turned to him, Josh felt free to look at her as much as he wanted. He knew he should look away, but he couldn't. When she turned back around, he still didn't look away. Their eyes locked. Josh tried to say something funny to break the tension, but that's not what came out. "You're beautiful."

Holly didn't know what to say. She was used to being complimented, but the way Josh said it made her feel like it was more than just flattery. "I don't want to be beautiful."

Josh touched her shoulder to get her to look at him. "Is that why you wear these clothes?"

Holly tensed up and shook him off. "All guys are the same, just like the one on the phone."

"I'm not that guy on the phone," Josh stood up. His stomach turned when he saw the look of terror that passed over her face. She quickly replaced it with cool reserve, but he saw it nonetheless. Josh sat down again. When the first-aid kit arrived, Holly fixed his foot. Josh didn't want to scare her anymore than he already had, so he didn't say anything else, not even to complain that his foot was killing him.

Holly finished and looked up. *Better to do this without her cowering below me.* Josh slipped off the bed and sat on the ground with her. "Holly, you don't have to tell me who that guy was or why he was calling you. Just know that I'm here for you, along with Sunny and Bret." Josh smiled. The pain that shot through his face was worth seeing her smile back at him.

"This isn't very fair for me to ask, but will you tell me what the fight was about?" Holly asked.

"Some of it was Bret finally laying it on me for being a creep for the past few weeks and the other…the other was about you. I've been a jerk. I'm sorry."

Holly couldn't believe what she was hearing. The guy was apologizing to her?

Josh didn't know how to take Holly's silence. Had he said too much? *She probably thinks I'm a wimp now. Way to go, Josh.*

"You're right," Holly said.

"That I'm a jerk?"

Holly laughed at the insulted look on his face, "No, you're right about what you said earlier. You're not like the guy who was on the phone."

She was only inches away from his face. *God, can I please kiss her?* Josh heard the answer loud and clear, but he wasn't about to give up so easily. *Well, I can't help it. So if You don't want me to kiss her, then You'll have to intervene in some way.*

Both Josh and Holly jumped when the door sprung open. "Hey guys! Are the two of you ready to eat?" Josh had never wanted to strangle Sunny so much in his life, and that was saying something. "Oh look, she has a key," Josh said mainly to himself, but Holly heard and chuckled.

"We're ready to go." Holly looked at the carpet. "I feel sorry for the maid. She's going to think we killed someone."

"Do you think the hotel is going to charge extra money?" Josh asked.

"Um, Josh," Bret choked on a laugh. "Holly's dad owns these hotels."

"Really? My grandparents own a chain of hotels too. What's your dad's name?"

Holly hesitated and then shrugged. "Steven Johnson."

Josh kept a straight face, but inside his head he was reeling as he began to connect the dots. *Tres Johnson is her father! Then she must be...No, it can't be her. Oh God, was that Bergenstein on the phone?* Josh had never felt cold hatred before, yet what flowed through him at that moment was powerful enough to drive any kindhearted soul to murder. *God, this isn't what You want. This isn't going to solve anything. Please help me. I can't handle this.* After a few minutes, Josh felt God's peace flow through him and wash away his anger. He knew it would come back if he let it, but that night, he didn't. Holly saw something special in Josh's eyes that night. She was comforted by it, even though she didn't realize that what she saw was God.

Sunny looked out the hotel window. It was hard to see anything with all the rain. "It looks like Fiesta Texas is out," she said primarily to herself since Holly was hiding in bed.

"Good, I'm going back to sleep."

"Holly, it's almost ten o'clock in the morning."

"I know." Holly pulled the covers over her head. "It's too early to be awake on a Saturday."

Sunny looked at Holly. Actually, she looked at a very big lump in the bed, same thing. She took her life in her hands and pulled off the covers.

"What the…? Hey!"

"Come on, get up."

"All right, and then I'm going to murder you."

"How much money do you have with you?"

"What? First you wake me up, and now you're going to rob me?"

"No, actually I think you need some new clothes, particularly new shoes because I want mine back. Besides, do you even have a dress or a nice outfit for tomorrow?"

"Tomorrow?" Holly was trying to make sense of what Sunny was saying, but her brain wasn't fully functioning yet. *Did she say shopping?* "Um, Sunny, I don't like shopping. I mean, I used to, but I don't anymore."

"Why?"

"Well, look at me. Can you imagine me walking into Gap?"

"Oh, well then, if that's how you feel, we definitely need to go shopping. Once we get you a new outfit, then you can change. By the way, do you want a hair cut?"

Holly groaned and reached for her covers, but they weren't there anymore. Therefore, she got up to get dressed and whacked Sunny with her pillow for a good measure.

Their first stop wasn't the mall. It was breakfast. "Look." Holly pointed at one of the buffet lines. "They still have Rice Krispies, and it's almost eleven in the morning."

"That must mean they're first class then."

Holly frowned at Sunny's sarcasm and grabbed some waffles. "See? I can eat other food."

"Yeah, as long as it isn't healthy for you," Sunny watched Holly douse her waffles in syrup.

"I don't criticize what you eat."

"Uh huh, is that why you're always telling me I don't eat enough?"

"Actually, that's criticizing how much you eat, not what you eat. Besides, you don't eat enough."

Sunny pretended to scowl. "I eat plenty. It's just that if I ate as much as you, you would have to roll me out of here." Holly laughed. "So are you ever going to tell me what that call was about?" Holly stopped laughing.

"Maybe someday, but not right now."

"Holly, are you in some kind of trouble?"

Sunny looked at her eyes. They looked so much older all of a sudden. How could they change so fast? "True or false . . ." Holly asked, "we should run from what we're afraid of."

God, I don't know how to answer that. I don't know what she's afraid of. Suddenly, Sunny had the answer, "For me, the answer is false, because there is nothing my God can't overcome. Without God, though, Holly, I can't tell you."

"I've lived without God my entire life. I don't see why I need Him now."

"Then you're braver than you think."

chapter seventeen

"Do we have to go to the mall?" Holly realized her voice was bordering on whining, but she was too distracted to care what she sounded like.

"In this case, Holly, I would definitely say 'face your fear.' "

"Everyone looks at me strangely."

You are not going to feel sorry for yourself. "People always look at you strangely, but that's never stopped you before. Don't tell me you're mallophobic, because I'm not buying it."

" 'Mallophobic' isn't a word," Holly mumbled.

Sunny ignored her. "Come on. I see a hairdresser up there."

Holly groaned again. She looked over her shoulder when she heard a screaming toddler who was mercilessly being dragged alongside his mother. *I feel for you, kid.* Holly dragged her feet. *Well, I do need new shoes, but why do I have to get a haircut?*

When they walked into the salon, one of the hairdressers looked at Holly and shook her head. Before either Holly or Sunny could say anything, the hairdresser—Jamie was her name—pushed Holly into a seat so fast she was surprised she didn't get whiplash.

"Lose a bet?" Jamie asked as she set to work on Holly's hair.

"I guess you could say that."

"Don't worry, honey. I'll fix it." *That's what I'm worried about,* Holly thought as she looked over at Sunny. "Don't move your head." Jamie jerked Holly's head back where it was. This time she did get whiplash.

"Sorry," Holly mumbled. *Why am I doing this again?* she thought. To distract herself from the horrifying sight of her hair falling to the ground, Holly watched the second hand tick away on her watch. It must have hypnotized her because before Holly knew what hit her, she jumped at the sound of a hair dryer.

When Jamie was finished with her, Holly almost didn't recognize herself. All of a sudden, she could see her face again, but that meant everyone else could as well. "Honey, what were you hiding that gorgeous face for?" Jamie asked while she swept hair off the ground.

"I...um."

"Oh," Jamie's eyes suddenly softened. "Honey, whoever he is, he isn't worth it. You can't run from what you're afraid of forever."

How could she? How did she know? Holly looked over at Sunny who was reading a fashion magazine and well out of earshot. "Um, did Sunny talk to you earlier?"

Jamie looked puzzled. "Who's Sunny?"

"The girl I came in with."

"Oh, no, she didn't talk to me. After doing people's hair for thirty years, you just catch on to things like this. I've seen your type before. You're beautiful, but don't let that frighten you."

"How can you know that? How can you know exactly what to say to me?"

"Well, some people call it luck. Personally, I call it God," Jamie started cleaning up the counter space in front of Holly.

"I've been hearing a lot about Him lately," Holly said, still wondering if this was all some sort of conspiracy to drive her mad. Her logical mind reminded her that the likelihood of that was slim to none. Sunny wouldn't have had enough time to set this up.

"Don't you think that He might be trying to get your attention?"

A couple of days ago, Holly would have been insulted by such a question, but now she wanted the answers too. "I'm not sure if I even believe He exists. It doesn't make sense."

"Yes it does. You're just using the wrong formula." Jamie took the cape off Holly and scooted her off the chair. "Well, you're done. You have great hair by the way. You remind me of some actress when she was younger. Shoot, what's her name?" Jamie looked at the ceiling, trying to remember.

"Let me guess, Anne Tricony?" Holly asked blandly, already knowing the answer.

Jamie snapped her fingers. "That's it. How did you know?"

Holly forced a smile. "I get that a lot. Thank you for cutting my hair." Holly tipped her and walked towards Sunny. Sunny looked up and beamed.

"You look great!"

"Thanks," Jamie's words ran through her head. *"You can't run from what you're afraid of forever."* Holly shook her head at the absurdity of the conversation. It couldn't be a coincidence, could it? "Sunny, did you talk to Jamie earlier?"

"Who's Jamie?"

"Never mind." Holly gave up trying to figure out what was going on. *First the radio, and now this.* One thing was for certain. She wasn't about to let Sunny know how fazed she was. Not only that, but she could feel something melting inside of her. No, Sunny definitely couldn't know what was going on inside of her heart. *If God is real, could He?* "Sunny, how long do we have until we meet the guys for lunch and then leave?"

"About three hours, why?"

Holly didn't answer her question. After paying for her haircut, she grabbed Sunny's arm. "Let's go." Now it was Holly's turn to drag Sunny along.

"You make me sick."

"Sorry," Holly said as they walked out of a department store.

"You look good in everything." Sunny slumped against the nearest wall.

"I didn't look good in these." Holly held up the clothes she'd been wearing that morning.

Josh would beg to differ. "Hmmm…how come you were so lucky in the gene pool?"

"I'm a good swimmer."

It took Sunny a moment to figure out what she meant, but then she snickered. "That was really corny."

"Yeah," Holly said, "but you're smiling—mission accomplished."

"Humph, I still can't believe you spent three hundred dollars on make-up."

"Well, I threw all my other stuff away about two years ago. That reminds me . . ." Holly walked over to a trashcan and dumped her old clothes into it. "I don't need those anymore."

While Holly's back was turned to her, Sunny beamed. "Okay, Miss America, we need to go. The guys are always grumpy on an empty stomach, and if we're a minute late, they'll complain." Suddenly, Holly stopped walking. "Holly, what's wrong?"

Holly bit her lower lip. "Maybe I shouldn't have thrown those clothes away."

"Holly, what are you afraid of? You look great."

"That's what I'm afraid of. Guys are weird around me when I look like this."

Sunny laughed. "Guys are weird, period. What happened to that cool, confident girl I knew who didn't care what anyone thought about her."

"She's in the trash can."

"Holly, the clothes you wear don't change who you are."

"Oh, really," Holly said sarcastically. She couldn't come up with anything better to say, so she left it at that. *What will Josh think of me? Will he think I did this for him? Did I do this for him?*

"Holly, snap out of it. You look perfectly fine. Now come on."

Holly sent Sunny a pathetic look. "Fine."

Holly and Sunny saw Josh and Bret sitting at one of the tables in the underground food court. Just as Sunny had expected, they looked moody. "Hey," Holly said coolly. *Just act like nothing's different.* Bret looked up first, and his mouth dropped. Josh was checking his watch, which informed him the girls were three minutes late, a grave sin against his stomach.

"It's about time the two of you got . . ." He stopped mid lecture when Bret elbowed him. "What did you do that for?" Josh forgot about Bret. In fact, he forgot about everything. His entire universe ceased to exist, and there was only Holly. For the first time in his life, Josh had to order himself to breathe. *It can't be her.* "Wha…what happened to you?" *I did not just say that.* "I mean, you look good, but why?" *That was worse.* "I mean, um, are you guys hungry?" Josh jumped up and started to go outside.

"Josh," Bret was trying not to laugh but failed miserably "the food is that way."

Josh turned around and glanced at Holly. She still looked the same, gorgeous. Because he seemed to be the only one making a fool of himself, he sent Sunny and Bret death looks and walked off before he could humiliate himself further.

Josh didn't realize he was at a pizza place until it was too late. He hated pizza, but he wasn't about to make an even bigger fool of himself by sporadically changing lines and getting a hamburger. That's what he'd planned to eat before Holly walked in, but he was staying right where he was. Josh didn't know who to be madder at—Holly, Sunny, or God. He settled on blaming Bret. It was easier that way.

When Josh walked back to the table, he didn't look at Holly. In fact, he didn't look at anyone. Had he looked in Holly's direction, he would have seen her failed attempt to bolt. Josh would be the first to say that Sunny didn't look very strong, but she had an iron grip. Holly couldn't have gotten away without making a scene. While she struggled to escape, Josh took a bite of his pizza and tried not to make a face.

"I thought you didn't like pizza, Josh?" Sunny casually remarked. That earned her a kick from under the table. "Ouch! Fine, be a creep," Sunny rubbed her shin.

Josh looked at the ground. He refused to feel guilty for taking his frustrations out on Sunny. Okay, he'd feel guilty, but he would not under any circumstance repent. This was all God's fault anyway. *That's mature,* he thought as he glanced at Bret. How come he wasn't making a fool of himself? Since when was Bret better with girls than he was? *Ever since Holly walked into my life.* Josh looked down at the ground and noticed bags of what had to be more clothes designed to torture him. "How much stuff did the two of you buy?"

"We would have gotten more if we'd had the time," Sunny smirked at him. She was enjoying watching her friend make a fool of himself. It happened so rarely that Sunny couldn't help but watch and grin.

It was Bret who saved Josh from further embarrassment. Well, sort of. He started talking about how good Holly looked and joked about how she needed to hang out with him more often.

Sunny got sick of looking at Josh glare at his food. "Earth to Josh." She waved her hand in front of his face. "What are you thinking about?"

One word came to Josh's mind—Holly. "None of your business, Sunny." He leaned over and whispered in Holly's ear. "I was thinking about you. I'm sorry I'm such a klutz around you. Bret's right. You do look great. You always have to me." Josh looked at her face to read her reaction.

When Holly smiled, her whole face lit up. She leaned over and whispered back into his ear. Josh had to concentrate to hear what she said. Her hand on his shoulder was distracting him, "Thank you," she whispered. "If it makes you feel any better, I almost acted the same way the first time I met you."

Sunny and Bret just looked at each other. Bret whispered loudly to Sunny so that all could hear, "Don't you hate it when people whisper at the table." Josh smirked, and Bret kept whispering. "Darn! I think she said something nice to him because I can see his ego swelling from here. It's going to be a long ride home."

The four of them laughed, and all of the previous awkwardness vanished. A few minutes later, they left for Austin. Before they got into their cars, Sunny spoke to Josh. "By the way, we're going to church tomorrow. I know you're dying to see me again, so I guess you'll just have to put up with Holly being there too." Josh turned red, and Sunny smiled. "Josh, I'm really happy for you, but be careful, okay? She's still not a Christian," Josh started to interrupt her, but Sunny stopped him. "You know, as well as I do, that neither of us can make her accept God. It will be God who opens her heart, and finally, it will be Holly who makes the choice."

"I know you're trying to warn me, but...," Josh looked over at Holly. She was a ways away and talking with Bret. She was laughing at something Bret had said. Josh felt something move inside of him, something he couldn't explain. "Sun, pray for me. I think I might be falling in love with her."

Sunny stared at him in silence for what seemed like an eternity, but then she finally spoke, "Josh, whatever you're feeling is not something to be afraid of, but if my parents taught me anything, it's this: 'Falling in love is like jumping out of an airplane. Gravity will bring us down no matter how much we want to fly, but a smart person, a godly person, will open up his parachute. It might not feel as exhilarating at first, but when you reach the ground, you'll still be alive.'"

"In other words," Josh said, "God created people's feelings for a reason, but don't allow them to control you."

"Exactly."

"You have really cool parents."

"We have a really cool God."

"Amen to that."

chapter eighteen

arry Harris was a small man. His growth plate had been damaged when he was ten, which left him looking a bit like a midget. Harry was the type who told anyone who would listen that he was a free agent "who didn't work for nobody but hisself." Although he had no idea that he would be dead soon, all five foot one of him was shaking from head to foot. He was currently standing in front of a man who was half his age, but that didn't make him any less formidable.

Harry watched the man behind the desk tap his cigar on an ashtray with a little Buddha in the middle. Harry didn't care much for religion. He believed that it was all a trick to get people's money, but if he had been a religious fellow, he would have said that the devil had his hand on this man. He had dark eyes, the kind that could creep into your dreams if you weren't careful.

"I don't see what the problem is Mr. Bergenstein." Harry almost squeaked. "I got you the information you wanted."

"Yes, Mr. Harris, but I gave you a new assignment. One of which you claim to be incapable of performing."

Bergenstein's blatant attack on Harry's pride did not go unfelt. "It's not that I can't do it, sir. I got them numbers and information that you was wantin' fo,' but I can't do what you is askin' me to do now. You could do hard time for somethin' like that. 'Specially it bein' the daughter of an important fella."

The man laughed. "Trust me, he won't lift a finger to help her. She's the black sheep of the family. The only reason he doesn't disown her is because she's the only child he has." The man leaned back in his chair seeming at ease with himself. "Now I want you to think carefully about the decision you are making. You are aware of how much money I'm offering you, are you not?"

"Yes, sir, but that money won't do me no good in prison."

"It won't do you any good in hell either." Albert picked up his phone and dialed extension seven. Less than a minute later a gruff looking man in his early thirties walked in. "Harry, I'd like for you to meet Tony Valasquez. Now, Tony, you were talking about a raise, and I think the amount you requested is more than reasonable."

"Why, thank you, sir."

"Of course, I need you to prove your loyalty to me first." Albert casually twirled the cigar through his fingers. "I see now," Albert looked at Harry, "that without loyalty, no business engagement can be done properly. Do you agree, Tony?"

"Um, yes, sir."

"Come closer then." Tony walked over to Albert. Shielded by the desk, Albert handed Tony a gun. "Kill that man over there, and I'll double your salary."

Tony raised the gun and fired. Harry Harris was dead before he hit the floor.

chapter nineteen

"Holly, get up." Sunny put her hands on her hips. It was the dawn of a new day, and thus they began their daily ritual. "Holly, don't pretend to be asleep. I know you're awake."

"Go away. It's bad enough you turned on the light."

"It's eight o'clock. Time to get up."

"It's Sunday."

"I know, and you promised to go to church with me."

Holly attempted to burrow further under the covers. "Isn't there a later service?" she groaned.

"Yep, but this is the one Josh, Bret, Elizabeth, and I always go to." Just as Sunny expected, Josh's name got Holly's attention. *Sorry God, but it's the only way I'll get her up. She's bigger than I am, so I can't drag her to church.*

Holly forced herself to sit up, but when Sunny's back was turned, she scrambled under the covers again. "Oh no you don't,"

Sunny crossed her arms and stamped her foot. "Come on, we only have thirty minutes to get ready."

"Fine." If there was a God, then Holly had a bone to pick with Him. How could He give her a roommate who was a morning person? Holly thought about what her life would be like if she had never met Sunny. Was it really just a lucky coincidence, or was there someone or something out there who really did have control over everything? *If You are real, then thank you for Sunny. She's the best friend I've ever had.* Holly felt something pass through her. She couldn't explain it, but it felt good.

All thoughts of the supernatural left her when Holly saw herself in the mirror. She felt the shock, but this time she was prepared for it. For the past twenty-four hours, she'd been getting more and more acquainted with her new look, or maybe she should say, her old look. Her biggest surprise was that she liked it. For once in her life, Holly was starting to like herself. If that didn't prove miracles could happen, then nothing would.

Thanks to not wearing heels for two years, Holly had to concentrate on not falling on her face. She was so focused she hardly noticed Josh and Bret walk in. She also didn't notice the way Elizabeth and Bret tripped over themselves to sit next to each other. Josh looked at Holly with indecision. *To sit next to Holly, or not to, that is the question.*

Sunny plopped down on the nearest seat and let the rest of her friends make fools of themselves. Perhaps, Sunny thought smugly to herself, she was the only one who hadn't lost her mind.

The preacher's name was Tyler Reaths. He was in his late forties and looked like a beach bum. In fact, Sunny thought she'd heard something about him growing up along the coasts of California. That was something to investigate later. She would have been glad to have a former surf dude for a preacher. Although, as it would turn out, he wasn't giving the message that day.

"I have treat for the congregation today," Pastor Reaths told them. "I won't be the one speaking."

"Is that the treat?" one of the deacons called out from the front row, and everyone laughed.

"Just for that, I should make you get up here," Pastor Reaths said with a twinkle in his eye, and then he cleared his throat. "The treat is that a buddy of mine, Mr. Mark Tayne, is giving the lesson. Those of you who don't know him yet ought to be ashamed of yourselves. He's our new youth director, which is a bit scary considering he looks like he just got out of diapers himself. Also, once you young ladies see him, you're going to be asking me anyway—so I'll tell you now. He's single, adorable on his better days—we don't talk about his bad ones—and he only has about three incurable diseases." A couple of the bolder girls cheered.

As the whole congregation laughed, a very red Mr. Tayne walked on stage. "Thank you, Ty for that embarrassing introduction. I wouldn't have wanted the people here to actually take me seriously. I . . ." He didn't remember what he was going to say. It was her, and she was looking right at him. Did she recognize him? Mark suddenly remembered he was standing in front of five hundred people who were waiting for him to talk about God.

"...I suppose that I could never live up to Pastor Reaths here, being ancient and all, but I will definitely try. I want to start this off with a question. Why are we here, on earth that is? Some people might say, 'Well, Mark, people have been asking themselves that question for years and still haven't figured it out. So how can you expect us to know?' " Mark paused and glanced at Sunny. She was still staring at him. *Of course she's staring at you, you half-wit. You're the speaker.*

He continued. "What if I told you the answer to our lives has been right in front of our noses for thousands of years?" Mark knew he had their attention now. "We were created for fellowship with our Creator. Now our Creator, God, didn't want robots to talk to Him because, after all, where's the fun in that? So He gave us free will. In other words, we have the choice of whether we have a relationship with Him or not.

"God created every human being with a need for Him, and this need can only be filled by Him. Unfortunately, we don't want to need Him or anybody. So we try to fill that hole with other stuff like friendships, money, dating, cars, sports, or school. You name it; we do it—anything to keep ourselves from the one relationship that would truly fulfill our need to be whole. We're human; we're contrary like that." That got a laugh from the audience.

"Some of us realize that it's God we need. Some of us don't. Yet no matter if you do or you don't, you will never be truly content without Him. You might be happy, even joyful for brief moments in your life, but why have only moments when you could have a lifetime of joy? People who seek a relationship with God can be going through the worst time in their lives and still have it made. On the other hand, you can have the world and still be miserable. Trust me; I've seen it. What we need is a relationship with God, but what we seek will be, as it always has been our choice."

Mark talked for thirty minutes. Sunny was going to tell Holly it was the guy from the store, but Holly looked like she was hanging onto his every word. Therefore, Sunny kept watching him. She tried not to notice how his shirt matched his eyes perfectly or how his smile was the cutest thing she'd ever seen. She couldn't like him; she refused. She'd heard someone behind her say he was twenty-five years old, which meant he was at least six years older than she was. Sunny didn't have a problem with people going out with guys who were years older than them, unless it was her. She never pictured herself as the type of girl who would go out with an older guy. Sunny looked at Mark again. *Why does he keep looking at me?* Sunny shook her head. *I'm probably just imagining things.*

When the service was over, Sunny, Holly, and Elizabeth went to the bathroom. They ignored Bret's comment about girls needing moral support to go to the bathroom.

"Hey! I think I've seen the two of you here before."

Josh and Bret turned around and found themselves face-to-face with the speaker. "Hey, great sermon." *Especially since Holly was listening.* Josh was ready to kiss the guy's feet.

"Thanks. I'm Mark." Mark stuck out his hand.

"I'm Josh, and this is Bret." The three shook hands. Maybe Josh was imagining things, but Mark seemed to grip his hand a bit harder than necessary.

Suddenly, Mark stuck his hands into his pockets and looked a little uncomfortable. "So um, that girl who was sitting next to you…the blonde?" This was aimed at Josh, "I met her once. She spilt her coke on me, but then she was gone before I had the chance to get her name."

"Oh," Josh laughed. *So that's why he almost broke my hand. Well, I guess Sunny could do worse.* "That's Sunny. She's not the most graceful girl on the planet, but she has a killer arm. So now I've told you her name, I wouldn't suggest making fun of it."

Mark lifted his eyebrows. "Have you ever been on the receiving end of her arm?"

"Well, only a few times, but that was mainly when we were little. I was shorter than her then," Josh explained. *I might as well let the guy breathe easier.* "We've been best friends since before I can remember. She's like a sister to me."

"Oh," *Thank you, God. One down, now this other goofball to go.* "So who were the other two girls?"

"The one with curly hair and glasses was Elisabeth, and the other was Holly."

Mark grinned at Bret and hoped his smile didn't look as forced as it felt. *Here it goes.* "So are you going out with Elizabeth?"

Bret smiled, "I'm working on it."

Yes! "So" Mark said to Josh, "how about you and Holly?"

"Well, I can't, if you know what I mean. Considering her life, it's strange she even came to church."

No way! She's gay? "What about Sunny?" Mark turned pale.

"Sunny!" Josh couldn't imagine going out with her. Hadn't he made that clear yet? Josh turned and looked at Bret who broke out laughing. "Sunny is worse than Holly."

God, what on earth is going on? Mark saw the three girls coming towards them. Sunny and Holly had linked their arms. If they'd known their sexuality was being questioned, they would have walked ten feet away from each other. Unfortunately, they didn't have a clue.

Sunny smiled at Mark and wondered why he looked so freaked out. Maybe he was just slow. Poor guy. Sunny smiled at him. "You're the guy I creamed with my drink, aren't you?"

"Um, yeah. Are you a Christian?"

Sunny was taken aback. "Yes, I'm assuming you are too." Sunny looked at Josh and tried to figure out if Mark's question had been as random to him.

"Yeah, I'm a Christian. Do you believe in the Bible?"

Thank God he's not asking Holly these questions. "Of course I do. Why?"

"So you believe everything it says?"

"Yes," Sunny was starting to get annoyed. "Is there particular reason you want to know, or do you always interrogate people when you first meet them?"

"Actually, I've already met you, and I'm not interrogating you. Have you read Leviticus?"

Sunny lifted her eyebrows. "Is this you not interrogating me because you're not very good at it?" When all Mark did was stare at her, she threw up her hands in surrender. "Yes, if you must know, I have read Leviticus all the way through. Though, I can't say that I enjoyed it very much."

"No one ever does," Josh mumbled.

"Both of you," Mark pointed at Sunny and Holly, "should read Leviticus 18 again. I think you'll find it very interesting. Well, I have to get ready for the next service. It was nice meeting you guys." He stormed off, leaving them staring at each other.

"Um, Josh, do you have any clue what all of that was about?"

"Sorry, Sunny, he seemed fairly normal until you walked up. Now I'm going to go back to the dorms to read Leviticus 18. I'm curious."

"Yeah," Sunny said, "well, I'm hungry. Let's go." Sunny refused to be angry about the way Mark had acted toward her. What had all that been about anyway? He had looked and treated her as if she were a little kid who had gotten her hand caught in the cookie jar. Sunny plastered on a smile. She refused to let him ruin her day.

Cold water hitting his face did little to cool him down. How could he have been such a moron? Love at first sight was for saps, and to think he'd actually thought she was "the one" was humiliating. Mark had never felt so stupid before in his life, and he abhorred stupidity. He'd come to know Christ when he was seventeen when a cop had saved his sorry tush after he'd picked a fight with the wrong crowd. Mark had been in and out of the system since he was three and had a knack for finding trouble wherever it lurked.

His life had been a downhill rollercoaster. You name it—he'd done it, but Mark had always been one to see an opportunity when it came his way. The cop, Randy was his name, had given him a choice. Either he could come quietly with him for dinner and allow Randy to speak freely about God, or he could go down to the station in handcuffs. Obviously, Mark had taken the prior choice. He'd expected to hear that Jesus loved him, that he should turn from his sins, and all the other stuff he'd "listened" to before.

Mark figured he could sit and listen to the old man huff and puff about God. He had to run out of breath eventually. What Mark hadn't counted on was coming to Christ that night. For the next three months, Mark wrestled with God for control over his life. In that time, he learned something very important. God was lovingly relentless when it came to doing what was best for His children. Eventually, Mark gave it up to God—his will, his drugs, his friends, and hardest of all, girls. For eight years, Mark had waited patiently, and sometimes not so patiently, for God to bring the right girl to him. Two days ago, he'd been sure God had finally done it, but now it looked like he'd been wrong.

Mark threw the pillow he'd been strangling at the door, and it made a satisfying bang. In the back of his mind, Mark could feel God trying to tell him something. *Leave me alone,* Mark said. He could almost hear God sigh. *I know You know what's best for me, God. I just don't want to hear it right now.* Mark slid down a wall onto the ground and sat there for a long time. No matter how hard he tried, he couldn't get Sunny's face out of his mind.

chapter twenty

After lunch, Holly and Sunny headed back to their dorm. Sunny got to her "key" first and opened the door. Before she'd taken two steps, she let out a huge sneeze and knocked Holly out the doorway.

"Bless you . . ." Holly stepped into the room stunned. *What on earth?* Their dorm was covered with sunflowers. Sunny's eyes were watering so much that she looked like she was crying. On top of that, she couldn't stop coughing and sneezing. "Sunny get out of the room before you collapse. I'll find out who had the bright idea to send these." Holly looked around the room. There must have been over a hundred of them. After sifting through a mountain of flowers, she finally spotted the culprit's note. Holly picked it up and groaned when she saw the name.

"Dilbert? Why is he…Ahchoo!…sending me flowers?" Sunny looked at Holly and then realization struck. "Oh no," she moaned, "this cannot be happening."

Holly put her hands on Sunny's shoulders and tried to look seriously concerned for her red-nosed friend. "It's happening, but we have bigger problems."

"What's that?"

"You can't go back into our room until it's been deflowered."

"That didn't sound right," Sunny said with a grin.

Holly rolled her eyes. "You just have a sick mind."

"No," Sunny sniffled, "I'm just sick period. I hate to say this, but you're going to have to clean the room by yourself."

Holly made a face, "Dilbert's the one who did it. Why can't he clean it up?"

"Well," Sunny said, "considering the fact he's a guy, and this is a girl's dormitory, I think there might be some legal issues we'd have to work through. By the way," Sunny peered inside of the room, "how did he get the flowers there in the first place?"

Holly laughed as she pictured Dilbert scaling three stories with a hundred sunflowers strapped to his back. "I really don't want to think about that right now. How exactly am I supposed to decontaminate the room?"

"Well, you can start by getting all the flowers out. Then vacuum and open up the window. I'll be back in about three hours. The room should be habitable by then. By the way," Sunny smiled, "thanks Holly."

"Yeah, yeah, yeah, I'd better be getting a really good Christmas present. Oh, wait, Sunny. How do you use a vacuum?"

Sunny stared at her for a moment without saying anything. "You're kidding, right? You've never used a vacuum?" Sunny laughed, and Holly scowled at her. "On second thought, you probably haven't. It shouldn't be hard, especially for a genius like you." Holly stuck out her tongue. "Oh, that's mature. Just hit the 'on' button and push the thing around the room."

It took fifteen minutes for Holly to track down the blasted machine. By the time Holly finally rolled it into her room, she was in a foul mood. "Just hit the 'on' button and push the thing around the room," Holly parroted Sunny in a disgusted voice. It took her a moment to locate the on switch. *See, it's not a button.* She hadn't been prepared for the loud noise. Holly jumped and bumped her elbow against the sink. "Just call me Cinderella. Oh, I'm going to kill Dilbert." Dilbert, it seemed, had taken the cheaper route and pulled the sunflowers out of the ground. Where he'd found them, she didn't want to know. On the other hand, Holly did want to know why he hadn't bothered to remove the roots.

On top of having a garden, dirt and all, inside her room, vacuuming was not as easy as it looked. It was difficult to get it go in the direction you wanted it to go, and Holly kept bumping into things that seemingly appeared out of nowhere. She didn't see the electrical cord either, but she definitely heard the machine try to suck it up. Panicked, Holly kicked the vacuum. When that didn't turn it off, she did the next best thing. She jerked the cord out of the socket. Holly screamed when the plug came flying at her face. It was turning out to be a glorious day.

This is pathetic. Machines only attack people in 'The Terminator.' Holly flopped down onto Sunny's bed. She thought she could use a rest before she started round two. "Ouch!" *Now what?* She had sat on something with a pointy edge. The culprit was a book with the letters NIV on it. *So this is the Bible,* Holly thought as she read the title. She looked around to make sure no one else was looking and then remembered her door was closed. She didn't want Sunny to get the idea she was starting to buy into that God thing. *Am I?* Holly shrugged and turned to page one. *"In the beginning, God created the heavens and the earth."* Holly felt something akin to excitement flow through her as she absorbed verse after verse. There was something different about this book. *"So God created people in His own image; God patterned them after Himself; male and female*

He created them. God blessed them...the Lord God formed man's body from the dust of the ground and breathed into it the breath of life. And man became a living person . . ."

When Sunny walked into the room later that evening, she was relieved she didn't sneeze. If she was surprised to find Holly on her bed, then Sunny felt full-fledged shock when she saw what was in Holly's lap.

Holly slowly looked up from the Bible. She sent Sunny a piercing look. Sunny didn't say a word. She just stood there. "Sunny, I don't understand. What was so special about Abraham? Out of all of the people on earth, why did God choose him?"

Sunny took a deep breath and sat down next to Holly. She wished Josh were there. He was so much better with this kind of thing, but God had chosen her. *God, please give me wisdom.* "Abraham was no better or worse than anyone who has ever walked the earth. You're right about that. The difference between him and the rest of the world was that Abraham had faith in what he couldn't see. While everyone else was worshiping trees and idols they'd carved out of stone and wood, he searched for the living God, the only One who was worth his time."

Holly looked skeptical. She started to ask something but then stopped. Sunny kept silent. She'd wait for Holly to make the next move. Sure enough, Holly finally gave into her own curiosity, "If God is real, and He's so great, then why doesn't everybody know Him?"

"God can't be seen the way people want to see Him. Therefore, they don't want to acknowledge that He exists. I hate to say this, but Mark was right. We want to live life our way. If we say there is a God who is better than us, then we are forced admit He can do a better job at running our lives. Yet if we pretend He doesn't exist, then we can fool ourselves into thinking we are the masters of our own lives."

Pride. She's talking about pride. Holly felt her own ego deflate somewhat at Sunny's words. "But wouldn't I have noticed by now that God was real?"

"Holly, the fact you're sitting here asking questions and listening to me proves you've noticed something is up. You must have realized that life isn't just a game of chance. Holly, do you think it was just coincidence the two of us were born in the same generation, accidentally bumped into each other in an airport while both our planes were delayed, then applied for the same college and became roommates?" Sunny couldn't tell what Holly was thinking. She seemed to neither accept nor deny what she was hearing. Sunny's assumptions were correct.   Holly didn't know what she believed anymore, so she did the only thing to do in moments of confusion. She asked more questions, "Mark was talking about being joyful even in bad times. What's that all about?"

"That's the one of the coolest parts. You see, once you realize that there is a God, you become conscious of the fact that He loves you. You realize you aren't an accident or a fluke of nature. You're here for a reason. God created you to love you and for you to love Him."

Holly held up her hands as if they could halt the onslaught of information. "Wait, wait, are you trying to tell me that the God who created this entire universe actually loves me? Why? What did I do?"

Sunny smiled. "Nothing you can do could take away or add to His love. He loves you because He made you. He wants to have a relationship with you."

Yeah right. "Well, here I am. Why doesn't He?"

God, how do I explain? "Well, there's a glitch. It all started with our earliest ancestors, Adam and Eve. They disobeyed God and thereby allowed sin to enter into the world, and the Bible says that sin leads to death. Now every child is born with the natural inclination to sin. In other words, you don't have to teach a toddler to say 'no' to his parents, he'll do it anyway."

"Does that mean we don't have a choice?"

"The toddler has a choice, and so do we, but the Bible says that at one point or another everyone has made a bad choice and has sinned."

Holly looked offended. "Are you saying I'm a sinner?"

"Have you ever lied about something?"

"Of course, I'm only human."

Sunny smiled. "Exactly."

Holly looked incredulous. "If you do one thing wrong, then you're a sinner?" Sunny nodded her head. "Well, then everyone has sinn...Oh, that's what you just said." Sunny smiled, and Holly looked confused again. "What does sin have to do with our relationship with God?"

Sunny took a deep breath. She wished she could just tell Holly about God's wonderful love, but she knew that if she didn't explain the fault of man, then Holly could never understand the true love of God. "Sin has everything to do with our relationship with Him. God is perfect. He, unlike the fictional Grecian gods, isn't like a human with super powers and everlasting life. He is what the Bible calls 'holy.' In other words, He is blameless, pure, and perfect. A holy Being cannot be with non-holy beings like us. That leaves us in a really bad fix. By our own bad choices, we have disassociated ourselves from the One whom we were created to be with. We're like star-crossed lovers. We're destined to be miserable because we don't have a shot at living life together. Thankfully though, God came up with a solution. . . ." Sunny went on to tell Holly the story of Jesus. She told Holly how God sent His Son, whom He loved very much, to earth to die so that man could have a relationship with God and eternal life in Heaven.

Holly leaned closer to Sunny. Once again, Sunny noticed how intense her eyes were. She had so many questions buzzing through her brain that she had a hard time asking one of them. Holly settled with the one bothering her most. "Why did Jesus have to die? If God is all-powerful, then why couldn't He just take away our sins with the snap of His fingers? If He has fingers, that is?"

Sunny chuckled. "God is a just God, a fair God. It would

be against His nature to be anything else. God isn't two-faced. Someone had to pay the price for our sins, and we couldn't pay it. Jesus, on the other hand, could pay it and He did."

Something was moving through Holly, urging her to find out more. Questions were coming to her that she knew hadn't come from herself. Something was leading her, and Holly was determined to find out what. "Sunny, what would have happened to us if Jesus hadn't paid for our sins?"

Sunny looked down. She didn't answer her right away, "Then we would have been thrown into the worst debtors' prison ever created, hell."

"That place is real?"

Sunny laughed at Holly's outburst. "Where do you think people got the idea from? You'd be surprised how many stories and concepts have been taken from the Bible and twisted to fit into our everyday lives."

"But we won't go to hell, right? I mean, since Jesus died, we're covered."

Sunny studied her sheets again. How do you tell your best friend that she's going to hell? God's voice resounded through Sunny's heart. "How can you *not* tell her?" Sunny's breath was caught in her throat.

She had to tell her. "Holly, if you died right now, you wouldn't be covered."

"What?" Holly didn't know why she was so scared. Since when did she believe all this stuff? She couldn't help but think, though, *what if it's true?* "Why wouldn't I be?"

"It's one thing to know God exists, that you're a sinner, and that Jesus paid the price for your sins. It's another thing entirely to accept God into your life."

If Sunny had been anyone else, the conversation would have ended there. Yet Holly couldn't help but trust that Sunny wouldn't say something like this to her if she didn't believe it with all her heart. "Sunny, what do I have to do?"

"You have to tell God that you know you messed up, and you're sorry. Tell Him thank you for sending His Son to die for you, and that you want Him to take over your life."

Warning bells went off through Holly's mind. "Take over my life—what do you mean?"

"I mean, give the wheel over to Him, and let Him drive. Your life will no longer be your own. It's worth it, Holly. It really is, but I'm not going to lie to you. It is a sacrifice. Every relationship has sacrifice in it."

"What happens if I give my life over to Him today, but then tomorrow decide I want it back?"

Sunny laughed, "I fight with God about running my life every day, but I have given my life over to Him and nothing can ever change that. I might defy Him and try to run away, but He always accepts me back. He loves me too much to ever let me go."

"If life with Him is so great, then why do you try to run away?"

Sunny smiled. "Because, like a little kid, I want to do things my way. I think we all still want to run out into the middle of a busy street. Why? I don't know, probably because it's forbidden."

"What you're saying makes sense, but Sunny, I don't know if I can give my life over to someone else."

"There's the real answer to your earlier question then."

Holly smirked, "Which one?"

"You asked why, if God was so great, doesn't everyone know Him? The truth is that the people who do know about Him don't want to give up what little control they have on their lives. What they don't realize is that the control they think they have is an illusion. God, on the other hand, is real and in control. The world spins and you draw your next breath because He wishes it. God is the only thing worth living for." Sunny heard herself speaking, but she knew the words were not her own. She was shaking down to her core. When God moved, He made sure He was felt. Sunny tried to read Holly's expression to see if she felt Him too. Yet there were too many emotions on Holly's face for her to pick just one.

"I'm going to bed," Holly said with stubborn resolve. Sunny tried not to sigh.

When they were both in bed and the lights were out, Sunny spoke again, "Holly, you know I want you to accept God into your life, but please also know that whether you do or you don't, you are the best friend I've ever had and I'll love you no matter what you choose."

"Thank you," Holly whispered. A tear slipped unnoticed down her cheek. She'd never had a best friend. Somehow, Holly knew without a doubt Sunny loved her. Maybe she was crazy, but it felt like Sunny always had loved her—despite the horrible way she'd treated her in the beginning. *If only God was as crazy as Sunny.* Holly told herself she was out of luck. If there really was a God, then He knew all of her faults. Suddenly, Holly remembered a man from her past. He'd spoken to her about God too. What was it he'd said? Holly searched her memory banks. *'You will never be too bad for God to love you.'*

But it doesn't make sense. If God had any brains at all, then He couldn't possibly love me. As if by magic, Holly remembered something she, herself, had said to her mother, *'Intelligence has nothing to do with love.'* Then Holly remembered what Jamie the hairdresser had said, *'It makes perfect sense. You're just using the wrong formula.'* Holly tossed and turned for hours. She would bring up an argument, only to have it shot down by her own photographic memory. She couldn't escape herself, not even to sleep. By the end of the night, Holly knew two things beyond a shadow of a doubt. God existed and God loved her. There was just one more thing left to do. Holly realized she had to choose. Either she could accept God or she could deny Him. It was as simple as that. Holly got up from bed and stumbled over to the light switch. She flicked it on and heard Sunny mumble something as she wakened from her blessed dream world.

"What? What's going on?" Sunny rubbed her eyes.

"It's morning, Sunny," Holly said as if in a daze. Truly, though, had she ever been more alive?

Sunny looked at the clock and saw it was three in the morning. After her eyes adjusted to the intrusive light, Sunny looked at Holly. She was smiling. "Who are you, and what have you done with my friend?"

Holly laughed. "Very funny, get up. I want you to help me. How do I tell God I want Him to come into my life?"

Oh, God, I can't believe this is happening. Am I still dreaming? "You pray to Him. Praying is another word for talking to God. You can pray aloud or in your head. Either way, He can hear you."

"How can I be sure I did it? Do I get a receipt?"

Sunny smiled at the joke. At least, she thought it was a joke. "You'll know."

Holly closed her eyes. *Okay, I feel sort of dumb, but I don't care anymore. God, I know you exist, and I know you created me. I'm sorry that I've messed up. Thank you so much for giving me another chance through Your son, Jesus. Please come into my life.* What was happening to her? She had this incredible feeling that washed through every cell in her body. It was as if she'd jumped into cold water on a hot summer day, but the water was inside her. Her skin tingled and her heart started beating faster and faster. Even her senses seemed to perk up. She felt overflowing joy and peace at the same time. It was the most wonderful feeling in the world. She wasn't alone anymore.

"What's happening?" Holly asked. Sunny's eyes were watering. She knew what had happened. "God's Spirit just united with yours. The Bible says that whenever someone accepts Christ, the angels in heaven sing praises to God."

Holly's eyes were wide with shock. "Why?"

"One of God's children made it home. Welcome to the family, sister. We're in this together for all eternity." Sunny reached over to embrace Holly and didn't let go. The music had just begun.

chapter twenty-one

Monday morning was not a pleasant experience for Holly or Sunny. Both girls were running on only a few hours of sleep and weren't the better for it. At breakfast, Elizabeth and the other girls left them alone. After a few months in college, they had all learned not to mess with those who've had no sleep. The ones that didn't learn that lesson ended up dead—or worse.

After breakfast, Holly mumbled what sounded like "goodbye" and headed to class. It took a lot of effort, but Sunny was finally able to get up from the table and walk outside. She looked forward to when her classes would be over and she could crash on her bed. Sunny knew she could crawl back in bed right now, but years of discipline kept her putting one foot in front of the other as she trudged off to class. The sun seemed especially bright that morning, as if nature were trying to keep her awake. Was it just her imagination, or was someone calling her name?

"Hello, Sunflower White. Why did you not respond?" Unfortunately, it wasn't her imagination, for no imagination could conjure Dilbert from thin air.

Sunny yawned, "Oh, hi. I really can't talk right now. I need to get to class." *I can't talk period.*

Dilbert carried on as if he hadn't heard her. Perhaps he hadn't. Multitasking wasn't his forte. "Did you receive my flowers?"

"Oh, yes, um, thanks." Sunny stifled another yawn. She wished she could run away, but she had the feeling if she didn't do something now, he would follow her around forever. The tricky part was figuring out how to get him to leave her alone without damaging his ego in the process. *I just wish this fog would clear from my head so that I could think straight.*

Dilbert straightened his bow tie. "I was hoping you would do me the honor of accompanying me to the show four days from today."

Or, Sunny thought, *you could ask, 'Hey, do you want to go the movies Friday night?'* Sunny silently moaned. *Shoot! I have nothing going on that night. Maybe if I say no, then he'll leave it alone,* "I'm sorry, Dilbert, but I can't."

He pressed her further. "Why not?"

Darn it. "Because, I, um, have a boyfriend." Sunny tried to ignore her mother's voice in her head telling her lying was never good, regardless of the situation.

"Oh really, your Texas friend Elizabeth Warner told me that you did not."

Oh shoot. Mom was right. Why didn't I just tell him the truth? Sunny thought as she dug herself deeper into her hole. "Well, that would make sense." Sunny bit her lower lip. "I just started going out with the guy this weekend, and I haven't seen Elizabeth since then." *Note to self: Warn Liz.*

Sunny couldn't figure out what was going through Dilbert's head. Then again, she wasn't sure what had been going through hers when she'd claimed to have a boyfriend. Sunny hadn't wanted to hurt Dilbert, but it looked like that was inevitable. "So who's the lucky guy?" he asked.

Uh-oh, he's using contractions. This can't be good. "His name is—Mark Tayne. He's already out of college." Without another word, Dilbert walked off. Sunny's conscience nagged her all the way to calculus.

Holly sat at her desk and tried for the hundredth time to focus on the calculus problem in front of her. Her mind kept wandering back to that morning. It was hard getting used to guys staring at her again. They would smile and nod at her, not in a bad way, but it unnerved her nonetheless. She tried to smile back, but Holly was afraid it was more of a grimace than anything else.

On top of that, she found people were friendlier to her, which meant she had to be friendly back. By the end of the day, she was exhausted. Actually, she'd started out exhausted. Now she was above and beyond. The euphoric feeling that had swept through her the night before was gone now, but in its place was the comfort that she wasn't alone. She hadn't been a Christian for a full day, and already she was wondering how she had ever faced life without God. Every time she started to feel worthless or ugly on the inside, Holly reminded herself she was none of those things because the God of the universe loved her and called her His own. Unfortunately, all of this didn't change the fact she was about to fall asleep on her math book.

Holly heard Sunny walk into their room. Sunny took one look at the books scattered on her desk and then crawled into bed. Holly glanced at the clock. It was two in the afternoon. Holly looked back over at Sunny who was already falling blissfully into a coma. *Well,* Holly thought, *if you can't beat'em, join'em.* She turned off her lamp, closed the shades, and went to bed barely taking the trouble to kick off her shoes.

Neither of them woke up until two hours later when Sunny's phone went off.

Holly whimpered and put her head under her pillow. "Make it stop."

The phone was vibrating across Sunny's desk away from her. She nearly fell off her bed trying to reach it before it went crashing to the ground below. Sunny looked at the caller ID and decided to answer, "This had better be important, Josh."

"Well, I don't know how important it is, but...wait a minute. Are you asleep?"

Why do people always ask that once they've woken you up? "I was." Sunny rubbed her eyes and looked at her clock. "What do you want?"

"Well, I'm here with Bret and Elizabeth at the library, and I'm starting to feel like the third wheel." Sunny thought she heard Bret laughing in the background. "So I was wondering if you and Holly want to come and study with us."

So I can be the fifth wheel? Sunny laughed to herself. "How long will you be there?"

"Considering all the work we have, I'd say we'll be here until around eight. Then we're going to go grab some hamburgers for dinner."

Sunny tried to remember if she'd had lunch that day. "Um, okay, Holly and I are going to sleep for another hour. We'll . . ."

Holly surfaced from underneath her pillow and interjected, "Two hours."

"Fine," Sunny said to Holly. Then to Josh she said, "We'll be there in about an hour and a half."

"Okay, see you," Josh hung up.

"Happy?" Sunny asked Holly after she'd hung up.

"No," Holly grumbled and then went back to sleep.

Sunny shrugged and turned off the power on her cell. Obviously, making everyone happy was impossible.

Surprisingly, it was Holly who got up first. She turned on the main lights, which induced some unintelligible comments from Sunny. "Hey, Sun, get up."

"Fine," Sunny grumbled and wished she could sleep until Christmas.

They walked downstairs together in silence, neither was in the mood to talk just yet. Once they were outside, Sunny suddenly stopped. "Oh, shoot."

"What?" Holly asked.

"I left one of my books up in the room. You go on. I'll meet you there."

"Okay. See you."

"Bye." Sunny walked up to her room, grabbed her book, and then headed back to the library. She had just stepped outside when she saw a familiar face who she first thought was Holly, but since when did Holly wear sunglasses? Sunny stopped dead in her tracks. "Are you Anne Tricony?" Anne sent her a dazzling smile, and Sunny no longer needed an answer. "Are you looking for Holly?"

Sunny's question seemed to throw the woman off balance. Obviously, she didn't think Holly told very many people who her mother was. She would have been right. In fact, Sunny didn't think that anyone else knew but her. "Um, yes, I am. Do you know her?"

"Yes, we're friends."

That seemed to shock the poor lady even more. "Really, I didn't know that she had, um, never mind. What's your name, dear?"

"I'm Sunflower White. Holly and I are roommates."

"Oh, what luck," Anne clapped her hands together and smiled. *Well,* Sunny thought, *she seems harmless to me, but she's definitely not like Holly. Maybe they just don't understand each other.* "I came here to invite Holly over for Thanksgiving weekend. I was wondering—would you like to come with us?"

Anne reminded Sunny of a kid at Christmas morning. *At least she's trying to become closer with Holly.* "Thank you. I'd love to, but let me see what Holly wants first."

"Oh, okay. Well, could you tell me where she is?"

"I'll take you there," Sunny smiled at Anne. *Holly's going to kill me.*

"This will be so much fun," Anne said. "It's so nice to get to know one of Holly's little friends." Anne looped her arm through Sunny's as they headed off to the library. *So much for studying.*

Where is she? Holly checked her watch again. It didn't take twenty minutes to get from the dorm to the library. *She'd better not have gone back to sleep.* Just to make sure, Holly called Sunny's cell. Sunny sounded awake when she informed Holly she'd be there in less than a minute. There was something funny about how she sounded, but Holly didn't think much of it. Holly glanced over at Josh. He was still hunched over a book and looking adorable. He looked up at her. *Oh shoot, think of something to ask him so he doesn't think you've been staring at him.* "So what's your major?" *That was lame. Besides, he's already told you. Just play dumb. No need to act,* Holly grumbled to herself.

If Josh noticed her blush, he didn't show it. "Bret and I are majoring in kinesiology and getting a minor in business." Josh looked like he was going to say something more, but then he stopped and reverted his attention back to his book.

You're not getting off the hook that easily. "Kinesiology, isn't that just a fancy word for a major in P.E.?"

Elizabeth giggled and elbowed Josh. "Busted."

"Ingrate," Josh said to Holly. "I'll have you know it's not very easy."

"Yeah, right," Holly was enjoying teasing him, "I suppose it's really hard to study to become a high school coach."

"I . . ." Josh began but then backed down. "Bret, tell her what we're going to do." Josh quickly looked at his book again.

Bret was momentarily thrown off guard. So were Elizabeth and Holly. It was obvious Josh was avoiding talking to Holly, but why? "Well," Bret started, trying to cut through the awkwardness, "we want to start our own line of fitness centers . . ." Bret went on to tell them their plans. Holly was impressed, but she didn't let on. She knew Josh was waiting for her to say something, but she refused to say anything until she knew why he was acting so strangely. Holly smirked when she noticed he'd been staring at the same page for the past fifteen minutes.

"What are you going to call it, Josh?" Holly aimed the question at him with deadly accuracy.

Josh looked up and caught Holly's eyes. She was surprised at what she saw. It was a mixture of excitement, longing, and regret. He was about to speak when his mouth dropped. "Is that Anne Tricony?" Elizabeth, Bret, and Holly all looked in the direction he was pointing. Holly's heart jumped with the rest of theirs but not for the same reason.

"What is Sunny doing with her? Do you think she knows her?" Elizabeth asked no one in particular. "That would be so cool. I wonder how they met."

How indeed. Holly was surprised the others couldn't hear her teeth grinding. She suppressed the urge to take off running, but that would make her a coward. Holly tightened her fists and stayed glued to her seat. When Anne finally saw her, she waved. Holly wasn't a coward, but she definitely didn't have the will to wave back. She concentrated on Sunny and thought about what she would do once she got her alone.

"Dude!" Bret exclaimed, "I think she's waving at us. Should we wave back?"

"Too late," Josh whispered. "She's almost here."

Well, there went my life being normal. Holly reluctantly stood up to greet Anne. "Hi, Mom." As if the collective gasps behind her weren't bad enough, Holly heard Bret choke on his soda. *Classic.* Elizabeth slapped him on the back, but that only worsened his dilemma. As Holly gave her mother a hug, she tried her best to ignore him. "What are you doing here?" she asked with a stick-on smile.

"Oh, I was in the neighborhood and thought I'd drop by. Who are your friends?" Anne could tell that something about her daughter had changed. Obviously, her outward appearance had, but though Holly would never believe it, Anne had never cared what Holly looked like on the outside. She'd always been proud of her daughter. Anne now realized she'd made the mistake of not being there for her Holly as a child, and it sickened her to remember the way she'd acted the first and last time Holly had come to her for help. She could never get those years back, but Anne wouldn't make the same mistake again. That was why she was here.

Holly wished she could disappear. She really did love her mother; Holly just didn't like being known as "the daughter of Anne Tricony." She had been completely unprepared for this. That was the reason, she told herself, she was angry. It was definitely not that her newfound conscience was suddenly telling her to forgive all Anne had done—and not done. "I see you've already met Sunny, though I think the word 'friend' would be pushing it at this point." Sunny stuck out her tongue from behind Anne's back. Holly turned around to face her other friends who were still slack-jawed. "This is Bret Thatcher, Liz Warner, and Josh Timberlaigh. They, unlike Sunny, didn't know you were my mom, which is why they're all gaping at you."

Anne smiled and instantly reminded Josh of her daughter. "It's nice to meet the three of you."

Holly shook Bret's shoulder to snap him out of his trance. "Oh, uh, it's nice to meet you too. You're a good actress."

Anne put on her humble face. "Why, thank you. You're very sweet."

Holly mentally rolled her eyes, and when Anne wasn't looking, she sent Sunny a "you're toast" look. Sunny wasn't easily intimidated, though. Having Holly as a friend, she'd acquired nerves of steel. Sunny smiled and jovially sat down with Anne at the table.

They talked for over an hour. *So much for studying,* Josh

thought. Not that he minded. Holly's mom was really cool. She looked a lot like Holly, but it was clear from the get-go that Holly had class, while her mother only had flash. Josh sat at the end of the table next to Holly, and since everyone was listening to Anne talk, he could watch her daughter without anyone noticing. Well, someone noticed. Anne could always tell when someone wasn't paying attention to her. Her own mother had said that skill was ingrained into her at birth. Yet instead of annoying her, as it usually would have, it intrigued her. She would have to look more carefully at this boy when she had the chance. For now, she'd allow him to look at her daughter.

"I can't believe you didn't warn me!" Holly yelled at Sunny the second they got into their room.

"Cool down. It wasn't my idea in the first place." Sunny didn't think Holly would physically come at her, but she stayed an arm's length away, just in case.

"So now you listen to my mother instead of me? Is that it?"

I can't believe she's so wound up. "No. You never said that if I ran across your mother, I had to warn you she was here."

"Do you think this is funny, Sunflower? Is this all just another joke?"

Sunny was about to make some crack about Holly's name, but when she saw tears start to form in Holly's eyes, the situation suddenly wasn't humorous any longer. "Wow, wait a minute. Holly, are you okay?" Sunny tried to hug her, but Holly pushed away.

"Go away," Holly sobbed.

"No way am I leaving you like this. Tell me what's wrong."

"I already told you what was wrong."

Sunny shook her head. "You seriously expect me to believe you're crying because your mother showed up?"

Holly wiped her eyes. "No, I'm crying because she was so nice to me. Sheesh, she even invited me to spend Thanksgiving weekend with her. She's never done anything like this before, and I don't know if I want her to. I was okay with the way things were." Holly searched for the right words. Sunny didn't understand how much pain placing trust in the wrong person could bring, but Holly knew. She still had the scars. "I'd accepted she would never be the kind of mom other people had." Holly threw up her hands. "Now she's acting as if she wants to be my mom."

Sunny prayed for wisdom, but all she felt was ignorant, ignorant to what Holly was going through and what to say to help her. "Holly, isn't that a good thing? She wants to change."

"I know it sounds stupid, but it's so much easier to hate her. Why should I try now, when she didn't try before? How can anyone expect me to give her a second chance?"

"Holly, no one expects you to give her a second chance." Sunny took a deep breath. "You're right. She doesn't deserve it, but do you think any of us deserve it?"

"What do you mean?"

Lord, please let this be the right thing to say. "God gave us all a second chance. Did we deserve it?"

Holly looked at the ground, trying to catch up with this new way of reasoning. "But He's God. It couldn't possibly have been as hard."

"You're right. It was harder. In order to give us a second chance, He had to give up His own Son. In order for you to give your mom a second chance, all you have to do is show up for Thanksgiving weekend." Sunny smiled and put her hands on Holly's shoulders. "That's all she's asking for, Holly."

But what if she's too busy for me when I get there? Then what? Holly shook off her fear. She had God now and a best friend. Maybe she would be hurt again, but she would never have to face the pain alone. "Will you come with me?"

Sunny hugged her, "Of course I will. Will you spend Thanksgiving day with my family in Salem?"

Holly smiled. "As long as you're talking about Salem, Oregon, it's a deal."

"Great!" Sunny grinned at her. "So does this mean you forgive me?"

Holly pretended to glare, but then her solemn face cracked into a smile, "All right. Just don't do that again." Holly poked her. "I don't think I'm up for third chances quite yet."

"I'll remember that. Oh, by the way, I ran into Dilbert today."

Holly laughed. "I hope you told him no more sunflowers."

"Actually," Sunny looked at the ground, "I sort of told him I had a boyfriend."

Holly choked on air. "You what?"

Sunny groaned. "That's not even the worst part. He kept pestering me about it. So I told him my boyfriend was Mark Tayne. That was the only name I could think of aside from something dumb like John Smith." Despite Sunny's desperate look, Holly laughed so hard she hiccupped. Sunny scowled, "I'm glad you find this so amusing. Now what do I do?"

"Frankly, I have absolutely no idea. At least he doesn't go to school here."

"Good point," Sunny said. Holly stared at her with a smirk. "What?"

"I was just wondering if you said that because, secretly, you do want to go out with Mark."

"Holly! That's disgusting. The guy is almost a decade older than me, and he's weird."

Holly rolled her eyes, "Sunny, six years is not a decade."

"I said 'almost.' "

Holly crossed her arms. "It's not even almost a decade, but you're right. He is weird. He's also very cute."

"Hmmph, I thought you liked Josh." Sunny mirrored Holly and crossed her arms.

"I do like Josh, most of the time. It's as if he's bi-polar or something. One minute he's talking to me, acting as if he's having a great time, and the next second he gets this weird look on his face and completely ignores me. It's really irritating." Sunny bit her lip. Holly had known her long enough to tell she was hiding something. "Spill, Sunny." Sunny stood up and paced. Holly stayed on the ground looking up expectantly.

"Now, don't take this in the wrong way," Sunny said, "but remember how I told you earlier this morning that one of the reasons I was so happy you were a Christian is because now we can be even closer friends?"

Holly thought a bit. She remembered Sunny saying something along those lines, but not in that context. "Yeah, you said God commanded Christians not to become too close to non-Christians because it always ends up badly for both parties involved." Sunny's shoulders seemed to relax a little. She started toying with some of the stuff on her shelves, probably hoping Holly would drop the subject of Josh all together. Her stalling tactics had the opposite effect on Holly's curiosity. "Sunny, come on, tell me what that has to do with Josh acting like a dork."

"Well," Sunny said, " 'friends' includes girlfriends and boyfriends; actually, it's even worse for a Christian to go out with a non-Christian."

Holly's eyes narrowed as she put the pieces together. "I think I understand now, but what has he been doing, avoiding me?" Holly stood up in a huff.

"Holly, I'm not saying Josh has been doing everything right, but imagine what it's been like for him. He's liked you since the beginning of the semester, but he hasn't been able to do anything about it." Sunny saw she was getting nowhere. "Even when you started to like him, he still couldn't ask you out. Half of his bad moods have been because he's frustrated about not being able to date you."

Holly sighed in exasperation, "Then why didn't he just ask me out? God would forgive him anyway."

Sunny smiled. *You so remind me of myself.* "Because, Holly, after a while, we all learn there's a reason God that has rules for us. It isn't to make our lives miserable. It's to make them complete. In fact, the Bible says that following God's way leads to the best kind of life, one filled with peace and joy."

Holly lifted an eyebrow. She wasn't sure about this complete obedience thing. *What does God know anyway?* Holly or God, she wasn't sure which, answered that question for her. God knew everything. Holly sighed in momentary surrender. "So I'm guessing you haven't told Josh I'm a Christian yet."

"No," Sunny said slowly, "do you want me to?"

"Absolutely not. I think I'm going to mess with him a little first."

Sunny's face was classic. "Holly!"

"I'm only joking. I wish I wasn't, but I am. Seriously, though, please don't tell him. I have to figure some stuff out first, and I'd like to be the one to tell him."

"You have a deal," Sunny said, already thinking about the fact Josh would crucify her if he found out what she was keeping from him. "How long are you going to wait before you tell him?"

"I don't know." Holly sent Sunny a mischievous smile. "How long before you let Mark know you two are going out?"

"Ha-ha," Sunny said dryly. "By the way, have you read Leviticus 18?"

"No, I'm still working on Genesis."

"Well, you're not missing much. The whole chapter is disgusting. I can't believe he told us to read it."

Hmmm...Weird Mark strikes again, Holly thought. *What's with that guy anyway? He's worse than Josh.*

Exhaustion crept in again on both of them, and before ten o'clock, they were asleep. Neither had a clue who was walking the campus that night. If they had, they wouldn't have fallen asleep that night.

chapter twenty-two

The week went by quickly enough. Holly got over everyone following her around as if she, not her mother, were a movie star. For such a large campus, it was sickening how fast news spread. It looked like she would never lead a life of anonymity no matter how hard she tried. Luckily, her friends still treated her the same way. On the downside, Elizabeth's roommate, Jasmine, was suddenly interested in becoming her new best friend. It was almost laughable, except Holly wasn't laughing. Jasmine, along with two Jasmine clones, had become Holly's constant shadow. Once Holly told them off, but she'd felt so bad afterward that she had apologized immediately. Darn her new conscience. Sunny told her it was the Holy Spirit. If Holly had known how meddlesome God was, she wouldn't have signed on. On second thought, she would have. *I just would have grumbled more about it.* Holly could almost hear God laughing.

Truthfully, though, Holly wouldn't trade God for anything. She searched the Bible to find out everything she could about Him. The more she read, the more she understood that He was what she'd been missing. It thrilled her that there was Someone in this world who would never bore her and never let her down.

God was the reason Holly had been hesitant to tell Josh she was a Christian. She knew that once he found out, it would only be a matter of time before they started dating. She had no objections to going out with Josh, but she wanted to learn more about her Heavenly Father first. She felt like that was what God wanted, but she couldn't shake the feeling she was hiding something from him. In addition, Holly had read verses about how Christians were supposed to declare their faith to other people. Did Josh fit the profile of "other people"? Holly shook her head in denial. *I'm not ready yet.*

The more she thought about Josh, the more confused she became. All Holly knew for sure was that with every fiber in her being, she wanted to know more about God. Had she not felt so at peace with herself, Holly would have run in the opposite direction. The only fear she had now was that He would go away. *Please don't leave me.* Sunny's words resounded through Holly's head. *'Once God has you, He'll never let you go.'*

Something out of the corner of her eye caught her attention. It was Josh. He was quickly walking out of the gym and didn't seem to notice her. Holly smiled despite herself, until she saw why he was walking so fast. There were three guys right behind him, and they were yelling something. Holly got closer so she could hear.

"Hey!" One of them yelled, "Tampon, come back."

"Yeah! Why are you running away, Tampon?"

Why are they calling him—oh no, God, what have I done? Holly felt anger bubbling inside her. It was her fault they were doing this. These guys were jerks. Holly wasn't violent by nature, but she seriously wanted to hurt them. What dumbfounded her was Josh wasn't standing up for himself. *I get it. He's trying to do the right thing by not fighting them.* As good as it sounded not to get into a fight, Holly could tell they weren't going to stop by getting the silent treatment. *I got him into this mess. I'll get him out.* She didn't have time to think her plan through, but Holly knew it would work.

Holly tried to picture Anne when she was trying to get attention. The image wasn't hard to conjure up. While Josh still had his back turned to the group, Holly walked up behind one of them and "accidentally" brushed up against him.

"Oh," Holly giggled, "excuse me."

The guy turned and looked her up and down. He smiled appraisingly. "Aren't you Anne Tricony's daughter?"

"Yes," Holly's stomach turned at the sight of him, but she put on her sexiest smile. "I am." She now had the attention of the other two blockheads.

"No offense to your mom, but you are definitely hotter than her." This glowing remark came from jerk number two.

It's 'hotter than she' you bonehead, and, duh, I'm younger. "Oh," Holly giggled again, "thank you." Holly pretended as if she were going to say something else, but then suddenly "noticed" Josh. Holly beamed; this time she didn't have to fake it. "Joshua!" Holly yelled as she ran up behind him.

Josh turned, and his eyes bugged out when Holly jumped into his arms and quickly kissed him on the mouth. He stared at her in shock, but nothing could compare to the looks the three stooges wore. Their mouths hung wide open. "What are you…?" Josh began, trying to assimilate what had just happened to him. He was sure he wasn't dreaming. At least, he hoped he wasn't. Had Holly just kissed him?

Holly leaned over and whispered into his ear, "I'm getting you out of the mess I put you in. Just play along."

Josh had no problem playing along as they walked back to his dorm hand in hand. He couldn't help but notice all the guys who saw them together. Josh knew he was now the envy of half of the guys in his dorm, and he didn't mind a bit. Josh told himself that it didn't bother him, since it was all for show. He was still faithfully praying to God to make Holly a Christian. God had to relent sooner or later, didn't He? Josh hoped it was sooner than later, especially after today. It touched him that she'd step out of her comfort zone to help him. Wait until he told Sunny.

From the dreamy look on Holly's face, Sunny should have known something was up that night. Yet it wasn't until Holly started giggling that she became suspicious. "What's so funny?" Holly was sitting in her desk trying to keep her pencil from wiggling.

She kept laughing. "Nothing, um, just math homework."

"Well, if you find it so amusing, feel free to do mine."

Holly snorted. She gave up on the problem and let the pencil fall. When it rolled off her desk and into the trash can, she laughed so hard she could scarcely breathe.

Okay, she's lost it. "Um, Holly, are you on something?"

"No," Holly hiccupped and tried to draw in oxygen. When she heard her cell ring, she nearly jumped out of her skin. Holly looked at the number and turned pale.

Sunny's heart skipped a beat. "Holly, is it that guy again, the one who called in San Antonio?" Holly never told Sunny what the call was about, but she wasn't stupid. The guy on the other end had been bad news.

"No," Holly said slowly, "it's not him. It's Josh." Saying nothing more, Holly turned off the power on her phone.

Sunny looked at her in amazement, "Did you just hang up on him?"

Holly shrugged and started snickering again. Sunny heard her own phone ring and looked at the caller ID. "It's Josh."

Holly's eyes widened, "Sunny, don't pick up!"

Sunny rolled her eyes. "I'm going to answer it. I don't know what's going on, but you're acting really weird." When Sunny hit the talk button, Holly squeaked and ran out of the room. Sunny stared after her in amazement. "Hey, Josh."

"Hey, Sunny, is Holly there?"

She was. Sunny rolled her eyes again and leaned against the wall, "Nope, you just missed her. By the way, she was acting stranger than usual." Sunny paused when she heard thunder boom outside. "You wouldn't happen to know why, would you?"

"I think I might have an idea."

Sunny could hear the smugness in his voice. *This can't be good.* "What happened?"

"She kissed me, and I . . ." Josh was about to tell Sunny that he was calling to thank Holly for getting him out of trouble with the creeps from his dorm. They were all but bowing down to him and asking for his forgiveness.

"Oh good," Sunny said with a sigh of relief. *Now I don't have to hide anything from him.* Sunny had always hated keeping secrets from Josh. This time had been no exception.

"Huh?"

"I'm just glad she finally told you she's a Christian. Though I have to admit, kissing you was a weird way to break it to you. On the other hand, I'm sure you didn't mind." Sunny heard thunder again. "I'm glad you're not mad at me. I thought you'd be furious when you found out she's been a Christian for a week, and I didn't tell you. After I told her why you'd been acting so weird around her for all these months, she asked me not to tell you. I think she wanted to do it, and now she did." Sunny waited for Josh to say something, but there was only silence on the other end, "Josh? Are you there?" Sunny heard the rain begin to fall and checked to see if she was still getting reception.

"Yes, Sunny. I'm here." Sunny heard the strain in his voice. She could have cut through the tension with a knife.

"Um, Josh, she did tell you, right?" Sunny already knew the answer.

"Sunny," Josh said her name in a steady tone that meant only one thing. He was furious. "I want you to take Holly downstairs and outside. I want to talk to her face to face."

Sunny looked out the window. Buckets of rain were illuminated by the lightening. "Josh, that's crazy. It's pouring outside."

"Do it, Sunny, or I'll come in there and drag her out myself!" Sunny had no doubt he would.

"Josh, listen to yourself. You're in no mood to talk to anyone. Yelling at Holly isn't going to make things better." Sunny tried to sound reasonable.

In Josh's mind, things couldn't get worse. Holly didn't care about him, and Sunny had sold out. "I want to talk to her—now. You said she wasn't in the room. Is that true, or were you lying to me then too?" His tone hurt more than a slap on the face ever could.

"No, Josh," Sunny said quietly. "I wasn't lying."

"Good, then I expect you to give me the same courtesy you gave her. Don't tell her what's going on."

"Josh, please pray before you come over here."

"You mean the way you prayed before you decided to keep secrets from me?"

Tears rolled down Sunny's face. "No, Josh, don't make the same mistake."

"Just have her meet me downstairs in ten minutes." Josh hung up. For thirty seconds, Sunny stared motionless at her phone. Her heart hurt too much to cry.

Sunny walked outside her room and found Holly sitting on the ground. Holly looked up at Sunny and her face immediately turned from giddy to concerned. "Sunny, what's wrong? Are you okay?"

"I'm fine," Sunny said.

Holly arched her eyebrow. "I'm not buying that. Tell me what's wrong."

"I can't. Will you come downstairs with me?"

"Yes, but why. What's downstairs?"

Sunny felt her heart break. It was as if she was trading one friend's loyalty for another. "I can't tell you." Sunny hesitated and then finally said, "You don't have to come down. You'll probably wish you hadn't."

Holly looked up at Sunny. She'd never seen her look like this before. It frightened her. "It's okay, Sunny. I trust you." Holly held out her hand for Sunny to pull her up.

Sunny looked like she was going to burst out in tears. Holly didn't know how to act. It was usually she who was having the mental breakdown. Sunny was supposed to be the strong one.

"Go outside, Holly."

Holly jumped when she heard the clap of thunder. It sounded like cannon was being shot two feet away. Wide-eyed, Holly looked at Sunny. "Are you crazy?"

"Just do it." Holly would have outright refused if she hadn't seen the pleading look in Sunny's eyes.

"Okay." Holly turned around and saw Sunny rooted to the spot. Obviously, she was not coming. Resolved to see what was going on, Holly marched out into the rain.

It was getting dark fast. If it hadn't been for the lightening, Holly might not have seen Josh standing there, soaked and leaning against a tree.

"You dolt," Holly yelled over the sound of the pounding rain. "Don't you know that you could get electrocuted standing under there like that?"

Josh didn't answer her comment. "Come with me." He grabbed her by the arm and led her to shelter in the form of a parking garage. By the time they got there, Holly was soaked and not very happy about it. If she'd wanted a shower, she would have taken a hot one, inside.

"What's this all about?"

"When were you going to tell me, Holly?" Even with the deafening rain, Holly knew by his tone Josh was yelling at her. Unfortunately, she had no clue what he was yelling about.

"Tell you what?"

"That you are a Christian? Darn it, Holly! What were you doing? Did you want to see how big of a fool you could turn me into?"

Holly just stared at him for a moment, taking it all in. "So Sunny told you."

"Yeah, she told me. She thought you had already clued me in. She also told me you knew why I haven't asked you out yet." Josh, if possible, became more furious. "If you don't want to go out, then why did you kiss me? Is this your idea of fun?"

Holly couldn't believe what she was hearing. "No, Josh, it was exactly what I said it was. I wanted to get those guys to leave you alone."

"Thanks a lot," Josh said sarcastically. "So do you usually do this for guys? You know, kiss them in public to make them feel better about themselves."

Despite the chill of the night, Holly felt herself turn red. "First of all, I didn't kiss you because I thought you needed an ego booster. Trust me, it's already big enough to serve you for three lifetimes. Secondly, I've never kissed anyone else but you."

Josh felt something try to melt inside of him. He didn't let it. "Somehow, I find that hard to believe. Remember Albert? He's a friend of yours, isn't he?" Josh froze. *Oh God, what did I just say?*

Holly's eyes widened, and her entire body started to shake. She slapped him across the face so hard Josh could have sworn he saw stars. "How dare you!" Holly tried to run away from him, but Josh grabbed her around the waist. "Let go of me!" Holly kicked his shin and thought she heard a crack. Still, Josh wouldn't let go.

"Holly, Holly, I'm so sorry. I'm so sorry." Instead of continuing to fight him, she turned and sobbed onto his shoulder. Josh felt the hot tears seep through his shirt. He knew he deserved so much more than a bruised shin and swollen face, and yet here was Holly in his arms. The fact she was crying because of him was more torture than any broken bone could ever be.

Holly was crying so hard that she was shaking. Josh kissed the side of her head and rocked her. When she finally caught her breath, she asked, "How could you say that to me, Josh?"

Josh was speechless. If he'd ever doubted he had a mean streak, tonight it had been confirmed. He knew he couldn't take the words back, but he wished to God he could. "Oh, Holly, I'm so sorry. I know that doesn't change anything, but know this, Holly, I didn't mean it, and I will do everything I can to prove that to you."

"How did you find out?"

There was no going back. "I've known ever since you told me who your father was. My grandparents do business with him sometimes. They were there the night it happened. I overheard them telling my mom how horribly your father treated you after everything happened. When my mom caught me listening, she said she'd skin me if I ever told anyone. It looks like you did that for her."

"Does anyone else know?" Holly pulled away from him so that she could look him in the eye. "Josh, tell me the truth."

"I swear, Holly. I never told anyone. I was never going to tell you, but I lost my temper. My feelings were hurt, and I lashed out at you."

Holly saw blood on his face where her ring had hit him. "It looks like I lashed back."

Josh winced when she touched his face. "I deserved it."

"You're right, but I wish I hadn't done it." She was still confused about one thing. "Josh, why were you so upset that I didn't tell you I was a Christian?"

Josh kicked a rock that was on the ground. He watched it roll off into the darkness. "It's not that important."

"Obviously it is," she said softly. "I've never seen you so upset."

Not many people have. "Becoming a Christian is the most important experience in a person's life. I wish that I could have shared it with you."

Holly smiled and hugged him. "Well, guess what? I'm still a Christian. Share it with me now."

Josh held on tight, etching the moment into his head. Holly finally pulled away, and Josh reluctantly let her go. "So" Josh shoved his hands into his wet pockets, "will you be my girlfriend?"

Holly blinked. "That was straightforward, but no."

"Oh," Josh felt his heart drop. He knew that after what he'd said, she probably didn't want him to even be around her. "I understand."

Josh started to walk off, but Holly put her hand on his shoulder. She hated that he immediately tensed. "No, I don't think that you do. What you said was a horrible thing, but I know you didn't mean it." Holly took a deep breath. She couldn't believe what she was about to say. God had changed her so much in the past few days. "I forgive you, but I want you to be my brother in Christ for a while before you become my boyfriend."

"Can't I be both?"

"Yes, eventually you can, but Josh, I don't feel like I'm ready. What do you think God wants us to do?"

"Darn it. Did you have to bring Him into this?" Josh smiled when he heard the thunder. *Yes, God, I hear you.*

"I think that keeping Him out of it is what's gotten us into trouble."

Josh smiled. If he hadn't been in love earlier, then he was now. "You know what, Holly? Even if you hadn't told me you were a Christian, I would have known from the way you're talking that you're sold out to Him." When Holly looked down, Josh clarified. "That's a compliment. You're already allowing Him to work in your life. I know tons of people who get saved and then completely shut God out." Josh knew he'd been guilty of just that.

Holly smiled at him, "It's not easy to do what He wants over what I want."

"No," Josh said, "it's not, but I'll make it easier for you. From now on, we're friends until you say it's okay to move on."

Holly beamed and gave him a big hug. "Thank you, Josh! Oh," Holly backed away from him, "would you rather we shook hands?"

Josh grinned mischievously. "Don't even think about it," he said and pulled Holly into a bear hug. *Thank you, God. I'm finished running this relationship my way. I'll do whatever you tell me to do.*

Josh heard, "Let the girl go" loud and clear in his head. *Fine,* Josh thought reluctantly and let Holly go. He imagined a picture of

God taking the place of Holly's dad. He was standing on the front porch with a shotgun waiting for His little girl to come home from a date. Only instead of a shotgun, God was holding a lightening bolt. Josh gulped, and after it stopped raining, he took Holly back to her dorm immediately. Josh made sure he didn't so much as brush against her the entire way back. God was a strict chaperone, and He would not be ignored, even if it took electrocution to make Himself known.

Holly walked into the dorm and up the stairs to her room. She was soaked, freezing, and ready to fall asleep, but none of that dampened the joy she felt. Holly knew that this was the beginning of a great friendship and, if everything went well, more. Holly opened her door and almost tripped on Sunny when she walked in. She'd forgotten how troubled her friend had looked when she'd left. It looked like things had only gotten worse. Sunny's eyes were puffy, and she looked miserable. Holly crouched on the ground next to her friend and tried to give her a hug, but Sunny stiffened. Had Sunny been the type of person who was constantly emotional, Holly might not have been so worried, but this wasn't like her at all.

Sunny spoke without looking at her, "Holly, I'm so sorry I didn't tell you Josh was waiting outside. Are you mad at me?"

Holly could have kicked herself. Did her friend really think she would be mad about something so small as that? Holly then remembered the way she'd thrown a fit when Sunny hadn't told her about Anne. If Holly had felt any lower, she knew she would have sunk through the carpet. "Sunny, of course I'm not mad at you," Holly gave her friend a hug again, and to her relief, she felt Sunny relax. "Is that what this is all about?"

"No, Josh is mad at me too." Sunny burst into tears again, and then told Holly everything Josh had said over the phone.

That no-good, little jerk, Holly thought. Though she didn't let on, Holly wished she had something to strangle. Josh's neck would have done quite nicely, but since he wasn't available, Holly settled with clenching and unclenching her fists. Holly could tell by the way Sunny was talking that she blamed herself. *Well,* Holly thought, *at least I can cure her of that.* "Sunny, this isn't your fault. I asked you, as a friend, not to tell him because I wanted more time to work things out. This has nothing to do with you, and I'm sorry we dragged you into it." Sunny didn't look convinced. Holly put her hands on Sunny's shoulders to get Sunny to look at her. The fact she was looking down made Holly wish she'd hit Josh harder when she had the chance. "Sunny, I mean it. This was not your fault." *It's not all Josh's fault either,* Holly reminded herself.

Sunny seemed to believe her this time. "Thank you, Holly."

"I should be the one thanking you. Now I'd love to stay and tell you just exactly what I'd like to do to Josh at this moment, but I'm drenched and freezing, so I'm going to go take a shower."

"Don't catch a cold," Sunny joked. "Josh might blame that on me too."

Holly laughed, glad that Sunny seemed like she was back to her normal self again. "If anyone's to blame, he is. I'd probably be asleep and warm right now if it weren't for Josh."

"Good point. Speaking of bed, I'm going to sleep."

Holly sent her a fake glare and walked out.

chapter twenty-three

osh walked with a limp the next day. He also sported a long red mark on the side of his face. *You deserve to be shot.* Holly and God seemed to have forgiven him, but it looked like forgiving himself would take more effort. Josh detested cruelty, and what he'd said the night before was no less than that. No matter how angry he'd been, nothing should have brought that out of him. It was grating that something so trivial could make him lose his temper. Worst of all, Holly was the last person he wanted to blow up in front of. *Why does it always work that way?* Needless to say, he could have handled the situation better.

Guilty or not, Josh couldn't wait to see Holly that day. After talking to Elizabeth, he learned that she would be going to the library early that morning. He decided to wait for her to come outside of her dorm.

He was about to give up and stalk someplace else, when she

walked out of the building. Josh smiled and waved to get her attention. When he did, he wished he hadn't.

A guy didn't study a girl for months and not know how that girl looked when she was angry. From the way she walked to the firm set of her jaw, Josh knew he was in big trouble. She wasn't angry. She was furious. Call it courage or fear, Josh was rooted to the spot.

"Joshua Timberlaigh, how dare you show your face around here?"

This can't be good. Josh knew he probably shouldn't notice how great she looked right now. Instinct, survival tactics, kept him from smiling at her. "I guess this means you're still mad at me. Sorry, I'll go now." Josh turned to leave, but Holly grabbed the back of his shirt and physically turned him back around. Josh prayed no one had seen her do that. It was embarrassing.

"You're not getting off the hook that easily." Holly tried not to feel bad about the mark on his face, tried and failed.

Josh shoved his hands into his pockets. "Listen, Holly, I feel really bad about what I said to you last night, but I don't know what I can do about it. If you don't want to see me anymore, then I understand. Trust me, that's torture enough." Josh looked at Holly. He knew he wasn't playing fairly, but he put on his most adorable face, the one he always used on his mom whenever he knew he was in trouble.

Holly stared at him for a moment with a perplexed look on her face. Then she laughed. *Talk about a way to shoot a guy in the foot,* Josh thought to himself. *Laugh at him when he's pouring his heart out. Then again, at least she's not aiming higher, like at my chest.*

"Josh, I already told you. I'm over what you said last night. I know you didn't mean it."

Now it was Josh's turn to be confused, confused and frustrated. He threw up his hands in surrender. "Then why are you mad at me?" *Honestly, God, why did you make females so complicated?*

Holly glared at him. "I'm mad about the way you treated Sunny last night. You owe her an apology, a very long one with lots of groveling." Holly wore a stubborn face and got into her battle stance.

Never one to turn down a challenge, Josh fought back. "Why do I owe *her* an apology?"

Holly didn't have to pretend to be mad at him anymore, "You treated her like dirt last night, when all she was doing was what I asked her to do." Holly could see Josh start to look a little guilty, but a little guilty was not what she was aiming for. "Last night was the first time I have ever seen her cry, and she was crying because you made her feel bad." Holly jabbed a finger at him. "The least you can do is give her an apology."

Josh refused to think about the fact he'd made Sunny cry. In his mind, he'd been wronged. "But she left me high and dry. What am I, chopped liver when it comes to her friendship with you?"

God, why did you make guys so complicated? Holly rolled her eyes. "It wasn't about you! I just wanted some time to think about my relationship with God before I jumped into a new one with you. Sunny did what I asked, not because she likes me more than you, but because she didn't think she was hurting you."

"Well, she did hurt me."

You can be such a baby. "Are you forgetting what you said to me last night?" Josh winced. He'd fallen right into that one. "You hurt Sunny, intentionally, just as much as you hurt me last night. It's worse on her, though, because not only were you a jerk, but she still thinks you're mad at her." As Josh shifted from foot to foot, Holly remembered he wasn't the only one who'd treated Sunny badly. "Sunny has been a much better friend to you and me than either of us have been to her. So like I said, the least you can do is give her an apology."

Josh knew he could refuse, but he wasn't that stupid. Wise people admit it when they're wrong. "You're right."

Josh heard God speak to him, '*That took you awhile.*' Josh sighed. "The next time I see Sunny, I'll tell her."

"Tell me what?" Josh jumped and looked behind him. Sunny stood less than ten feet away.

"How long have you been standing there?" Josh asked.

"I just walked up." Sunny looked suspiciously from one friend to the next.

"What's going on?"

"Nothing," Holly said breezily. "Josh just wanted to talk to you. That's all. I'll leave the two you alone." As Holly walked off, she could feel Josh glaring at her. Sunny looked at him warily.

"Sunny, I'm sorry for being a jerk on the phone last night."

Sunny narrowed her eyes at Holly's disappearing figure. "Did Holly tell you to say that?"

Josh laughed. They knew each other so well. "No, she demanded that I say that, but she was right. I'm sorry, Sunny."

"You're forgiven."

Josh looked at her in surprise. "That's it? You're not still upset?"

Sunny shrugged. "No, should I be?"

Josh smiled. "Holly was right about something else."

"Hmmm…do tell."

"You're a much better friend to me than I am to you."

Sunny reached over and hugged him. "It's not a contest, Josh. Besides, you're a great friend."

"I am?"

"Yeah, you're taking me and the gang out to lunch tomorrow after church. It's so nice of you to offer."

Sunny smiled sweetly, and Josh groaned. "What is it with girls and making guys pay for lunch?" Sunny just laughed and hooked her arm through his. As they walked off together, they didn't realize they were being watched.

Josh's alarm went off at eight o'clock the next day. He looked over at Bret who was holding his teddy bear, fast asleep. Josh had sworn under pain of death not to tell anyone about Mr. Floppy. "Hey Bret, wake up." Josh threw a towel across the room at his friend.

"Huh? Is it already morning?"

"Yep, sun's up."

"Let's go to the later service today. I don't want to fall asleep in church."

That was all Josh needed to convince him. He rolled over and grabbed his phone. Luckily, Sunny's number was on speed dial. Josh didn't want to worry about numbers so early in the morning. "Hey, Sun, we're going to the later service today."

"Okay. We're still on for lunch, right?"

"Right," Josh mumbled. "I'll probably kick myself later, but you can choose the place. I'm not falling for that menu trick, though. So don't try it."

"Wasn't gonna," Sunny said sweetly over the phone. Josh hoped that didn't mean she and Holly were cooking up something else. He'd better be on guard just in case.

"Call me once you get out of church, and let me know the plans."

"All right," Sunny yawned over the phone. "Oh, Holly says good night."

"Tell her she has a bad sense of humor early in the morning."

Josh heard Sunny yell at Holly, "He says good night to you too. Goodbye, Josh."

Josh grunted and went back to sleep.

After church that day, Josh ran into Mark again. "Hey, how's it going?"

Mark shrugged his shoulders. "Not bad," Aside from the weird conversation he'd had with Sunny the week before, Mark seemed like a really cool guy, one who Josh wanted to get to know better.

"So I know you're out of college now, but did you go to UT before?"

Mark chuckled. "No, that would have required me actually trying in high school, which I thought was a waste of time back then."

Josh shrugged. He wasn't a big fan of judging people by where they went to school, but he was still curious. "Where did you go to school? I know you have to have a theology degree to be the youth minister. At least, you did back at my old church in Oregon."

A strange look crossed over Mark's face, but it was gone as quickly as it came. "Yeah, you do here too. I went to school in the backwoods of Tennessee. Don't tell anyone, though; people might think I'm a hillbilly."

Josh laughed. He knew Mark didn't give a darn what people thought of him. "Hey, some friends of mine and I are going to the football game next Saturday. Do you want to come?" *Sunny is going to kill me.*

"Sounds great," Mark said. *I wonder if Sunny will be there?* Mark quickly reminded himself he didn't care.

"Okay, I'll get you a ticket. We get them cheaper with our student ID."

"Thanks, I'll see you there."

"Holly, it won't be that bad."

"What's your definition of bad?" Holly shivered against the wind. For a New Englander, she wasn't very warm blooded. Apart from her eye color, that was one of the few traits Holly inherited from her father. Texas' warm climate was one of the reasons Holly decided on UT, though now she wished she had looked closer into the benefits of the University of Hawaii.

"Josh will be at the game," Sunny waked Holly from her dream of palm trees and tropical heat.

Holly shot Sunny a look stating she was less than amused.

"Him and half the student population. I can think of better ways to spend my Saturday than jumping up and down, screaming over a few sweaty guys hitting each other. Where's the challenge? All they do is run an egg-shaped ball made out of pig skin from one end of the field to the other."

Sunny rolled her eyes, "Whatever you do, don't repeat that to the guys. All that will come from that will be an hour-long lecture on the importance of football in a well-rounded education."

"You see, that's why there shouldn't be college football. Education and sports just don't mix."

Sunny chuckled. "Don't repeat that either. So are you coming?"

Holly kicked a rock on the ground, "Do I have a choice?"

"Nope."

Holly plastered on a smile. "Fine, I'd love to go, but I am not under any circumstances wearing the school colors."

"Oh, but, Holly, burnt orange goes so nicely with your complexion," Sunny teased.

"Humph," Holly pretended to be insulted, "I don't have to take this." Holly walked back to their dorm. Once inside her room, she decided to change into something more comfortable—sweats. Holly reached back to shut the door, but her hand only met air. Her heart stopped when she heard the door behind her close and lock. Holly slowly turned around and came face to face with a man she'd never seemed before. As frightening as that was, it was the gun pointed at her head that caught her full attention. Holly instinctively held up her hands. She knew if she yelled out, she would be dead.

"Sorry about the gun, Miss. Johnson. I needed to make sure you didn't do something stupid." There was a sneer in his voice and violence in his eyes.

Stay calm. God, where are You? Like taking a hot shower on a cold day, God's voice flowed through her soul. *'I'm right where I've always been, right by your side.'* Holly took a deep breath and calmly asked, "Who are you, and why are you in my room?"

Tony was momentarily caught off guard by her cool confidence. "I'm an employee of Mr. Albert Bergenstein." The frigid air seeped through her skin when she heard Albert's name. "I'm here to confirm that you will be at the New Year's Eve party."

Bile crept up into the back of Holly's throat, and her stomach churned, but she hadn't sat through etiquette classes for naught. "The fashionably bored" look was one of the first lessons. "And what, might I ask, does your 'esteemed' employer intend to do if I decide to attend another event that evening?"

A look of delighted malevolence crept onto the man's face. If possible, Holly became more ill. "I was hoping you would ask that. While I was waiting for you, I took the liberty of looking at your bulletin board over there beside what I presume is your bed. You have such nice pictures. It's a shame one will be terminated for this demonstration." Before Holly understood what he was talking about, the man raised his gun and fired four silent shots. "You'll be there," he said knowingly, and then without another word, he left.

Holly quickly locked the door behind her. Her whole body shook as she walked over to the bulletin board. There was a picture of Josh, Bret, Sunny, and Elizabeth. Had Holly not taken the picture, she wouldn't have recognized them because they no longer had heads. Holly jumped when she heard someone unlock her door from outside. She held her breath as the door slowly opened. It was Sunny.

"Hey, Holly, you won't believe it. There was a guy coming down the staircase as I was coming up. I know guys sneak in sometimes, but this guy looked like he was almost forty. Isn't that gross? He was too well dressed to be maintenance."

Oh, God, she was so close to him. She could have been killed. Holly remembered the picture on her bulletin. Sunny wasn't blind; she wasn't stupid either. It wouldn't take her very long to realize something was up. "Sunny, get out of here."

"What?" Sunny looked at Holly as if she'd lost her marbles. "I just got here."

"Just leave for a little while, okay?" Holly heard the tone in her own voice and grimaced.

"Is this about the football game, because if it's that big of a deal, you don't have to go."

"It's not about the stupid game!" Holly knew she was yelling, but she wanted Sunny out of there before she saw the picture. It was obvious Sunny wasn't leaving. If Holly knew her as well as she thought she did, then she was sure Sunny would stay in the room because she would think Holly needed her help. Holly did the only thing she could think of. She went over to Sunny, yanked the key out of her hand, and shoved her startled friend out the door. Holly slammed it shut before Sunny could come to her senses and barge back in.

Ignoring her friend's angry banging, Holly quickly took down the picture and looked for something else to put over the gaping holes in her bulletin board. She settled on a goofy-looking photo of Josh and Bret. *Well,* Holly glanced warily at the door, *I have to open it sooner or later.* Holly heard her stomach grumble, so she opted for sooner. As it turned out, she should have waited. Sunny had been about to bang on the door again when, instead of the door, she slammed her fist into Holly's face. She let out a howl of pain. "You broke my nose!" Blood was everywhere. It was the perfect ending to a Monday.

chapter twenty-four

"*I* still can't believe you punched her in the face."

"I didn't punch her! Well, not intentionally at least."

Elizabeth laughed. They were standing in line for hot dogs at the game. "You're lucky that Holly doesn't know anything about fighting. She could have knocked you all the way back to the first grade."

"She's not that big," Sunny mumbled.

"You'd have to be blind to call Holly big, but she is tall. She could have sat on you."

"Can we talk about something else, please?" It was enough that Bret and Josh had been teasing her about getting into catfights all week, without having Elizabeth make fun of her as well. She wished she'd slugged one of them instead. That would wipe the smiles off their faces.

"You're not going to like my change of subject."

"What's that?" Sunny asked.

"Well," Elizabeth said, "isn't that the guy from church, the one who was so strange around you?"

Mark? Sunny turned around and, sure enough, there was Mark standing with the rest of her friends. *What is he doing here?*

Sunny marched over to Mark with Elizabeth tailing behind her. "What are you doing here?"

"Sunny!" Elizabeth hissed and then glanced at Holly who was obviously enjoying the whole scene. "You're a big help," Elizabeth jabbed Holly in the ribs.

"Ouch, what did I do?" A smile still played on her lips. The day had taken an interesting turn. "I'm just an innocent spectator."

Sunny sent her a "yeah right" look and then turned her disgust towards the person of the hour, namely Mark. Why did he have to look so cute? It made her want to dump her drink on him again just to wipe the smirk off his face. Unfortunately, the line was too long to get another one. Sunny glared at him. He had a twinkle in his eye that made her wary. "I'm sorry," Sunny said through gritted teeth. Just because the guy was a creep didn't mean she had to be rude. "I hope you didn't take that the wrong way. I was just surprised to see you." Sunny shot Bret a warning look. She could tell by his expression he was about to contradict her. She looked at Mark again. He stared back at her as if she had horns, as if she were the weird one. Well, if he was going to stare at her, then she would give him a taste of his own medicine. Sunny scowled at him. Soon, though, she'd forgotten she was trying to scare him off. She couldn't tear her eyes away from his. Knowing looks passed between her friends, but they went unnoticed. When the announcer came on, Sunny and Mark jumped, as if being set free from a spell.

Soon the six of them headed to their seats. The small aluminum stands made Holly's imagination run into overtime. She could easily see herself tripping and rolling down them, breaking every bone in her body on the way down. It wasn't a comforting image.

They did finally get into their row without any major casualties, unless you count Sunny's death glares. Of course, they all seemed to deflect off their intended target, Mark. He perversely enjoyed the attention.

A very large man with half the concession stand in his lap guarded the path to their seats. He was remarkably unmoved by their approach. Holly was in the lead, so she was the first to try to forge a way past him. Holly was almost passed the man when everything seemed to go in slow motion. Holly's foot caught under his, and she screamed as she began to fall toward the concrete below. Holly put up her hands to shield herself from the impact, knowing full well that they would do little to break her fall.

Arms grabbed her around the waist and jerked her back. Once Holly knew she was no longer in danger of falling, she turned, and there was Josh. He was busy staring down the man she'd tripped over. The man seemed indifferent to her near death experience, indifferent and slightly annoyed for being bothered. Holly touched the side of Josh's face to get his attention. Josh looked at her, and his features softened immediately. "Are you okay?"

"Yes, thank . . ."

"Tell your girlfriend to be more careful next time, shrimp," the fat, muscle man spoke.

Josh's jaw set. "Next time," he said quietly, "you can move your foot so that a lady can pass."

The man laughed loudly. Even the roar of the crowds couldn't drown out the sneer in his voice. "I don't see any ladies around here."

Uh oh, Holly thought. She wasn't offended. The guy was obviously goading Josh for the fun of it, but she saw something in Josh snap. "Listen, you piece of scum," he said, "either you apologize right now or else . . ."

"Or else what?" Obviously, the muscle man didn't like being called scum. As he stood up, the food on his lap fell to the ground. The man must have been six inches taller than Josh and twice as big.

Idiot! Holly wanted to scream at Josh. She did not want to watch him get beaten up, especially not because of her. Holly looked at him, expecting him to be terrified, but Josh wasn't. He stood his ground. Either he was really dumb, or else he was very brave, probably both.

"I'm not going to fight you," Josh said evenly. His eyes barely reached the man's chin.

"Too late, you little weasel." The man ran his fist into Josh's stomach knocking the wind out of him. Josh doubled over for a second and then, with difficulty, stood up straight again.

"What are you, a wimp?" the man taunted. *What luck.* He had his own football right here in the stands.

"No." To Holly's dismay, Josh had gotten his wind back and could talk again. "I could fight you, but what would that prove? You're obviously bigger than me. Like I said, I won't fight you."

The man's face turned purple. Holly thought he might kill Josh. As he wound up to punch him again, Holly saw Mark come up from behind, grab the guy's head and twist. Immediately, the man slumped backwards. It took both Mark and Josh to push him back into his seat.

"Is he dead?" Sunny asked, who'd only seen a little from her line of view, looking at the man in horror.

"No," Mark looked around to see who had noticed what he'd done, "he's just unconscious."

"Where did you learn to do that?" Bret stared back and forth between the unconscious man and Mark.

"No place you'd want to go," Mark mumbled. "Are you okay, Josh?"

"Yeah," Josh winced, "you didn't have to do that."

"What kind of a guest would I be if I allowed my host to be turned into a bloody pulp?" Mark asked smiling. He was obviously the only one who was currently amused at having an unconscious man in the seat next to them. "By the way, what you did took guts, guts and a whole lot of stupidity."

"Thanks, I think."

Mark slapped him on the back and didn't seem to notice Josh

wince. "Don't mention it, really. Well, now for the exciting part—football."

"Great," Holly mumbled unenthusiastically. She'd had enough excitement for one day. In fact, compared to what she had just witnessed, football looked like a rather calm sport. At any rate, the players weren't trying to kill each other, or so Josh assured her.

Sunny looked to her left and saw Holly on the edge of her seat. *Who would have thought she would be the little football princess.* More than once that day Holly had stood up to yell at the ref while the rest of them quietly stayed seated. Josh was proud.

After the third quarter, it was obvious the Aggies would be crushed by the Texas Longhorns. Sunny, who had grown up around men, had seen her share of football games. She figured she could miss five minutes of this one. "Hey, guys." No one looked up except for Mark. "Guys!" Four very perturbed faces turned towards her. Mark just smiled. "I'm going to get a drink. Does anyone else want anything?" They all wanted something, but there was no way she could carry back five cokes, two popcorns, and a pickle by herself.

"One of you is going to have to come with me." Sunny first looked at her friends. They were ignoring her again.

"I'll come," Mark said.

Great, Sunny thought. "All right, but you're carrying the pickle."

"How generous of you," he smiled and rose from his seat.

"Humph," was all Sunny had to say as they walked off together. Holly wondered vaguely if she'd ever see Mark again, alive that is. Thoughts of funerals were soon forgotten, though, when Texas intercepted the ball at the 20-yard line and ran 60 yards. Holly was sure that she would be hoarse the next day, but it was worth it. Who would have guessed football could be so exciting?

Sunny and Mark stood in an impossibly long line at the concession stand, and after ten minutes of complete silence, both were on edge.

"Stop doing that."

Mark held up his hands in exasperated surrender. "What am I doing?"

"You're looking at me."

"Well, sorry," Mark said sarcastically. The fact he knew he'd been watching her more than the game only added to his aggravation.

"Listen, Buster, I…oh no." Sunny grabbed Mark by the shoulders and turned him to face her. "Hide me."

"What's going on?" Mark whispered, startled by the sudden change of events. The fact Sunny had her head buried into his shoulder made no impact on him in the least. He was tired; that's all. Mark heard someone call Sunny's name from about twenty feet away.

"Greetings, Sunflower White. I did not know that you enjoyed football. It is a grotesque game, is it not?"

"Um . . ." Sunny started. She was clearly at a loss for words.

Dilbert suddenly noticed Mark standing there and narrowed his eyes. "Who are you?"

"Mark Tayne." Mark held out his hand, which Dilbert, of course, ignored. Instead, he gave him a death glare that even Holly would have been proud of. They made a wonderful trio—one seething, one confused beyond words, and the last wishing she hadn't been born.

"Oh, you're her boyfriend. I didn't think you existed." Dilbert stomped off.

Mark watched him go and then slowly turned to a very red Sunny. He looked at her archly. "*I'm* your boyfriend?"

God, just kill me now! Sunny bit her lower lip. "I'm sorry. Dilbert was pestering me to go out with him, and I told him I had a boyfriend. He wouldn't let it go, so I gave him your name." Sunny waited for him to yell or laugh. Mark did neither.

Sunny blurted it all out so fast that Mark had trouble keeping up. "So you said that I was your boyfriend?" he asked slowly.

"Yes." Sunny looked at him guiltily. "Yes, I know, I know. I should have told the truth."

"Yeah, why didn't you just tell him you were gay? That would have gotten him to leave you alone."

Sunny laughed, "And that would have been better than telling him I had a boyfriend?"

Mark shrugged, suddenly feeling uncomfortable. "At least it would have been the truth."

If Sunny had had anything in her mouth, she would have choked on it. Instead, she just gaped at him. "You're joking, right? Do I look gay to you?" Sunny's cheeks burned.

Mark was taken aback and momentarily speechless. "Bret and Josh told me that Holly and you were gay." *Didn't they?* Mark desperately tried to remember the conversation.

Sunny was almost seething. "They told you what? Why would they say that? Even more importantly, why would you believe them?" She poked Mark in the chest.

"Well, I, um, I…" *Now what?* His biggest nightmare was proving to be just a dream and here he was talking like an inarticulate imbecile. The last time he'd felt like such a fool was back in second grade when he'd wet himself. Correction—that was less embarrassing.

"So that's why you had me read Leviticus 18. Now that I think about it, there was a verse in there about homosexuality." Sunny stared at him waiting for him to say something; Mark just gulped. Suddenly, Sunny burst out laughing.

Well, Mark thought, *it's better than her yelling at me.* It was his turn to turn red.

"So?" Sunny asked, "does this mean you'll stop staring at me?"

Mark smiled. "Nope, in fact, I think I'll be staring at you a lot more from now on."

Sunny tried to blow off his comment as lame. "Is this you hitting on me?"

"Do you want it to be?" Mark grinned and lifted his eyebrows.

Sunny laughed. "You're pretty good at this. Actually, you're too good and too old."

"What do you mean I'm too old? I'm only twenty-five."

"Yeah, and I'm only eighteen. Forget about it, Mark."

I can't believe she thinks I'm old. I'm not old. I'm in the prime of my life, aren't I? Sunny was staring at him, "What? Are you looking for gray hair?"

Sunny chuckled. "I can't tell if you're more insulted that I won't go out with you, or because I just called you old."

"I think it's a mutual thing," Mark said blandly. "You don't really think I'm old, do you?"

"Old? No, not old. Just too old for me."

We'll see about that. "Okay," Mark said with a smile that he knew worked wonders. When Sunny stopped smirking, he knew he hadn't lost his touch. They were finally at the front of the concession line. Sunny reached for her wallet but then nearly jumped out of her skin when Mark lightly took her hand.

"I'll pay," Mark sent her another smile. Just because he hadn't used his skills in years didn't mean he couldn't revive them from the dead. He hadn't become a lady's man by age twelve for nothing. Mark grinned to himself. Sunny didn't stand a chance.

What is he up to? Sunny had grown up with guys. She could tell when they were cooking something up in those conniving brains of theirs. She'd just have to be more cautious around him—that or stay away. Sunny quickly glanced at Mark again. That was a mistake. How the guy didn't trip while watching her was a mystery. One thing was for sure, she wouldn't be able to stay away from him, not even if he was the devil himself, and with that smile, he just might be. She'd have to check for horns later.

"Sunny! We were supposed to leave half an hour ago!"

A week had passed since the fateful football game. Since then,

Sunny was constantly on the alert for what Holly liked to call "Mark attacks." Sunny told herself she wouldn't be annoyed if he weren't so good at it. Monday morning, he'd appeared bearing gifts in the form of Starbucks. Coffee was her Achilles heel. It was then that Mark asked her to have lunch with him on Wednesday. He did this, of course, after she'd accepted the coffee. She would have loved to have thrown his sneaky invitation back in his face, but she couldn't. Darn her parents for teaching her good manners.

Mark told her he knew a nice place to eat, and Sunny, who was already ready to ring his neck, left it at that. To ask where they were going would have, in her mind, shown a sign of interest, and this boy obviously didn't need any more encouragement. Of course, Mark had failed to mention that the spot was located on Canyon Lake, an hour and a half away from Austin. Sunny was furious that she enjoyed the ride. He was a great person to talk to—too great. Secretly, she had been sad when they arrived at his friend's condo for dinner. She didn't want to share him with others, but of course, Sunny would never admit that to herself.

Unable to find anything remotely wrong with him, and she had looked, Sunny settled on the next best thing. She blamed everything that went wrong in her life on him. After almost a week, she'd gotten fairly good at it. For instance, it was his fault she was running late and hadn't completely packed because she kept thinking about him, thinking about him in a bad way, of course. It was all his fault Holly and she were going to miss their plane to Salem. Now how was she going to explain *that* to her parents?

"Sunny! I said hurry up, not daydream."

"Be quiet and pack something." Sunny threw her a dirty look and stuck out her tongue.

"I already have," Holly mumble to herself. "In fact, I've packed everything."

"You don't have to brag about it."

Holly leaned back against her bed and watched her friend hurriedly stuff clothes into her bag. She'd tried to help earlier, but that had nearly earned her another black eye. This one would have been intentional. "This trip with you is looking more and more appealing by the minute," Holly said dryly.

Sunny smiled, "Yes, it'll be amazing if we not only get there on time but also alive."

"I promise not to kill you, if you promise not to kill me."

Sunny laughed and shook Holly's hand, "Deal."

Eight excruciatingly long hours later, Sunny and Holly walked into Sunny's house in Salem. Compared to Holly's parents' homes, the place was a closet, but she wouldn't have had warmer feelings toward Buckingham Palace. For the first time in Holly's life, she felt like she'd stepped into a home. She knew it was Sunny's mother, not a hired servant, who had arranged the flowers on the table. It had been Sunny's father, not a photographer, who was behind the lens in the family photos. What was more, everyone was happy to be there. A few months ago, Holly would have balked at the place, but now, it made her feel good, and a little jealous. The envious feelings passed, though, when Holly quickly found herself treated like one of them. Hollywood Rose Johnson, daughter of a millionaire and a Hollywood Star, had found her place in the White family household.

Dinner was an exciting event. Holly sat between Sunny's two older brothers Matt and Kip. They were twins. Holly quickly found out she had been strategically placed there to keep WWIII from going nuclear. Sunny's oldest brother, Zachary, sat across from Holly looking bored. His equally bored wife, Melissa, sat next to him. Without being told, Holly knew that Melissa and Sunny had it in for each other. Holly could tell Sunny's mother was what kept her daughter and daughter-in-law from going at each other with their steak knives. Holly sized Melissa up from across the table and decided she'd place her bets on Sunny.

Loud banging on the table brought Holly's full attention back to a bigger problem, namely the twins. "I am not a sissy!" Matt bellowed. "Just because I want to be an artist doesn't mean I'm afraid of life. I just like to paint it!"

"Oh really," Kip was truly enjoying himself, "and what would you do if you ever got into a fight? Would you stab the other guy with your paint brush?"

"It's an interesting thought," Matt gritted his teeth. "Why don't we go outside and try it?"

"Oh please, I wouldn't want to make you cry. Sunny can do that."

Matt turned red. "I was sick and only ten years old. I hadn't hit my growth spurt either."

Melissa was aghast. "You beat up a sick child?"

Sunny scowled at her, "Um, hello, I was six when he was ten, and he was well enough to give my Barbie a Jacuzzi ride in the toilet."

"You played with Barbies?" Holly looked shocked.

"Shut up, Holly," Sunny sent her a don't-mess-with-me-while-I'm-at-war smile. "For your information, Melissa, I . . ."

"That's enough." Mrs. White spoke up. Actually, she spoke very softly; nevertheless, the entire White population cowered, including the new Mrs. Melissa White. "I won't have all of you being childish in front of our guest." Melissa smiled victoriously at Sunny. Sunny's mother rolled her eyes. "I'm not talking about you, Melissa. I'm talking about Holly." Sunny smirked right back at Melissa.

After a few moments of silence, Mr. White must have felt it was safe to speak. He cleared his throat and said, "Well, since everyone here is so intent on killing each other, on Thanksgiving Day of all days, why don't we play Risk later on and save ourselves the trouble?"

"I'll play!" Jacob, Sunny's younger brother, said eagerly.

Matt looked mutinously at his twin. "Let the games begin."

After that comment, Kip was definitely going to play. Zachary and Melissa said that they had places to go, people to see, etc. Later Sunny translated for Holly. Basically, they wanted to go somewhere else to be bored because life was too exciting there. Sunny was the last to concede to play. Mrs. White only wanted to watch, and Holly decided to join her on the sidelines since she still had nightmares from the first time she played at UT. Her friends had slaughtered her. So much for beginner's luck. Holly preferred less brutal games, like hockey.

Watching the game was an amusing diversion. After three minutes, Matt was already hitting Kip over the head with the rule-book yelling, "Read it, you imbecile!" Holly also observed Sunny's younger brother, Jacob, surreptitiously removing his opponents' men from the board. Jacob looked at her, smiled, and put his finger over his mouth in a silent, "Shush."

The game lasted for over three hours. By the end, Holly could barely keep her eyes open. Even the twins were too tired to yell at each other. Then the game was over.

"Man! Jacob always wins," Matt complained. Jacob looked up at Holly and winked. Holly just shook her head. She knew the next time she played she would watch her men like a hawk.

chapter twenty-five

Sunny's alarm went off at five o'clock the next day. Even Sunny wasn't cheerful that early in the morning, especially after staying up past one talking to Holly. Unfortunately, Mrs. White was a firm believer in being at the airport two hours early. Sunny told Holly that it was just in case alien life forms took over the airport and the plane left early. Therefore, they were there at seven. Due to the bad weather, the flight crew for their plane was delayed in another city. The two-hour wait slowly dragged into four—typical.

While they waited, Holly did her best to choke down some eggs at an airport café. She wasn't sure, but Holly didn't think scrambled eggs were supposed to be runny. Holly knew she should have stuck with McDonalds. She glanced over at Sunny who looked like a robot as she drank her coffee. Holly could have timed her watch by it. Sunny took a sip every ten seconds while she stared off into the oblivion. Maybe Sunny wasn't actually awake yet. Holly smiled mischievously.

"Hey, Sunny, look. I think I see Elvis over there."

"That's nice." Sunny took another sip.

She must be drinking decaf. Holly grabbed Sunny by the shoulders and shook. That got her attention. "Holly! What's the matter with you?"

"I just told you that Elvis is back from the dead, and you just sat there."

Sunny looked confused, "Have you been reading those weird magazines again?"

Holly rolled her eyes. This conversation was going from dumb to dumber. "That's not the point. I . . ." Just then, Holly heard their flight number called over the loudspeaker. *Finally.* "Okay, Sunny, it's time to go."

Sunny was back into her coffee autopilot. "Go where?"

God, keep me from strangling her, please. I'm almost positive I'll regret it later. "No where, Sunny. Just pick up your bag and follow me."

"Okay," Sunny followed her in blind obedience.

Something was wrong. Holly couldn't put her finger on it, but something was definitely wrong. Then it hit her, "Sunny! Sunny wake up." Holly roughly woke up her sleeping friend.

"What? What's going on? Where am I?" Sunny looked around the cabin frantically. Then her eyes fell on Holly, and with blinding speed, everything came back to her. They were on a plane headed for Los Angeles. "What's wrong?"

"Sunny, we're heading in the wrong direction."

"What do you mean we're heading in the wrong direction?"

"I mean, we're heading north instead of south. The sun is on the wrong side of the plane."

"Oh, is that all?" Sunny attempted to fall back asleep.

Holly shook her again, this time more urgently. "Sunny, the sun is on the wrong side of the plane!"

Sunny didn't show any sign of comprehension. She just blinked and then made a very intelligent sound, "Huh?"

"If we were heading south, then the sun would be on the left side of the plane, not the right."

Sunny looked over her shoulder, "But, Holly, the sun is on the left side."

Holly rolled her eyes, "You're other left, Sunny."

Sunny rubbed her eyes. "Are you sure?"

Holly raised one eyebrow. "I happen know my right from my left."

Sunny gritted her teeth. Not only was she tired, but fear was starting to seep in. "I'm not talking about being directionally impaired. I'm talking about the direction we're heading in." *Did that make any sense?* Sunny couldn't be sure, but Holly got the message.

"Oh, sorry," Holly said. "Yes, I know what direction we're heading."

Sunny was starting to grow worried. Why would they be heading north? Her eyes suddenly widened, "Do you think it's terrorists?"

Holly forced herself not to laugh. Sunny was serious. "Don't worry, Sunny. I don't think Alaska is a prime target for any terrorist group, and that's where we're going. Personally, I think there's something wrong with the plane. It keeps jolting, like it can't maintain speed or something."

"Are you trying to ease my vivid imagination? Because if you are, stop." She hated flying. Why did this always happen to her? *Trust in Me,* Sunny heard God say. *I won't let any harm come to you. Be brave.* "Holly," Sunny said steadily, "whatever is happening, we're going to be all right."

As it turned out, there had been something wrong with the plane, and it was just what Holly had expected. The pilots couldn't control the speed and had been circling around the airport trying to override the system. Once they realized they couldn't, they scheduled an emergency landing. Even with God's assurance, Sunny didn't enjoy being welcomed back to the ground by fire trucks and ambulances.

The next available flight was an hour later. They had to ride in what Holly accurately deemed a sardine can. Sunny was sure it was God's grace alone that allowed them to rattle their way across the sky and arrive in Los Angeles in one piece. What an experience. Thank God it wasn't her last.

The luggage was late, which was no big surprise considering the circumstances. Sunny was surprised though, when a limo picked them up. She'd been in a limo before, but obviously not as much as Holly had. Somehow, that wasn't shocking.

Sunny had never been to Los Angeles, so she stared out the window like the tourist she was while Holly slept. "Hey, Holly, wake up." Sunny elbowed her friend.

"What?" Holly mumbled without opening her eyes.

"It's your name." Sunny pointed out the window.

"Huh?" Holly opened her eyes and looked out the window to see the legendary white letters. Holly glared at Sunny. "You woke me up for that, Sunflower?"

"Sheesh, Holly, don't be so excited. People might be able to see through the tinted window. You wouldn't want them to think critically of you." Holly rolled her eyes and then put her pillow over her head to ward off any more unsolicited cracks about her name.

When they arrived at Anne's home, a burly looking man of about fifty knocked on the outside window. Holly rolled it down and glared up at him.

"Oh," the guard said unenthusiastically, "it's you." Sunny

started to smile, but then she realized the guy wasn't being rude to be funny. He was serious.

Holly returned his sentiments cue for cue. "You're still here? What a shame." Holly spoke to the chauffeur lazily, "Drive on, please."

Once the window was up, Sunny asked Holly, "What was that all about?" She indicated toward the guard who was still glaring holes into the back of the car.

"Oh, him? That's Earnest Rankin. He works for my mom, unfortunately."

"Why don't you like him?"

Holly shrugged. "What's to like?" Sunny just stared at her, and Holly rolled her eyes. "What do you want me to do, be nice to him?"

"Yes, that's exactly what you should do."

"Give me one good reason why I should be nice to that creep."

Sunny just stared at her and then looked away. Holly sighed dramatically, "Whatever you want to say, say it."

Sunny smiled and shook her head. Holly grumbled to herself, "Let me guess. God would want me to be nice to him even though he is a vile creature."

Sunny's smile widened, and she nodded her head. "Fine," Holly said belligerently, "since I'm new at this whole 'being nice' thing. You're going to have to help me."

"You've got it."

After a few seconds, Holly let out a pathetic whimper and laid her head on Sunny's shoulder, "Are you sure God created him too?"

Sunny laughed. "I'm sure." That got another groan from Holly. "Hey look," Sunny tried to distract her. "There's your mom." It was strange. Holly's face went from playful and childish to mature and sophisticated. She straightened and brushed back her hair. Sunny was reminded of a soldier putting his armor on for battle. If Sunny hadn't known better, she would have mistaken the worry in her eyes for self-assurance.

Mask or no mask, Sunny saw fear. "Holly, did you know I didn't learn to ride a bike until I was thirteen?" Holly shook her head unbelieving. Even she, who was afraid of anything with wheels, had learned to ride before that. "My brothers all chipped in to buy me a bike for Christmas and said I would be riding it before the sunset if it killed me. I was afraid it would, but Matt gave me this Bible verse. It's Isaiah 41:10, 'So do not fear, for I am with you; do not be dismayed, for I am your God. I will strengthen you and help you; I will uphold you with my righteous right hand.' I don't know if that helps you, but it's gotten me through a lot of things in my life."

"Did you learn to ride that day?"

Sunny smiled. "I won our school triathlon the next year."

Holly smiled back. "Thanks, Sunny."

The night with Anne Tricony was anything but boring. Holly's stepfather said about three words the entire evening, but he seemed to enjoy being quiet around Holly's mother. To Sunny's way of thinking, it was a good thing because there was no way Robert would get a word in otherwise.

The old grandfather clock rang eleven, jolting Sunny out of her catnap. She looked over to see that Holly was having a hard time staying awake as well. Holly held her chin up in her hands to keep it from banging onto the table. Sunny tried to listen as Anne prattled on, but she couldn't keep her eyes open much longer. Actually, she didn't want to keep them open because the room was starting to shake. She hoped it was just her and not one of California's infamous earthquakes. What a great way to end a vacation, falling off into the Pacific. Sunny could think of better ways to die.

Anne let out a humongous yawn and stretched. The yawn seemed to be an epidemic that quickly passed around the table. "Well," Robert tried to stifle another yawn, "I think we've stayed up long enough. I'm sure the girls are tired." He winked at Holly, and Sunny knew that if she'd had enough energy to move, she would have kissed him. Anne looked disappointed to quit her one-way conversation, but thankfully, she didn't protest. They all said goodnight and headed off in their separate directions.

Holly trudged up the stairs like a sullen tour guide. "We need to get an elevator," she huffed.

Sunny wasn't much better off. "How much farther is it?"

"Our wing is about a mile's walk from here."

From the looks of the place, Sunny wasn't entirely sure Holly was joking. When they finally did get to the room, Sunny took one look at her nice, comfy bed and all but wept in gratitude. It had been a long day.

chapter twenty-six

The next day was devoted entirely to Holly's old favorite sport—shopping. Sunny found that everything with Holly was an experience, and this was no different. Holly shopped like there was no tomorrow. She was, without a doubt, an impulse buyer who was intolerant of fussing with something as trivial as a price tag. After an hour of constantly fighting with her, Sunny stopped refusing gifts. By the end of the day, Sunny was sure she had just doubled her earthly possessions. Sunny realized Holly simply enjoyed giving. While they had been in a toy store, Holly had given a random little kid a stuffed animal. She was just that way.

After much inner debate, Holly decided to buy her mother's gruff security guard a Christmas present. Holly knew he was a big San Francisco Giants fan, so she bought him a baseball autographed by Barry Bonds. The sports salesman assured her he was a star player. Neither Holly nor Sunny watched the sport so they decided to trust him.

Lunch was an interesting affair as well. Holly and Sunny stopped at a little diner off the side of the road. It was called Lulu's. Lulu's made Holly feel like she'd stepped back in time. The walls were sporadically covered with pictures of Marilyn Monroe, James Dean, Elvis Presley, and other ancient big shots. There were pictures of L.A. back in her golden years, and most had colored lights sprouting out of them to give a vivid, live effect. Next to the pictures were old license plates, playing cards, and guitar picks. The rest of the restaurant meshed perfectly with its walls, from the high-backed booths to the multi-colored tiles and mushroom stools. It was just the kind of place where Holly and Sunny wanted to eat. That is, until they met their waitress.

The aging woman reminded Holly of the mistress of the keep. There was no funny business with her. She might not be the owner, but in essence, she seemed to be the diner itself. When she spoke, even the walls listened. Holly found herself saying "Yes, ma'am" and asking "Please" after every request. The workers in the diner were no less reverent. The younger ones looked absolutely terrified of the old dragon. Holly had to admit, though, the service was excellent, and the food was even better.

By the end of the day, Sunny felt like she'd run a marathon and wanted nothing more than to take a shower and climb back in bed for a month. Holly, on the other hand, looked like she was ready for round two. Well, she could go back into the ring on her own because Sunny's top priority for the rest of the day was sleep.

Sunny's waning energy was the reason Holly was downstairs that night in the kitchen. The kitchen had always been her favorite room in the house. She didn't know why, but it was. Later she would wonder if God had something to do with it because what was about to happen that night was nothing short of a miracle.

Holly rummaged around for the Rice Krispies. Just because it was nighttime didn't mean she couldn't have cereal, fine restaurants be darned. She just wouldn't mention it to Sunny who Holly was sure would never let her live it down. What did Sunny have against Rice Krispies anyway? She nearly dropped the milk when she heard the door behind her slam. Holly turned to see who it was.

"Oh, sorry dear, I forgot that door swings back so quickly."

"Hi, Mom. What are you doing up so late?"

Anne yawned, "I guess I came down here for the same thing you did—Snap, Crackle, and Pop."

At first Holly was confused, but then she looked at the little elves on the front of her cereal box. "Oh," Holly laughed and pushed the box over to her mom.

"You know, I don't think your grandmother ever did forgive me for getting you hooked on these."

"Why?" Holly asked with her mouth full. "How are *they* improper for a young lady of society?"

Anne rolled her eyes and mimicked Victoria. "Food is not to make noise in one's mouth." Anne took another bite.

Holly laughed. "So did she try to contraband them when you were around too?"

"Yes, but it was one of the few fights I did win with her. She actually refused to have breakfast with me, which wasn't a huge loss." Holly smiled. Her grandmother really was an odd old bird. With the exception of the crackling cereal, they sat in silence for the next few minutes. When Anne did speak, all humor was gone form her voice. "Thank you for coming, Holly. It really means a lot."

Holly looked up from her bowl and smiled. "I'm glad I came. I'm having a good time."

Anne seemed to brighten at that comment. "Did you have a good time with Sunny's family?"

"Yes, they're all very nice. Her family is so different from . . ." Holly was about to say the word "ours" but then though the better of it, ". . . from other families."

"Really, how so?"

Holly took her time. She didn't want her mother to get the wrong message. "Well, for one thing, they're Christians."

Anne lifted an eyebrow at Holly's mention of religion. "A lot of people are Christians."

Holly shook her head. "No, not like this. They actually have a relationship with God." *Well, it's now or never.* "So do I. I'm a Christian now." *I hope she doesn't think I've joined some sort of cult.*

Anne, who hadn't stepped foot in a church since she was seventeen, didn't look upset at all. "Is that why you're so different now?"

Am I, God? "Yes, I guess so."

"How do you become a Christian?"

Holly had to force herself not to gape at her mother. She couldn't believe this was happening. Holly felt excitement rush through her, and she knew it was God stirring in her. She was nervous too. What if she messed up? *Oh God, speak through me. I don't know how to do this, but You do.* "Well, first . . ."

Before the clock struck twelve, Anne Tricony was born again into the family of God. The music rose.

Anne went with Holly and Sunny to the airport the next day. She was full of questions for both of them about God and how to learn more about Him. It was exciting for all three of them. All too soon, though, it was time to head toward their gate. Holly started to say goodbye, but her mother hugged her instead. For the first time, she felt like they were really mother and daughter. Maybe all the suffering and pain she'd gone through as a child made this more special. Holly knew that had she had a "normal" upbringing, she wouldn't have recognized this relationship for what it really was—it was a gift from God to the His children whom He loved. Holly understood why real joy could only come from God; it was because real love could only come from Him.

"I love you, Mom." Holly started crying. She didn't want to leave.

"I love you too, Holly." Anne looked at her daughter's face. It was so like her own. When had she grown up? "I'm also very proud of you and so blessed to have you as a daughter." Anne kissed her on the cheek. "You'd better go. You wouldn't want to miss your plane."

"Yeah," Holly started to walk toward the gate.

"Oh, and Holly?" Anne said, "I know that it's not your style, but dare to be spontaneous sometimes and drop in."

"I'll do that." With one final wave and smile, she met up with Sunny on the other side of the barrier. Sunny didn't say anything. She just put her arm around her best friend, and they both walked to the gate.

chapter twenty-seven

After Thanksgiving, the heat was on to prepare for finals. Even Holly was stressed out. By now, she knew the Bible verses about not worrying. There were over four hundred to be exact, but Jesus hadn't had a linguistics paper, now had He? Holly blamed the people from the Tower of Babel. It was all their fault that she had to study.

Josh never failed to brighten up her day, though. She knew it was killing him not to ask her out. He didn't, though, and Holly loved him all the more for it. *Speaking of couples,* Holly couldn't help but wonder how much longer Sunny could handle the "Mark attacks." She had to admit the most recent one had been horribly unfair. When they got into their room that day, one of Holly's shirts had been mysteriously running around the room. When Sunny had poked the shirt, it yipped. Both Holly and Sunny jumped, but then Sunny finally got the nerve to pick up the shirt. As it turned out, there was a little puppy under it. It had a lopsided bow attached to its collar with a note. Sunny, a natural born dog-lover, picked up the squirming ball of fur and, with great difficulty, took off the note. It read, "*Dear Sunny, my name is Woof. I'm cute and cuddly and want to be your puppy. Your handsome friend, Mark, adopted my sister and says that I can stay at his house while you're still in college as long as you come to visit me. Please adopt me, because if you don't, I won't have a home.*"

"Why that scheming little . . ." Sunny growled and then the puppy barked as if to say, '*You're not giving me attention.*' Sunny looked down. The puppy had laughter in his eyes and a little bit of a forlorn look as well. He reminded her of Mark. All rational thinking went out the door when the puppy managed to wriggle its way up onto Sunny's shoulder and give her kisses. *At least Mark isn't that presumptuous.* She picked the puppy up and looked at it in the face. Woof gave her the saddest eyes she'd ever seen. Sunny laughed and hugged him.

"Does this mean you're keeping him?" Holly's curiosity had led her to read the note.

"No, Mark's going to keep him."

"You know he'll only take that as more encouragement."

Sunny smiled at the puppy. "I know."

Holly looked at her curiously, "Does this mean you'll go out with him now?" Sunny didn't answer her. She just kept playing with Woof who was now so happy that he was spinning around in circles. To Holly, she looked like she was in denial, but Holly didn't see the plan formulating in Sunny's head.

Mark looked at his watch again. Patience was not a virtue God had bestowed upon him. *Come on, Josh, where are you?* Josh had called him in the middle of the night saying he needed to talk to him, but would he settle with a quick chat on the phone? No, he'd made Mark drag himself out of bed and meet him in a dinky little corner store at one in the morning. *He'd better show up or else that*

little punk is going down. Christian or no Christian. "Ah!" Something cold and wet landed on his head and spilled down onto his clothes. His sweater was soaked before he knew what had hit him. Mark jumped up out of the booth he'd been sitting in and turned to face his attacker, fists raised. Imagine his surprise when he came face to face with not a surly truck driver looking for a fight, but Sunny. Well, it was a pleasant surprise, but that didn't change the fact he was now dripping wet with what he assumed to be coke, and thanks to his bath, he was freezing.

"Why did you…? What are you doing? I mean…oh, you found Woof. I thought you'd like him."

Sunny glared at him. "Mark Tayne, who do you think you are? Didn't anyone ever teach you that no means no?" Mark looked around the store. Luckily, there weren't too many people hanging around to see this embarrassing scene. "I said I don't want to go out with you."

Mark crossed his arms and tried to recover some shroud of dignity. "You do know that lying is a sin."

Sunny made an exasperated noise in the back of her throat. "Why are you so sure of yourself?"

"Why are you so against going out with me?"

"I have gone out with you."

Mark shook his head. "No, you've allowed yourself to be tricked into doing things with me. There is a difference. Personally, I think you enjoy it."

"Enjoy what? Being stalked by you?"

Mark smirked, which kicked Sunny's temper up another notch. "Let me ask you this," Mark said smoothly. "If you don't like me, then why did you set me up like this tonight? Why not just call me up and yell at me?"

"I thought I could make you mad enough to leave me alone." Sunny looked him straight in the eye, daring him to call her bluff.

"First of all, you could never do that. Second, that's not why you came here."

This was not turning out the way she'd planned, and, darn

it, she was happy about that. A part of her hadn't wanted him to be furious with him. "How do you know what I feel and what I don't?"

Mark smiled. "It's all in your eyes. Besides, I can prove it."

At that, Sunny lifted an eyebrow. "Oh really?"

"Really." Mark slowly bent down and kissed her. He forced himself to pull back, but not soon enough. His heart was racing, and for the first time in years, he was nervous, nervous that when he looked at her face, he would see disgust, or worse, disinterest.

What he did see was terrifying and wonderful. She was smiling at him, and though he'd never seen anyone look at him in this way, he knew now what he'd only caught whispers of before. She loved him, possibly as much as he loved her, but did she know? Probably not.

Sunny started to blush, "That definitely wasn't what I came here for." Sunny looked at the ground. Her brain told her she should slap him and run away. Her heart told her brain to shut up. "I've never kissed anyone before."

Mark felt two things, shock and relief. It shocked him because she was beautiful, and he was relieved because he wouldn't have to go to prison for first-degree murder.

Sunny didn't know how to take his silence. Was he disappointed because she didn't have any experience? "I guess you've had tons of practice." She couldn't look him in the face, but she had to know.

"I lost my virginity when I was thirteen."

Sunny tried not to look shocked. "Oh, I understand."

"No, I don't think you do. My mom abandoned my brothers and me when I was three and . . ."

"But what about that shirt? You said it was from your mom." *Smooth, Sunny, he's pouring his heart out to you and that's what you ask him?*

Mark didn't look like her question fazed him at all. "You mean the shirt you spilled coke on the first time?" Sunny smiled since he was drenched yet again, and this time, she'd done it on purpose and with great pleasure. "I was talking about my foster mom. I was adopted when I was sixteen."

"Oh," Sunny really wished she could say something more profound than that.

Mark smiled, sensing she was uncomfortable. "Growing up, I spent some time in the system, but most of it out and on the streets. I'm not saying it's right, but when you live that life, it becomes a part of you." Mark shoved his hands inside his pockets and prayed Sunny wouldn't fault him for who he had been. "I let it become a part of me. Luckily, someone told me about God, and for once, I listened. I accepted Christ at seventeen, and God got a hold of my life. That's when I made a promise to him that I would never even kiss another girl until the one that I would spend the rest of my life with. I've kept that promise."

"Until now?"

"No, Sunny, I haven't broken my promise."

Sunny's heart skipped at beat. "What are you saying?" *He's insane.*

Mark tried to look cool by smiling. Sunny could tell something was up, but the emotions passing through his eyes were too complex for her to read. "You should go home, Sunny. I might say or do something stupid."

Sunny surprised even herself when she reached out and hugged him. It felt so good to be in his arms, even if it meant getting coke all over herself. "I trust you," she whispered, and then without another word, she walked out. Mark stared after her. He couldn't believe what he'd just heard. She trusted him despite what he'd told her? Mark wanted nothing more than to thank God, but he couldn't think of anything to say. How could he think at all when he was so happy that he might explode at any second? Suddenly, Mark jumped up in the air, fist raised, and shouted, "Yes!" *I think God got the picture.*

Without saying a word, the clerk stared unblinkingly at him. As Mark walked by him, he smiled and said, "God's awesome, dude." Not waiting for the stunned man's reply, Mark floated out the door.

"So what happened?" Holly woke up when Sunny came in that night. She'd meant to stay awake but had crashed sometime after eleven. She wasn't usually so tired, but preparing for her evil finals was taking away her snooze time. Holly wasn't used to having to actually study. Unfortunately, it was beneath her dignity to get anything less than an A.

Holly noticed that Sunny turned a pretty shade of pink. "No way, did you two kiss?"

Sunny whirled around. "How did you know?"

"I didn't," Holly grinned at her, "until now." Holly ignored Sunny's scowling. "So did you kiss him, or did he kiss you?"

"He kissed me. Unlike someone I know," Sunny indicated at Holly. "I don't just walk up and kiss guys."

Holly let the issue go. She was not about to get into that discussion again. "Did you kiss him back?"

"Holly!"

Holly looked at her innocently. "What?"

"I don't ask you about Josh," Sunny was turning even redder.

Holly rolled her eyes as she watched Sunny squirt toothpaste onto her toothbrush. "First of all, you wouldn't want to know if we did anything because he's like a brother to you. Second, you already know we aren't going out."

Sunny spoke with her toothbrush in her mouth, "Speaking of which, when are you going to be nice and go out with him?" Holly mimicked the way Sunny sounded, and Sunny glared at her. "You know what I mean."

"Yes," Holly said with a smirk, "I know what you mean." After she'd finished brushing her teeth, Sunny turned out the lights. She had already climbed into bed when Holly asked, "By the way, was that coke on the front of your sweater?" When Sunny pretended to be asleep, Holly chuckled quietly to herself.

He did not have time for this. Josh pounded his frustrations into the heavy bag. It was the only thing he knew to do to loosen up. Heaven only knew he should be studying. Josh felt the sweat run down his face, and it felt good. At least he could control something. Josh smashed his fist into the deadweight. He knew if he didn't put gloves on soon, he would regret it later, but he was beyond caring. How much patience did God expect him to have? Didn't He know his control was about to snap? Deep down, Josh felt a promise, a promise that God knew exactly how much he could take. Josh knew he would just have to step out on faith and trust that God would never make him go past his breaking point. Breathing heavily, Josh dropped his fists and walked away. He wasn't in this alone.

Across the gym stood Tony. He'd watched the kid try to beat the bag to smithereens. Tony had waited in anticipation to see the kid break. He'd seen tougher guys go at a bag like that before. Eventually, they all lost control, yet the kid hadn't. In the midst of the heat, he'd regained his cool. What had happened? Tony knew one thing was for sure, he'd be watching Joshua Timberlaigh much closer from now on. People with control were the most dangerous ones to take out. Tony sneered at the kid's fading figure. *We'll see how cool you are.*

"Stop chewing your pencil. You'll chip your tooth." Holly and Sunny were in the library studying, as usual. Sunny looked down at her mangled pencil. If anyone asked her what she did when she was nervous, upset, or worried, this would be it. It was an annoying habit. At least no one ever wanted to borrow her pens or pencils.

"Why hasn't he called?"

Holly tried her best to be sympathetic. *Why is it that when I'm the most tired that those are the times being Christ-like is the most important?* Holly figured God had something to do with it. *All right God, I don't have any patience left for anyone, even Sunny. I could definitely use some help here. It's not her fault I'm tired. It is her fault she's spazzing over this guy, though.* Holly wouldn't let herself remember how often she'd thought of Josh in the past hour. "Sunny," Holly started slowly, searching for the right words, "how about you pray to God to let you concentrate on your finals, and leave the worrying up to Him? He put Mark in your life, and He'll take care of the rest. You'll see."

It took her awhile, but Sunny finally smiled. "Thanks, Holly. You're the best."

"No, I'm not, but I'm learning that God is."

Later on while Holly was working on her English paper, Sunny's hands caught her attention. She was signing. Holly gave her a strange look but then saw that someone was talking, actually he was signing, across the room to Sunny. Holly watched in fascination.

"That was so cool!" Holly said after they had finished. "Can you teach me?"

Sunny laughed. "It's not that easy. Besides, don't you have an English paper?"

Holly looked mournfully at her computer screen. She'd only managed to type a quarter of page in the past thirty minutes. It was taking forever. "You're right, but will you at least show me the alphabet?"

Welcoming the distraction, Sunny easily gave in. "Sure."

It wasn't as hard as it looked. Of course, all that she was learning was the alphabet. Still, Holly thought that she could get used to a language where you didn't have to learn a weird foreign accent. All in all, American Sign Language was pretty cool.

That night Holly checked her e-mails. Something that used to be a mere nuisance had turned into what she looked forward to every evening, and it was all because of Josh. Josh e-mailed her every morning before he went to class, and she e-mailed him every night. He never forgot, and neither did she. Most of the time they talked about absolutely nothing, but a whole lot of nothing was beginning to mean everything to her. That night, though, someone new had e-mailed her. It didn't look like spam, so she opened it. It read, *"Don't forget, Princess. I'll be waiting."* Holly must have yelled out because Sunny was instantly beside her. How could she have forgotten about Albert and the party? She'd pushed it to the back of her mind, and now New Year's was almost here. She would have to face him soon. She didn't have a choice.

Sunny looked at the screen, "Holly, what's wrong?"

Holly shook her head in horror. "I…I can't tell you."

"Holly, why not?" Sunny tried to remain calm, but her friend looked like she'd seen a ghost.

Holly slowly relaxed her face, "It's none of your business." Holly stood up, trying to use her height as an advantage. *You can't drag her into this.*

"Baloney, you're my friend, so it is my business."

Holly clenched her jaw to keep her teeth from chattering, "Maybe I don't want to be friends anymore."

Sunny looked at her, and Holly gulped. What she'd said was for the best, but that didn't mean she could stand seeing Sunny hurt.

Sunny didn't look hurt when she shoved Holly back into her chair. "Okay, I don't know what has you so frightened, but you're not leaving this room until you tell me exactly what's going on."

"Sunny, you don't know what you're getting yourself into."

"Tell me the truth, Holly. Am I already in it?"

Holly remembered the picture with the bullet holes. Holly looked down at the ground, "Yes, Sunny, you're already in it, but telling you will make it worse."

Sunny shook her head. "I don't see how. Holly, you have to tell me what's going on."

Holly looked up at Sunny. She looked so terrified Sunny had to force herself not to back off. After about a minute of silence, Holly took a deep breath and started from the beginning, the very beginning.

It was raining outside. *Perfect,* Tony thought to himself. It was bad enough he had to baby sit a couple of teenage brats to make sure they didn't do anything stupid, like disobey his lunatic boss, Bergenstein. He'd witnessed some major cases of obsession. You didn't spend a couple years in prison without seeing even harmless things like love turn into warped forms of their earlier selves. But he had never seen anyone rage like Bergenstein had when Tony told him about Holly's little rendezvous with that Joshua Timberlaigh kid in the parking garage. Tony shook his head. If he hadn't been armed, he would have been afraid of him, and Tony wasn't afraid of anyone. Once he got his money, Tony would get as far away from that maniac as he could.

Tony looked up at Sunny and Holly's window again, but the light was out. *There's nothing else here tonight.* Dripping wet, Tony climbed back into his car. He took out his last cigarette and reached for a lighter. It wasn't on the shotgun seat as it usually was. Tony grunted as he bent over and riffled through some old newspapers on the floorboard. No luck. Tony sighed and leaned back against the seat with his cigarette still in his mouth. It was the perfect end to a perfect day.

Suddenly, he saw a flame out of the corner of his eye. "Looking for this?" A low male voice came from the back seat. Before Tony had the chance to reach for his gun, he felt the barrel of one on his head. Tony slowly lifted his hands. "What business do you have with a couple of college kids, Tony?"

"Who are you?" He tried to turn his head but came face-to-face with the flame from his filched lighter.

"Answer my question. Are you on a job?"

"Yeah, a big job. It's worth a hundred grand. I'd be willing to split it with you." Tony could feel the sweat running down his back. He told himself it was from the fire, not fear.

"Now you're talking."

To Tony's relief, the flame died, and he was able to turn around. His mouth dropped. At first he thought he was seeing a ghost. "Mark, is that you?"

Mark Tayne continued to point the gun at Tony's head. "Just talk."

chapter twenty-eight

ttempted rape and death threats made Sunny realize taking finals wasn't really that traumatic after all. Despite Holly's ranting and raving, Sunny's mind was made up. So was Josh's. Both of them were going with Holly to Massachusetts for New Year's. Sunny found out Josh had arranged an invitation, via his grandparents, when he'd first learned Holly was going. He, of course, neglected to mention this to Holly until it was too late for her to say no.

Sunny wasn't so fortunate in relations, but once she'd made up her mind, Josh decided to take her as his escort. Of course, it was just a ruse to keep Bergenstein from breathing down Josh's neck. Appearing with Holly was out of the question. Soon after arriving at the party, Sunny would leave, hopefully unnoticed, and wait for Josh and Holly to return to their hotel. If she didn't see or hear from them by two in the morning, they would throw in all their cards and call the police. That was what Josh wanted to do to begin with, but Holly had her mind set on talking Albert out of his obsession. Sunny knew it was a stupid idea. *But what are Josh and I supposed to do, God? We can't tie her down and make her stay here while we call the police.* The thought was tempting, but she knew it would never work. As Sunny had explained to Josh, who had been very Neanderthal-like from the get-go, Holly had prayed to God about it, and this is what she felt like God was leading her to do.

On a happier note, they had a whole week and a half until the blessed event. At the moment Sunny, Holly, Josh, Bret, and Elizabeth were heading in the opposite direction toward Salem, Oregon. They were on a huge plane and loving every moment of their newfound freedom. No more finals! Sunny had passed calculus with an "A." Miracles, it seemed, never ceased.

Holly sat sandwiched between Josh on her left and Sunny on her right. Sunny had the aisle seat, which she figured was safer because that way she would be sucked out the window third. Yet as Josh so nicely reminded her, she would be first sucked out the door.

Bret and Elizabeth sat in the row across from them. They stopped pretending they were "just friends," but that didn't mean the practical jokes had ceased. Bret had made the mistake of falling asleep on the plane, and Elizabeth, armed with her cosmetics, decided to give her boyfriend a makeover. Josh had to admit, purple was not a good color for Bret, especially on his lips.

As amusing as this was, Sunny fell asleep about ten minutes after Bret did. All her friends knew not to mess with her face. About that time Lisa, the stewardess, came by to ask what they wanted to drink. Lisa had a high arch in her right eyebrow, which made her look forever cynical. Holly wondered if her face naturally made her look like she was in a bad mood or if she was just in a bad mood, period. As it turned out, she was in a bad mood. Holly shrugged and turned her attention to Josh. He was singing aloud and off-key to some song in his CD player. Luckily, the plane drowned most of his voice out. Josh had his eyes closed, which Holly figured gave her the right to stare at him as much as she wanted to. The more she watched him, the faster her heart beat. It almost hurt. Was it time to take their relationship to the next step? Holly started wishing Josh had never left it up to her. *Wait a minute. It's not up to me. God, is it time yet?* Holly heard the answer and smiled. She watched Josh a little longer and reached for his hand with the knowledge that things would never be the same. It was sad and exciting all rolled into one huge emotion that left Holly weak. Then fear of change gripped her throat, and she started to draw her hand back. Later Holly would realize God had had different plans. Sudden turbulence that only Holly seemed to feel surged her hand forward onto his. Josh's eyes opened and locked with hers. Holly knew it was her last chance to pull away. She could just say it had been an accident. It was a plane after all. *Let go and let God.* Holly slowly smiled and closed her fingers around his.

She couldn't tell what was passing through Josh's mind as he looked back and forth between their joined hands and her face, but he seemed to get the message. Josh smiled, closed his eyes, and then leaned back, relaxed, and enjoyed the rest of the ride. If their pastor was right and life really was like the ocean, then he was riding the waves.

Holly eventually fell asleep with the rest of her friends but was soon awakened by someone yelling. Bret had woken up, and he showed his appreciation for Elizabeth's artistic talents by grinding her lipstick into the pull down tray. The stewardess, if possible, had an even fouler face when Holly and the gang left the plane. Truthfully, though, she couldn't blame her.

chapter twenty-nine

If Holly had known what was awaiting her at the end of the terminal, she probably would have jumped right back on the plane to Texas. She definitely wouldn't have been holding Josh's hand. What could only be the younger, female version of her new boyfriend came running up to him. His sister, Jane, took one look at their connected hands and gave Holly the dirtiest look she'd ever received. Sunny told her later that Jane had always been the only girl in Josh's life, or so he'd led her to believe. Jane wasn't the only surprise family member. Nope. The whole Timberlaigh clan had arrived. Albeit, it was just his parents, but they were enough.

The next shock of the day was when Holly saw not only Sunny's mom but her own as well. Sunny told her that Anne had wanted to surprise her. Holly was surprised all right. Now all she needed was her grandmother to show up in a clown suit, and she would be set for life on surprises. Just to be on the safe side, Holly tried not to look to her left or right. This Christmas was going to be like no other.

The Whites offered their home, but Holly and her mother opted to stay with Elizabeth in a hotel down the road. Most of their time, though, was spent at the White's or the Timberlaigh's.

Holly quickly found out Josh was the beloved son of one formidable Mrs. Timberlaigh. With Josh's mom watching her like a hawk, Holly didn't have much time to work on her bigger adversary, Jane Timberlaigh. Holly knew she was in trouble when she caught Jane attempting to put gum in her hair. The kid was going down, but it seemed as if Holly would have to go through the mom first.

That night Holly had been tricked into eating dinner at the Timberlaigh's by herself. Everyone else was either at the hotel or at the White's. Holly suddenly became very suspicious of a conspiracy when, like clockwork, everyone evacuated the table, everyone with the exception of Mrs. Timberlaigh.

Feeling like this meal might very well have been her last, Holly quickly tried to escape, but Mrs. Timberlaigh was too quick.

Mrs. Timberlaigh cleared her throat and sent her a hard look. "Holly, I'm sure you're not used to cleaning up after yourself, but would you mind helping me with the dishes?"

Holly resisted the urge to say "no" flat out, not because of the request, but because of the way it had been asked. Just because she'd had people pick up after her, didn't mean she was spoiled. *The operative word is 'privileged.' Okay, Holly, what would Jesus do in your place?* "Sure, I'd love to help," Holly tried to say sincerely. "I don't get to help out that often where I'm from." Holly smiled. *Take that.*

Mrs. Timberlaigh lifted one eyebrow but didn't say anything. She handed Holly a dish to dry.

You know, you could at least attempt to be nice. "It was nice of you to let me stay for dinner." Holly saw Mrs. Timberlaigh's jaw set, but she politely nodded. They continued to wash the dishes in silence. Holly stared out the window. There was a beautiful sunset, but it was lost on her. As the time ticked by, Holly grew more nervous until she couldn't stand the silence any longer, "Ma'am, I'm sorry, but if you have a question for me, then please ask."

"Are you a Christian?"

"Yes. Didn't Josh tell you?"

"I wanted to hear it from you." Mrs. Timberlaigh stopped handing her dishes.

"I think that I understand. If I had a son, I would want to know the same thing." *See, God, I'm being nice.*

"Then you'll understand my next and last question. Who do you love most—God, Josh, or yourself?"

What? Holly didn't know what to say. She'd never admitted to loving Josh aloud, let alone tried to compare that love to her love for God. Holly thought about it and realized she needed to know the answer more than Mrs. Timberlaigh did. How much time passed before Holly spoke was a mystery to her, but when she did speak, it was with confidence.

"Mrs. Timberlaigh, I have been a selfish person my entire life. I think I can honestly say I never loved anyone until this year, especially not myself. I didn't understand love," Holly stared out the window and smiled, "but now I do. Love means giving and forgiving everything no matter the cost or return. Love means always thinking of the other person first." Holly stopped and studied her hands. "I can't completely answer your question, not truthfully at least, because God's still teaching me how to love. I do know, though, that I could never really love myself if I didn't love God, and the greatest way to love God is to love others. I love your son, Mrs. Timberlaigh, with all my heart, and that's all I have to give." As Holly stared at the woman in front of her, she realized what she'd said was true. All her life, she'd been a pauper disguised as a princess, but now she really did have everything.

Mrs. Timberlaigh didn't say anything for a long time. She just stared at Holly, as if trying to figure her out. Finally, she seemed to come to a conclusion. "My son has always been one of God's most precious gifts to me." Holly tried to speak, but she held up her hand and stopped her. "Let me finish. Josh has been the joy of my life, and I thank God that you're with my son. Just please don't hurt him." Her eyes filled, and she quickly walked out of the room.

Holly stood there in the kitchen. She didn't know what had just happened, but she knew it was something big.

When it came to the other Timberlaigh female, talking was definitely not going to work. Everyone got together the day before Christmas Eve for lunch at the Timberlaigh's.

"Holly, catch." Holly quickly jumped out of the way. *Whose brilliant idea was it to invent the Frisbee anyway?* The flying red disk looked like a weapon to her.

"Holly!" Sunny stuck her hands on her hips. "This is Frisbee, not dodge ball." Sunny sent both Jacob and Josh a look of annoyance. Frisbee was becoming more a game of throw and fetch with Holly around.

Holly scowled at Sunny. It wasn't her fault that she'd never played. "What's dodge ball?"

Josh looked at Holly shocked. He tried to speak, but no words came. Unfortunately, Jane decided to educate Holly on the finer points of the all-American sport.

Seemingly out of nowhere, a snowball flew towards Holly and hit her dead-on. For a split second, Holly thought her face was on fire. Then a fire lit inside of her. *That's it!* Jane saw the spark in Holly's eyes and tried to make a run for it, but she was too late. Holly grabbed the hood of Jane's jacket, and with strength she didn't realize she possessed, Holly brought her down. Then being the mature college student she was, Holly sat on her and dumped snow in her face.

Bret reluctantly dragged Holly off Josh's flailing sister. If Josh had been in shock earlier, then he was about to enter cardiac arrest now. Sunny looked over to see if Jane, unlike her older brother, was still breathing.

She was breathing all right. In fact, she was up and ready for round two. The game had gotten personal. Sunny barely had time to yell, "Holly! Watch out behind you!"

Holly started to turn but was quickly knocked to the ground by ninety-seven pounds of preteen fury. What started out as a snowball fight turned into something much deadlier, a catfight. Holly had the advantage in size and weight, but a downfall to being an only child was she had absolutely no practice fighting. Jane, having an older brother her entire life, did.

The grownups got over their shock faster than their kids and were able to pull the two apart before one of them was seriously injured. Mrs. Timberlaigh got a hold of Holly, barely, and Anne somehow managed to hold onto Jane. Mrs. White just sat back and thanked the Lord that, for once, it wasn't her kids.

chapter thirty

Not even Jane Timberlaigh could ruin Christmas Eve for Holly. Actually, ever since "the alien encounter" as Holly had dubbed it, Jane had become much more civil around her. Holly didn't know if it was respect, fear, or Mrs. Timberlaigh that was responsible for the miracle. She decided to chalk the mystery up to God and let it be.

Holly helped Sunny and Elizabeth prepare the living room for dinner. There were so many people that they had to put some tables together and scrounge around the house for chairs. In the end, they had to go over to the White's and snatch another one. It was either that, or they would have to use Mr. Timberlaigh's EZ chair. When Holly suggested that next time they should hire a party coordinator, Sunny didn't know if she should laugh or educate Holly the finer points of middle-class living.

"Don't give Holly the knives, Sunny. She might use one to carve a hole in Josh's sister," Elizabeth laughed at her own joke. Sunny tried not to laugh, but she couldn't help it.

"Sorry, Holly," Sunny chuckled, "but I can still see you throwing her to the ground and making her eat snow." Elizabeth made the sound affects, which made both of them laugh even harder.

"You two sound like a couple of hyenas," Holly mumbled to no one in particular and then walked out of the room. Actually, she stomped out. She stepped outside the house and slammed the door so hard that the old grandfather clock chimed. Holly nearly tripped over Josh on the steps.

"Hey," Josh stood up, "are you looking to fight another one of us Timberlaighs? We're a dying race, you know."

"Enough!" Holly threw up her hands. "That little thing, whom you call your sister, deserved it."

"I know. I'm just glad you did it because I'm not supposed to hit her. It's not fair being a guy sometimes."

Holly couldn't help but smile. Her temper began to cool. "I'm glad you are a guy." Holly leaned closer to him, "Because this would be kind of strange if you weren't." Holly didn't know if she kissed him or if he kissed her. All she knew was that they were kissing. For how long, she wasn't sure. She started to pull away, but Josh wrapped his arms around her waist and held her there.

Holly heard someone knocking on the window beside the door. Josh and Holly looked through the glass and saw their three friends grinning at them. Bret gave Josh two thumbs up and was quickly elbowed by Sunny.

Josh turned red, and Holly laughed. "Well, that was awkward," he said and ran a hand through his hair.

"It could be worse," Holly said. "It could have been our parents."

The thought made Josh's eyes widen. "Good point."

"Yes, very good point. Too bad we're standing right here." Anne and Mrs. Timberlaigh appeared around the corner along with Mrs. White who looked like she was having the time of her life.

This might just possibly be the most embarrassing thing that has ever happened to me. Holly wished she could sink through the ground. "What are you guys doing here?" she asked.

"I live here," Josh's mom said blandly.

"We were talking in the backyard when we heard the door slam," Anne still looked disturbed from seeing her baby girl kiss someone.

"Yes, we thought someone had gotten into another fight," Mrs. White said with a grin.

"Obviously, we were wrong, but I'm glad we were here for the show," Mrs. Timberlaigh laughed.

Josh's eyes bugged out. "Mom!"

"Oh, sorry, honey. Should we leave the two of you alone now?"

If possible, Josh turned redder. "I think I'm going back inside," Holly said. "It's safer in there." She quickly escaped, leaving Josh out in the cold with the moms.

Dinner was fabulous, but the best part was later when everyone got to open their presents. There were so many presents that the living room looked like it might not be big enough for people to fit too.

Anne didn't know what to get the kids, so she gave them money—lots of money. None of them, except Holly, could believe it when they pulled out a thousand dollars from their stockings. Bret vowed he would never miss another of her movies. Anne laughed at that, and then to Holly's astonishment, she invited everyone back to L.A. the day after Christmas. Everyone agreed, and after a gory battle, Anne finally talked Mrs. White into allowing her to pay for everyone's tickets.

Opening all the presents took about two hours, but the time seemed to fly by. Everyone was in such a good mood that even Matt and Kip stopped fighting. Jane couldn't believe it when she got a present from Holly. It was two new CDs she'd been dying to have.

As Jane expertly tore away the shrink-wrap, Josh whispered into Holly's ear, "I think you've just become her new favorite person."

"Doubtful," Holly said. "She practically worships you."

Josh looked skeptical. "Yeah, but I only got her one CD."

Holly laughed and gave Josh his present. It was a shirt, which Josh changed into the immediately. Sunny pointed out he'd forgotten to take off the tag. They all laughed while he attempted to pull it off with his shirt still on. Bret decided to put him out of his misery and yanked it off for him.

Towards the end of the day, Matt and Kip gave up their fragile truce and started a wrapping paper war. Soon, all the kids and Mr. White were throwing wadded balls of paper at each other.

"Sure," Mrs. White rolled her eyes, "we spend all this money on presents, and what do they do? They play with the wrapping paper." That comment made all the kids throw paper at her. Soon, the grownups had joined in, and the battle began.

"I didn't know wrapping paper could give you a paper cut," Sunny looked skeptically at Holly who was pitifully sucking her finger. "In fact, I think you're just trying to get me to pack your stuff, and I'm not going to. Besides, you've only spent two nights at my house. You can't have too much to pack anyway." Sunny looked around her room. There were clothes everywhere. "Then again, you change clothes every hour on the hour."

Holly ignored what she assumed to be an insult and continued to coerce Sunny into packing for her. It was worth a shot. "Where's your Christmas spirit?" Holly asked as she searched for a Band-Aid.

"Christmas is over," Sunny said dryly.

"Bah humbug to you too." Holly rolled up her sweater and shoved it into her bag.

Sunny watched in abject horror. "What are you doing?"

"What does it look like I'm doing? I'm packing."

"Holly, I don't know what you're doing, but that's not packing."

Holly sent her a "so what are you gonna to do about it" look and rolled up another shirt. Sunny glared at her. *Someone woke up on the wrong side of the bed*, Holly thought.

There was a knock on the door, and Mrs. White stuck her head in the room. "Girls, are you almost packed? We need to leave in thirty minutes."

"Mom, just for curiosity's sake, when does the plane leave?"

"Oh, in about three and a half hours." Mrs. White closed the door and left.

"And it takes less than an hour to get there," Holly heard Sunny grumble under her breath.

Holly walked over, closed Sunny's suitcase, and then sat on top of it. Holly cut Sunny off before she could protest. "All right, Sunflower, what's wrong."

"You're on my suitcase."

"And I'm not getting off until you tell me what's bothering you. You don't have someone stalking you too, do you?" Holly smiled at the fact she could joke about Albert.

"I wish."

Huh? "You wish you had someone stalking you? Would you like my stalker?"

Sunny laughed, "I was talking about Mark. It's been two weeks now, and he hasn't even had the decency to call and say, "Let's just be friends.'"

"Sunny, I don't know if this is a comfort to you or not, but the guy has never wanted to just be friends with you. Besides, it's not as if he's just avoiding you. He's disappeared."

"No, Holly, that's not comforting. What if he's in trouble?"

"I think Mark can take care of himself. Remember that big guy at the football game?"

"Holly, not even someone who's good at karate can win against a bullet."

"Sunny, Mark is a youth minister. How much trouble can he

get himself into?" Sunny sent Holly a look saying Mark could get himself into a lot of trouble. Holly rolled her eyes. "You are so in love with this guy."

"I am not!"

"Yeah, you are, but don't worry," Holly wriggled her eyebrows. "I won't tell anyone."

Sunny scowled and shoved Holly off her suitcase. *I am not in love with him.*

chapter thirty-one

At Anne's home breakfast was an exciting event for Holly simply because she'd never eaten with anyone other than her mother in the morning. In fact, she often wondered why Anne had bought such a long table for the dining room. It could easily fit twenty. Holly had always assumed it was just for decoration. Now that there were over a dozen people fighting for the pancakes, she didn't know what to think. It was loud, Sunny's brothers were obnoxious as usual, and Holly enjoyed every moment of it. Excitement turned into unease, though, when Matt asked Holly what they should do for the rest of the day. All the grownups were going to Malibu with Holly's mom, and as fun as hanging out with a movie star sounded, they would rather die than spend the whole day with their parents—boring!

"I really don't know. All I ever do is read or shop." Matt and Kip acted as if shopping were some sort of twenty-first century torture, and outside of school, reading wasn't a part of their vocabulary.

Holly racked her brains for something to do. She wasn't used to being the activities instructor. Suddenly, inspiration hit. "Do you guys like rollercoasters?" Twin smiles greeted her from across the table. *I'll take that as a yes.*

If someone wanted fantasy, they went to Disney Land or Universal Studios, but if they wanted excitement, Magic Mountain was the place to be. It was a theme park devoted entirely to roll-ercoasters. The faster they went, the better, according to the guys. Elizabeth seemed inclined to agree, but Sunny, Holly, and Jane were much more skeptical. They actually wanted to live to see their twenties.

When they walked into the park, the guys looked at the coast-ers with veneration and awe. "So" Holly asked, "where do you guys want to go first?"

"Let's follow the screams," Jacob said with a look of excite-ment.

Sunny whispered into Holly's ear. "How can there be any ques-tion that girls are smarter than guys? Wouldn't the sane thing be to run in the opposite direction of the screams?"

"Actually, I think we might be the dumb ones considering we actually have full use of our brains, yet we follow them anyway."

"Good point."

The first ride was a huge wooden rollercoaster. Sunny looked up and tried to see how high it went. She heard the people above her scream as they whizzed by in a cramped, little box on wheels. The entire rollercoaster shook. All it would take was one beam to break, and the coaster would come tumbling down like a house of cards. Sunny's eyes widened. "No way am I going on that thing."

Her three brothers looked at her in shock. "What are you

saying?" Kip couldn't believe anyone would pass up such a terrifying experience.

"I'm saying that I'm going to stay here on the ground while you guys go and get yourselves killed," Sunny told him matter-of-factly. "Go have fun," she added sweetly.

"Do you want me to stay here with you?" Holly asked. Sunny could tell she didn't really want to stay. She wanted to go on the ride too.

"No, I'll be fine. I'm hungry; I'll grab something to eat while you guys go."

Sister or no sister, Matt couldn't stand waiting any longer. "Okay, see you in twenty minutes, Sun."

"Bye." Sunny waved as they walked off and then headed toward the concession stand to buy an overpriced, greasy hamburger. Sunny stopped dead in her tracks. She could have sworn she heard her name. Sunny shrugged. Truthfully, someone probably had said her name. That was the problem with having a name people used in everyday life. For all she knew someone could be saying it was "sunny" outside.

Sunny quickly looked over to her left at a little walk-through park. Okay, now she was hearing both her first and last name. What were the odds of that? Yet weren't all of her friends on the ride? Maybe Holly had decided not to go on the rollercoaster after all. But what was she doing over there?

Sunny walked through the small entryway and then heard her name again. It was louder this time. She couldn't place the voice, but there was a familiar ring to it. She walked a little further. Now she was completely hidden from the rides by the trees and bushes. Sunny heard someone's foot scrape the pavement behind her. She started to turn but a hand came around her face and closed over her mouth before she could scream. Whoever it was, was dragging her away from the path. Sunny tried to fight back but couldn't. The person holding her was too strong. Panic swept through her, but what could she do?

"Sunny, it's okay," a voice whispered. "It's me, Mark." Now they were completely off the path and out of sight. Sunny didn't know what to think, so she did the first thing that came to her mind. "Oof." Mark grunted when Sunny elbowed him in the gut.

The second he loosened his grip, she sprang free. Her heart was slowly returning back to normal, but the adrenaline rush was far from gone. "First you don't call for like three weeks, and then you scare me half to death by dragging me over here. Feel free to start explaining."

Mark was taken aback by the sudden onslaught of accusations. "Sure, just let me get my wind back first."

"If you're talking, it's back." Sunny glared furiously at him, but Mark didn't miss the hurt in her eyes. "You just disappeared, Mark. I hate it that I care, but I have to know. Did you stop liking me?"

Mark looked surprised but then softly smiled. He reached up and brushed away a few loose strands from her face. They told him everything she was thinking. "Listen to me. No matter what happens, nothing will ever change the way I feel about you."

Sunny shook her head. "How can you promise that?" She tried to think clearly but was afraid she wouldn't be able to think at all if he kept playing with her hair.

"God set us apart for each other, and no one changes His mind. Nothing could change how I feel about you either."

"What are you saying?" Sunny's heart began to beat faster and faster.

Mark forced himself to keep his hands out of his pockets and his eyes off the ground. Now was not the time to develop a sudden case of shyness. *Here it goes.* "I love you."

"No," Sunny pushed his hand away from her face. "You can't be saying that to me. We barely even know each other." *This is crazy!*

Mark suddenly felt like she'd just stomped on his heart. "Why can't you give me a chance?"

Sunny was too emotional to see how much she was hurting him. "I was about to give you a chance, but then you left!" she shouted at him. "How can I trust you if you're going to just disappear whenever you feel like it? Where have you been these past few days, Mark? Here's the chance you wanted. Tell me." *Please,* she added silently.

Mark looked from the ground up to Sunny's face. There was a sad look in his eyes. "I can't tell you. I came here only to warn you to stay out of Massachusetts."

"What? Why?"

"It's dangerous for you. Sunny, please trust me. You told me earlier that you did."

"You broke my trust," Sunny felt pain mixed with anger boiling in her heart. All of it was his fault. She hadn't asked for this. "Give me a reason not to go."

"I can't! I can tell you everything when you get back to school." Mark put his hands on her shoulders. He wanted to shake the sense into her. "You know very well it's dangerous. There's no reason for you to go to Massachusetts, Sunny. You'll only be putting yourself and others you love at risk.

Sunny shoved Mark away from her. She couldn't take it any longer. "I don't want to see you when school starts back up. I should have never become attached to you in the first place." She felt her eyes ice over. Then before she could change her mind and make a fool of herself by going into his arms, she ran off.

Mark caught up to her right as she entered the mainstream of people in the park. "You're not going anywhere until you promise me you won't go with Josh and Holly to that party."

Sunny whirled around and narrowed her eyes suspiciously. "How did you know about that? Actually, do you know what? I don't want to know. Just stay away from my friends and me!"

Mark grabbed the front of her jacket and pulled her up close, almost to his eye level. Fire lit in his eyes. "You don't know what you're messing with."

Sunny tried not to be scared of him, but acting had never been her strong suit. "Let the girl go." The voice came from a park security guard. Mark hesitated but then let Sunny go and slowly backed away. The policeman's eyes went from hard to gentle as he shifted his gaze from Mark to Sunny. "Are you okay, Miss?"

Still shaken, Sunny answered him, "Yes, sir."

"Is there anything I can do for you?"

Sunny took one last look at Mark. He was currently shooting daggers with his eyes at her and the security guard. "Could you please get me a cab?" Sunny didn't want to stay at the park any longer. She didn't want to face her friends, not while her heart was breaking in two. Darn it, but Holly had been right. She loved him.

"What do you mean you're almost back to my house? What's wrong?" Holly held her cell up to her ear and waited for Sunny's response. "I'm not being nosey," Holly stamped her foot. "You just randomly decided to leave without so much as a goodbye?" Holly looked at her phone irritably when Sunny hung up.

"What did she say?" Josh asked.

"Goodbye," Holly said dryly.

Matt held his stomach. "I wish I'd gone with her. I don't feel so good."

"Yeah, me either," Kip said. "Hey, Jacob, if I start to hurl, come closer."

Instead of being insulted, Jacob just laughed. "You two are getting old. One ride and you're toast."

Matt groaned, "Don't talk about food right now."

Kip glared at his youngest sibling. "Mom was too lenient on you growing up."

"What are you talking about? I'm a perfect angel." Jacob smiled, and Jane sent Holly a "yeah right" look.

"So" Bret asked, "which ride next?"

Matt and Kip groaned when Elizabeth pointed to a tall steel rollercoaster with tons of loops.

By the end of the day, everyone except Josh and Holly had had it. First Sunny left, then Matt and Kip, and then finally, Elizabeth, Jane, Bret, and Jacob. Now Josh and Holly were trying to see who would fall first. Both were determined to win the unspoken competition.

"How about that one?"

Holly looked up, way up. It wasn't a roller coaster at all, but a giant swing that lifted its victims high above the earth's atmosphere and then dropped them. Holly gulped but then courageously turned to Josh with a grin. "You're on."

Butterflies turned into birds as they got closer and closer to the front of the line. *I must be very stupid to agree to do this.* When their time came, Holly was so nervous that she didn't notice Josh whisper to one of the workers.

All too soon, Holly was in a harness and at the front of the line. She was already squeezing all the blood out of Josh's hand, and they hadn't even left the ground. It would serve him right if she broke a few bones. He was the one who had suggested the ride in the first place.

"You'll be fine," Josh whispered into her ear and then kissed her cheek.

One of the workers walked up to them, "Okay, are you two ready?"

Josh looked at Holly who had turned pale. "Yes," Josh smiled, "we're ready."

"All right, once you get to the top, one of you needs to pull the cord to release you. Why don't you do it?" he indicated to Josh.

"Sure." Josh winked at the man. Holly was too nervous about being dropped hundreds of feet to notice.

After they were strapped in, Holly realized she was in the last place she wanted to be. Competition or no competition, she did not want to do this. "Um, I think you can go by yourself, Josh." Holly looked at the two guys who had tied them into the little contraption. "I don't want to do this."

One of the guys smiled, showing off his yellow, crooked teeth, "Too late, Miss."

Before Holly had the chance to protest, she was no longer standing. She didn't move, but the platform Josh and she had been standing on suddenly disappeared. In less than a second, they went from vertical to horizontal. Holly tried to break her fall, but her arms were tied down. She slowly opened her eyes and found herself parallel to the ground that was two feet from her face. The distance didn't stay so short for long. The ground was getting farther and farther away. "This is the dumbest thing I've ever done!" Holly turned her head toward Josh and yelled at him. "I want you to know that if I live through this, I'm going to kill you." Josh laughed.

When they reached the top, Holly estimated they were roughly twenty stories in the air, dangling by a few cables. The thought wasn't comforting. Holly waited for Josh to pull the cord, but he didn't. "Josh, what are you doing?"

"I need to ask you something."

"I think it can wait." Holly braced herself, but still nothing happened. "Josh, if you don't pull it, they're going to."

"No, they're not."

Holly panicked. "What? Are we stuck up here?"

"We are until you answer my questions." Holly could hear the laughter in his voice. Here they were about to die, and he sounded like he was having the time of his life. Typical guy.

"I am really going to hurt you." Holly kept waiting for them to drop. She could see people starting to point at them from the ground. "Fine! What do you want to know?"

"Do you love me?"

Her heart skipped a beat. She closed her eyes. Was it the height or Josh that was making her dizzy? "Yes." Her voice was barely audible.

"Good, that makes this easier. Holly, look at the park. Do you see all those people?"

"Yes."

"All of them were made by God. Not one is alike, but there is only one person in the entire world who I want to be with, and that's you. Hollywood Rose Johnson, will you marry me?"

How do you know my real name? She realized what he'd just asked her. "What? I'm only eighteen. Are you insane?"

"Probably, but that's not the answer I'm looking for." Josh suddenly let out a whoop.

Holly didn't have time to assimilate everything that was happening. All of a sudden, the ground was rushing toward her. She screamed out in excitement. The thrill of what had been said mixed with the euphoria of soaring through the sky with nothing more than a couple of straps, which kept her from falling to her doom. Her heart was filled with joy, while her head screamed in frustration.

When they got down from the ride, all the workers were grinning. This didn't happen every day. Holly wanted to kiss the ground; instead, she kissed Josh. She figured it was more sanitary that way. When she remembered what he had asked her, though, Holly took a step backward. "Josh, I do love you, but . . ."

"Shhhh . . ." Josh kissed her forehead and then laid her head against his shoulder, "I know it's a big decision. I've been praying about it for months now, but you haven't. So why don't you take a little while, okay?"

Holly's eyes started to water. Whether it was from being happy or sad, she didn't know. "Thanks, Josh."

Josh laughed. "You should be thanking me. Patience is not one of my stronger virtues. You have no idea how hard it is for me not to force you to tell me right away."

"I know." She held out her hand with a smile. Josh took it and they left the park. Neither cared anymore who could ride the most rides. They were perfectly content with a draw.

Once inside the gate at Holly's house, she got out of the taxi with Josh and told him she'd meet him inside. She had some unfinished business to take care of. Holly pushed her shoulders back, took a deep breath, and walked over to the security guard's station.

The guard saw it was her, so he reached over and opened the door without bothering to get up. "What do you want?"

Holly smiled. She could always depend on his foul attitude. She dug into her backpack and pulled out a colorfully wrapped package. "I bought you a Christmas present." Holly handed it to him. At first the guard was stunned, but then he grew suspicious. "What is it?"

"Open it, and you'll find out. Merry Christmas and have a great New Year." Saying nothing else, Holly left.

Holly knocked on Sunny's door that night. No one answered so she just walked in. Sunny was in there, and she looked as cheery as she had at the dinner table. Holly still didn't know what was wrong, but she knew Sunny well enough not to push for an explanation. If Sunny wanted to tell her what was up, she would.

With her back to Holly, Sunny asked, "Are you nervous about tomorrow?"

"Not yet, but I do feel bad about not telling the others."

Sunny sighed. "Me too, but you know we can't."

"I know." Holly, Sunny, and Josh had told everyone they were going back to Texas early to get ready for school. It was a lie, but they didn't know what else to do. The truth wouldn't be taken well. Holly walked over and hugged Sunny. "It's going to be okay."

"I hope you're right."

chapter thirty-two

The long plane ride to Massachusetts seemed to fly by. Holly was nervous now. She kept wringing her hands until Josh finally got a hold of one of them. He smiled at her with laughter in his eyes. Instead of smiling back, she just rested her head on his shoulder. Later she looked over at Sunny. She didn't seem nervous at all, but the look of determination on her face seemed to be set in stone. One friend thought this whole thing was funny and the other looked like she was ready to kill someone. *Am I the only sane one around here?* Holly tried not to feel guilty for dragging her friends into her mess. *But hadn't they volunteered themselves?*

Josh leaned over and whispered into her ear, "Relax, God will protect us."

"I hope you're right."

"God has control over everything, Holly. Nothing can happen unless He says so."

Holly squeezed his hand. "Thanks, Josh. I needed to hear that."

A couple hours later, they checked into their hotel rooms. It was seven o'clock, and fashionably late was at ten-thirty. Holly and Sunny decided to order room service and eat while they got ready. Josh crashed in his room and checked out the latest "On Command" movie. Unlike his friends, it only took a few minutes for him to get ready. For the life of him, he'd never understand what took girls so long.

Josh knocked on their door at precisely ten o'clock. He heard some shuffling, and then the door slowly opened. Holly stood in the doorway. Her dress matched her eyes perfectly, and it shimmered silver sparkles wherever the light touched. The dress was long, but it only took Josh a millisecond to notice the slit that went about three-fourths up her leg. He had mixed feelings about that. While he loved looking at her legs, so would every other sane male at the party. Josh worked his way up her dress until he finally reached her face. Normally, Holly didn't wear much make-up, if any. Tonight, though, she had taken the time, and Josh could only think one thing. "You're beautiful."

Holly blushed. "Thanks."

Sunny, who'd been putting her shoes on, walked out at that moment. Josh's mouth dropped. "What are you wearing?"

"A dress," Sunny said dryly.

"That's not a dress, that's a...um...I mean you actually look nice. I mean you're not supposed to look good."

Sunny laughed. Josh was so predictable. "Keep digging, and you won't be able to get yourself out." Sunny put her hands on Josh's shoulders. "Listen, Josh, we went through this at prom. I am a girl. Repeat that in your head." Josh scowled at her, and Sunny chuckled.

Josh kept glaring. He knew she was right, but . . ."Why can't you just wear jeans or something?"

"To a party?" Sunny laughed again, and this time he laughed with her. Josh took a deep breath and held the door open for both of them. When they got outside, it was freezing. Therefore, the girls walked back inside and stayed near the entrance while Josh hailed a cab.

"So" Holly asked Sunny once Josh walked away, "do you think he likes our dresses?"   Sunny smirked, "No, not at all."

Josh walked back to them, completely unaware they were making fun of him. "I think we should pray."

"You're right," Sunny said. "Holly, why don't you pray?"

"Me?"

"Yes, you."

Holly took a deep breath. She still thought it was incredible that the God who created the universe would listen to what she had to say. Still, praying aloud was new for her, but who better to do it with than Josh and Sunny? Holly bowed her head. "Father, thank you for being with us today. You know what kind of danger we're in, but we know that You take care of Your children. Please keep us from getting hurt, and let this conflict be over soon. Amen."

They all hugged and then climbed into their cabs. Holly and her friends had decided to go separately. Since Sunny was pretending to be Josh's date, she was riding with him. Holly tried to convince herself that being jealous of her friends' act was stupid. Unfortunately, she couldn't pretend away the fact that Josh was with Sunny and not her. When had she come to need his company so much? *This isn't the time for questions like that.*

All too soon the cab slowly came to a stop in from of the Bergenstein mansion. She had been there before but never since her grandmother's birthday party. Holly slowly walked toward the entrance. Why did she feel like she was stepping into a slaughterhouse? *God, be with me.*

When Holly walked into the ballroom, she felt as if she had stepped back in time. The room and the people were the same, even the grandiose air hadn't changed. *I bet the gossip has.* Holly knew all too well that she had been the object of their conversations two years ago when she, the belle of the ball, had suddenly removed herself from their society. As she stepped inside the crowded room, she could tell their memories were still in good condition. Holly heard the room go quiet, and for a split second, she felt like she was in a movie. Then everyone began talking again, and Holly had the sickening feeling it was about her.

"Holly, it is nice to see you have gotten over your childish rebellion." She had not seen her father in over a year, but she still recognized his voice and the chilling tone he always specially reserved for her.

Holly turned around and smiled. "You don't seem very surprised to see me, Father."

"Albert informed me you were coming. Though, I must admit I am surprised to find he was correct."

Holly kept her smile in place. "It's so good to see the two of you have become such good friends." *I always thought you were so much alike.* "Is he a business associate of yours now, Father?"

"Yes, actually, he is, and I aspire to a much deeper relationship. He is the son I never had."

Holly raised one eyebrow. *Interesting.* Maybe her father had more to do with this masquerade than she had previously thought. As for the low blow about Albert being his long lost son, Holly was used to little comments like that. Her father had never let an opportunity to express his disapproval of her go to waste. When she'd been young, she'd tried to please her father. After she realized she could never gain his approval, Holly had done everything she could to force her father to detest her. Now, by God's grace, she didn't care anymore. The only wish she had for him was for God to get a hold of his life as He had hers. Holly realized she didn't deserve salvation any more than her father. That fact alone kept her praying for him.

Holly felt two hands close over her shoulders. She didn't have to turn to see him. She smelt him. Albert still carried his old stench of alcohol with him wherever he went. "Hello, Holly." He whispered into her ear, "It was so good of you to come." He reminded her of a snake.

Forgetting her father, she turned to face him. He would have been handsome if it hadn't been for his cold eyes. Albert looked like he was ready to devour her. Holly took a graceful step back. Hopefully, to anyone watching, it looked as if Holly had propriety, not fear.

"What is this all about, Albert?" Holly asked.

"Patience is a virtue, my dear."

As Albert reached to touch her face, he looked over her shoulder, and his face contorted into the most demonic visage she had ever seen. Holly knew before looking what the object of his loathing had to be. It was time to play her part. She looked over her shoulder. Sure enough, there stood Josh and Sunny, arm in arm and looking appropriately bored.

"Oh, Albert," Holly purred, "how thoughtful of you to invite my friends." For a good measure, she gave him a quick kiss on his cheek. *Please don't kill me, Josh.* Holly sent Albert a killer smile. While he was still dumbfounded, she said, "I'm going to go over and say 'hello.'"

Holly escaped before Albert could get his breath back.

She found her friends with the Vancouvers. Instead of purple, Mrs. Vancouver was wearing red. Coupled with her jewelry, the color made her look like a shiny apple. Holly vaguely wondered why she always thought of fruit whenever the elderly woman was around.

"Holly, have you met my grandparents?" Josh asked.

Holly didn't have to fake her surprise. They were his grandparents? It really was a small world. "Yes, we know each other," Holly said and smiled. Out of all of the people in Salem, they really were some of the nicest.

"Holly? Is that you?" came from Mrs. Vancouver. "Why, I haven't seen you since . . ." She cut herself off, suddenly embarrassed. "Well, since the last time I saw you."

So that's how Josh knew about Albert. Surprisingly, she didn't care anymore. Holly smiled, and Mr. Vancouver covered for his wife, "It's amazing that you know our grandson." Mr. Vancouver winked at Holly to let her know he was in on everything. "He is quite a catch."

Josh turned red. "Thanks, Grandpa. Of course," Josh cleared his throat, "I'm going out with Sunny here. Remember?"

Mrs. Vancouver looked confused, "You are?" Mr. Vancouver sent her a look, "Oh yes! You are preten...I mean, um, yes, I remember." Mrs. Vancouver turned the color of her blouse.

Holly mentally groaned. It was the beginning of a long night. After two years of seeing neither hide nor hair of her, everyone wanted to talk with the new, and in their minds, improved Holly Rose Johnson. Those two years seemed to add mystery to Holly's impeccable social record. After an hour of grueling socializing, Holly was at the top of everyone's "A list" again, and wasn't it so cute how she and that Bergenstein boy were getting along? Holly knew they were already planning their wedding presents. *Over my dead body.* She hoped that wasn't going to be the case.

It should have bothered her that Albert was constantly by her side, but Holly didn't pay attention to him. She kept glancing over at Josh and Sunny. In Holly's mind, they were playing "boyfriend and girlfriend" too well. She glanced at the clock again. It was eleven forty-five. Sure enough, Sunny left just as they had planned. *Okay, just one more hour, and I can leave.* Holly was already bored with the party. Then again, what else was new?

Holly jumped out of her skin when people started shouting, "Ten! Nine! Eight...!" she shouted with them. When they got to "three," Holly noticed Albert was shifting toward her. It was then she remembered the old New Year's tradition to kiss someone at midnight. She tried to back away but was trapped by a wall of people. Albert grabbed her and pulled her toward him. When he kissed her, Holly felt like throwing up. All of her pushing and shoving got her nowhere as he held her there. When he finally let her go, she was too furious to say anything. Holly didn't know which part of him she wanted to hit first. *Oh no, did Josh see that?* Holly looked for him. She found him. Josh saw it all right and was heading their way. He looked livid.

"Ladies and gentlemen," Holly heard a voice coming from the speakers. It was Albert's. Holly looked at him and for the first time, she noticed the mike on his collar. *He must have had it in his pocket and just put it on, but why?* Holly's thoughts were once again broken by Albert's loud voice. "Thank you for celebrating the New Year's with me. Now I want you to share another special moment with me as I ask the most important question of my life." Albert turned to face her, and Holly's heart caught in her throat. "Holly Rose Johnson, you're beautiful, and I have been in love with you since you were sixteen. Will you marry me?" There was a collective awe, and then everyone was silent. No one even had the audacity to breathe loudly.

"You know, Albert," Holly began, as her mind filled with possible ways to get out of the mess he'd just put her in. She could downright refuse him, but as satisfying as that would be, she didn't come here to make Albert want to kill her. She was there to appease him. How could she do that now without embarrassing him? Holly could only think of one thing. It was worth a shot. "That's a really, um, great offer, but I'm afraid you're too late."

"What?" Albert turned pale.

"You see, I'm marrying Joshua Timberlaigh."

There was a gasp throughout the crowd. Through the buzz, one voice rang loud and clear. "I will not have my daughter marry a penniless nobody."

"That's my grandson you're talking about, you twit!" Mr. Vancouver yelled from across the room. "Unless you want to cease all our associations, you will do well to remember that."

Tres Johnson silenced his bellowing immediately. Nothing, it seemed, spoke louder than money to him. Holly wished she could see her father's face. Instead, she saw Albert's, which was reddened by fury. That triggered Holly's anger. Did that creep actually expect her to accept him after what he'd done? She'd played his game long enough. "That's right, Albert. Joshua Timberlaigh is the sole grandson of Mr. Vancouver. I don't believe I am marrying beneath my station." Some small voice of reason told her she'd gone a bit too far.

"Why you…!" Everyone gasped as Albert raised his hand to slap Holly. He swung at her but never made contact. A fist came seemingly out of nowhere and connected with Albert's face, sending him sprawling to the ground.

"Don't you dare touch her!" Josh turned to Holly. "Are you all right?" Before she had the chance to answer, he was suddenly on the ground with Albert on top of him. While Albert had the advantage, he tried to punch Josh in the face, but at the last moment, Josh moved his head. Albert smashed his own fist into the marble floor. As he howled in pain, Josh kneed him, and Albert rolled onto the ground. When Josh got up off the floor, he saw the security guards making their way toward them, and he knew the fight was over. Josh looked at Holly and without saying anything, quickly escorted her out.

During the cab ride home, neither said a word for the first ten minutes. Finally, Holly spoke, "Are you all right? Did he hurt you?"

"Only when he kissed you." Josh squeezed her hand. "Holly, did you mean what you said about the two of us getting married?"

So that's why he's been so quiet. Holly's heart pounded so hard she thought it might explode. Why was she more nervous now when there was only Josh than she had been earlier? "Yes, I was going to tell you when we got back to the hotel. I'm sorry I couldn't tell you earlier, but . . ." Josh cut her off with a kiss. Some things couldn't be expressed in words.

Not taking the time to wait for an elevator, Holly raced up the stairs to her room. She was so excited to tell Sunny that she could hardly stand it. Holly groaned in frustration as she fumbled with the plastic key. "Sunny! Sunny! You won't believe what just happened!" Holly stopped abruptly. There stood Sunny with a gun pointed at her head. The man who held the gun was the very one who'd been in her room at UT. Mark stood next to him, seemingly bored. Holly looked at Sunny. Physically, she looked like she was okay, but there was terror in her eyes.

Holly looked at Mark. What was he doing here with this monster? "What's going on?"

Mark smiled. "Well, we're kidnapping you. I told Tony here that you wouldn't put up a fight if we were holding a gun to your best friend."

He was right. Holly's eyes turned cold. "I thought you were her friend too."

Mark shook his head. Holly's stomach turned when she saw the laughter in his eyes. "Rule number one, never trust anyone. Now call Josh to let him know you're okay."

Think of something! God, where are you? "He doesn't think I'm going to call him tonight. He might think something's up."

Mark laughed. "People are often fools when they're in love. Besides, that's all the more reason to call. Let him know you're fine and are about to go to sleep. We wouldn't want him calling you later on, now would we?"

Holly reluctantly picked up the phone and dialed Josh's room extension. He picked up almost immediately. "Hi, Josh, I was just thinking about you...Yes, Sunny's thrilled." Holly's voice caught in her throat. "We can all have breakfast in the morning. How does that sound? No, you can't come over tonight because Sunny's falling asleep, and I'm about to crash too. I love you, Josh. Goodbye." Holly hung up and tried to swallow her tears. What if she never saw him again? This was all her fault! Why hadn't she just gone to the police?

"All right," Tony growled, "let's go. You first," Tony indicated at Holly with his gun. "Any attempt to escape, and your friend is dead."

"Um, Tony," Mark said, "I'll take care of Sunny. You just make sure Holly doesn't decide her friendship isn't worth it and bails."

Holly whirled around. "How dare you, of all people, say that!"

"I would suggest being quiet right now, Holly." Mark moved the gun from Sunny's back to her head. Holly walked through the door without saying another word.

Downstairs in the parking lot there was an abandoned cop car. Tony pushed Holly into the front seat and handcuffed her left hand to the barrier that was between the front and backseat. Sunny was put in the back. Holly heard Mark tell Tony he'd meet them there, wherever "there" was.

chapter thirty-three

They drove in silence. Holly didn't know what to do except pray. She knew without a doubt that Sunny was praying as well. God could get them out of this mess. Holly just didn't know if He would. *God, what can I do?* Sunny, unlike Holly, wasn't handcuffed but was trapped in the backseat where it was impossible to unlock the doors.

Holly estimated it was around two in the morning. There were more people on the streets than usual, thanks to New Year's. *What a great way to start out the New Year.* Holly looked down at the dashboard. There was nothing of particular interest down there, just a lighter and some old newspapers. A headline caught Holly's eye. It read, "New Improvements for the Hard of Hearing." Holly saw the traffic light ahead of them turn red, and they were slowly pulling up behind another police car. Inspiration hit Holly. She knew she'd have to work fast. After making sure Tony wasn't paying attention, Holly held up her hand for Sunny to see and finger spelled, "r-u-n (pause) w-h-e-n (pause) w-e (pause) c-r-a-s-h…r-u-n (pause) w-h-e-n (pause) w-e (pause) c-r-a-s-h."

By this time, they had come to a complete stop. There was no time for hesitation. The light would turn green soon. Holly shifted her body to where she was half in Tony's lap and stomped on the gas pedal, and the car lurched forward into the police car in front of them. If Holly hadn't been handcuffed, she would have gone straight into the windshield. Her arm screamed with pain, but she hardly noticed. Holly hit the automatic unlock. "Run, Sunny!"

Sunny didn't argue. She didn't want to leave Holly, but she knew she was no help to her if she was a prisoner as well. She sprung out of the car and barely dodged Tony who decided it was time to leave. Red light or no red light, he wasn't about to sit around and let the cops arrest him. Tony jumped the curb and was off with the police car chasing after him.

Sunny jumped when a man in the car parked in the lane next to her yelled her name. "Sunny, you harebrain, what are you doing?" It was Mark. Sunny was about to run from him but then saw that Josh was with him too.

"Sunny, Mark's a good guy," Josh told her. "He's been helping the police."

Sunny shook her head unbelievingly. Sunny noticed another man was in the vehicle with them. Ignoring the perturbed cars behind him, the man got out and walked over to her. Sunny knew she should have been afraid, but the guy looked old enough to be her grandfather. "Be quiet, you two. You're scaring the girl." He turned to Sunny. "Now it's going to be all right. I'm a police officer. You're friend there, Mark, is an undercover cop. He's been tracking Tony—that creep who was with you earlier—for months now. Here's my badge. I'm sorry, but for now that's all the proof I can give you. We're running out of time." Sunny started to look at the badge but was interrupted when Mark got out of the car.

"You," Mark told her, "are going down to the station where it's safe."

Sunny glared at him. Cop or no cop, there was no way she would take orders from him. "No, I'm not!"

Mark ground his teeth, "Yes, you . . ."

"Quiet, Mark," the other officer said to him. If Mark had had a tail, it would have gone between his legs. That alone was proof enough for Sunny that this guy was all right. "We don't have time to take her by the station. Besides, this isn't even our jurisdiction, and the police are already irritated we're 'vacationing' here. They know we're investigating a case." The man chuckled, "They can't prove it though."

"Fine," Mark said. It was not as if he had much of a choice. "Watch your head, Sunny." Sunny realized she was being put into the back of what looked like another police car.

She looked over at Josh, who had worry written all over his face. She couldn't blame him. Holly was still in the car with a potential killer. "Hi," Josh said blandly.

Mark started the car back up. "Are you sure you know where you're going?" the police officer asked him.

"For the hundredth time—yes. Tony took me there about an hour ago."

"And he bought your story?"

"Yes, he's a crook. He thinks everyone is like him and will do anything to earn a quick buck."

"Well, that's helpful. Now why exactly did you let your girl-friend come to Salem?"

Mark gripped the steering wheel so tightly that Sunny thought it would break under pressure. "She's stubborn and won't listen to me."

The elder officer turned around to face her. "I like you already."

Holly felt a black eye forming. It was the product of Tony shoving her off him. Luckily, he was too involved in trying to get away from the police car to do any further damage. To Holly's despair, he managed to elude the police. Soon Holly recognized where they were going. It was a place she'd sworn she'd never go back to. They were going to her old home.

God, I need you now. Holly felt a peace wash over her with the knowledge that nothing happened unless He let it. Thanks to God, Sunny was safe.

They pulled into her driveway, and Albert opened the door. His face hardened when he saw the handcuffs and her eye. Before Holly realized what had happened, Albert pulled out a gun and shot Tony in the head. Holly screamed.

"He won't be hurting you anymore." Albert took the cuffs off and dragged her out of the car into the house.

When they got inside, Holly's heart started pounding in overtime. She had to make him see reason. "Albert, why are you doing this? There are thousands of pretty girls out there who I'm sure would love to marry you."

Albert picked up a glass vase and threw it across the room. It hit the wall and shattered into a million pieces. "I don't want anyone else! We were made for each other."

He's insane. Holly knew then that Albert wouldn't hesitate to kill her just like Natasha and Tony, and Holly was sure there had been others as well. She turned when she heard footsteps coming down the main stairs. It was her father and grandmother. Victoria looked more archaic than ever, but still wore the same scowl on her face that she always had.

"We don't have much time," Tres said.

Holly looked back and forth between the three of them. "Time for what? What's going on?"

"We're getting married," Albert told her.

Holly knew she had to be dreaming when a priest walked in. It was like a bad movie, only it was really happening. Albert was going to force her to marry him. "This means nothing Albert. I don't love you. How can you possibly think this will change things?"

Albert slapped her across the face. "You will learn to love me."

Holly looked at her father. He was going to stand there and do nothing. *Leave him to his own fate, God. I want nothing to do with him.* Holly did the last thing they expected. She bolted toward Tres and shoved him into the priest. They both went tumbling backwards onto the steps. Victoria grabbed her wrist, but Holly was stronger and was able to pull away.

Holly suddenly had déjà vu that shot her two years back in time. *Now, now, now!* Now was the time for her escape. Just a few more stairs, and she'd be out of sight. Holly darted around the corner. She could hear Albert's pounding steps behind her. Holly saw the servant's staircase up on her left and bolted toward it. She flew down the stairs and into the kitchen. Holly skidded to a halt. *There!* She spotted the door that led outside and ran through it. She was now at the side of the house. Her best chance was to get to the street. Holly sprinted across the lawn. She could still hear Albert running behind her. He was gaining.

I'm so close. If I can just go a little farther… The wind was knocked out of her as she hit the ground. Albert was on top of her. "You're right, Holly," he gasped. "You're too much trouble, but if I can't have you, no one will." Albert stood and pinned Holly to the ground by putting his foot on her neck. He pulled out his gun and aimed it for her heart. *God, help!* A voice screamed inside her head as she watched Albert pull the trigger in slow motion. The gun went off, and out of the corner of her eye, she saw Josh sail through the air and tackle Albert.

Am I alive? Holly looked at the grass to her left. There was a black hole in the ground half an inch from her face. The bullet hadn't hit her! Josh had saved her life. *Oh no! Josh!* Holly looked at the two of them. They were still fighting. Albert was on the bottom and looking the worse for it, but he'd managed to get a hold of his gun. "Josh! Watch out!" Albert shot and missed by a millimeter, and then it was all over.

"Drop the gun," a police officer stood over both of them. He and five other officers had their guns aimed at Albert's head. Albert put the gun down and then slowly put his hands on his head.

Josh released him and ran over to Holly. "Are you all right?" Holly didn't say anything. She just went into his arms and cried.

Josh held her there for a long time. "Josh, don't ever do that again."

"That's funny. I was going to tell you the same thing."

Eventually, Holly was able to pull away and smile at him. "So when are we going to get married?"

Josh was thrown off by the question but not for long. "How about now?"

Holly shook her head and laughed. It felt so good, so right, with him. "How about next Christmas?"

"You've got a deal." Josh hugged her again. He'd almost lost her. They had arrived at the Johnson mansion only moments after Holly had. One look at the bullet hole in Tony's head had had Mark calling for backup. Soon after, Josh had seen Holly run out the side of the house with Albert close behind her, and Josh had flown after them. The rest was history.

Holly suddenly spotted Sunny coming toward them. "Sunny!" Holly ran to her and almost knocked her friend over when she hugged her so hard.

"I love you too." Sunny said as she tried to get her breath back. "That's why I'm going to wait until later to tell you how stupid it was not to call the police in the first place."

Holly was about to say something back when she saw Mark. "What is he doing here?"

"Rule number two," Mark grinned, "things are never what they seem."

"He," Sunny held out her hand to him, "is, believe it or not, a police officer. He was tracking that guy, Tony, and then pretended to be on his side so that he could help us." Sunny smiled proudly, all of her earlier frustrations temporarily forgotten. "It's because of him that we knew where to find you."

Holly looked at Mark who was turning red from Sunny's praise. "Thanks, Mark."

"Anytime...actually, I hope never again." They all laughed.

Holly agreed with him. If she never saw another gun for the rest of her life, she'd be happy.

"Hey! Holly, guess what?"

"What, Josh?"

"Mark's friend, the police officer, said I would make a good cop. What do you think?"

"No."

"What?"

"Absolutely not. You'd be great at it, Josh, but then you would get yourself shot. No way."

The police officer walked over to them smiling. "I doubt you'll win that argument, young man." There was a twinkle in his eye. He loved a happy ending. "I'm Jack Cannon. It's a pleasure to meet you, Holly." Officer Cannon held out his hand to Holly who, surprisingly, didn't take it.

Holly's jaw dropped. "It's you."

The officer's eyebrows furrowed together. "Excuse me?"

"Don't you remember me?" Holly asked. "I'm the girl you picked up out of the rain a couple of years ago in L.A."

Jack looked stunned. "Well, I'll be. You sure do get yourself into a lot of trouble."

Holly laughed and hugged the man. "You're my guardian angel. By the way, I know what you mean now about believing in what you can't see."

Jack smiled warmly. "Do you believe then?"

Holly looked at her friends smiling at her and saw her father and Albert put into the back of a police car off in the distance. Holly shook her head, "No, I don't believe. I know my God is real because He lives inside of me."

Jack Cannon beamed at her. "There are a lot of people in this world who will say otherwise."

Holly simply shrugged and held out her hands to Josh and Sunny. Smiling at them, she wondered how anyone could look at her life and still question if there was a God. Holly watched as the tree limbs got caught up in the wind. If she hadn't known better, she would have sworn she heard music.

Contact Katherine Adair at
adair_kat@yahoo.com

or order more copies of this book at:

TATE PUBLISHING, LLC

127 East Trade Center Terrace
Mustang, Oklahoma 73064

(888) 361 - 9473

TATE PUBLISHING, LLC
www.tatepublishing.com